THE RULE MAKER

BOSTON HAWKS HOCKEY
BOOK 4

GINA AZZI

THREE CITIES PUBLISHING LLC

The Rule Maker

Copyright © 2021 by Gina Azzi

All rights reserved.

No part of this publication may be reproduced, distributed, or transmitted in any form or by any means, including photocopying, recording, or other electronic or mechanical methods, without the prior written permission of the publisher, except in the case of brief quotations embodied in critical reviews and certain other noncommercial uses permitted by copyright law.

This is a work of fiction. Names, characters, businesses, places, events, locales, and incidents are either the products of the author's imagination or used in a fictitious manner. Any resemblance to actual persons, living or dead, or actual events is purely coincidental.

CHAPTER 1
CHLOE

"I've officially regressed," I lament to my best friend Abbi, as I kick my feet up on my bedroom wall. My bedroom wall in my parents' new house in Boston because at the ripe age of thirty, I've moved back in.

"It's just temporary, Chlo. Just until you get back on your feet," she reassures me.

I sigh, staring up at the ceiling fan which turns lazily, breaking the streams of light that flicker across the room. "I'm back in my childhood hometown, in a house eerily similar to my childhood home, being treated like a child, all because I—"

"Stop," Abbi cuts me off. "Don't go there. You didn't do anything wrong. *Steve* deserves the blame, not you."

Just hearing my ex-fiancé's name feels like a hot, fire iron is being plunged into my chest. Two months ago, Steve blew up our lives and the tidy, perfect future I'd envisioned for us. I never thought he'd cheat on me and most certainly not with Brittney, one of my most trusted and beloved friends who rounded out the trio along with Abbi and me.

"And Brittney," Abbi adds, as if reading my thoughts. The disgust in her voice alleviates some of the ache in my chest.

At least I still have Abbi, who was quick to cut Steve and Brittney off despite my delusional desire to make things okay between us all. *It's just the hurt talking,* Abbi said. She was right. As the weeks passed and Brittney moved into the airy, inviting farmhouse-styled condo I lovingly decorated for Steve and me in Hoboken, New Jersey, my hurt seeped into anger. Anger tinged with humiliation.

How dare my fiancé and friend have an affair behind my back? Were they planning to keep it up after Steve and I wed? Would I have ever caught on if Abbi didn't surprise me with a day of pampering for my birthday and I forgot my pedicure flip-flops at home?

The image of Steve and Brittney going at it like rabbits on *my* bed, with the wood paneled headboard and white coverlet from Pottery Barn, flares in my mind like a trumpet. I groan.

Abbi sighs. "Babe, I know you're hurt."

"I'm not hurt. I'm furious," I correct her, wishing I could bleach my eyeballs to unsee everything I saw. "I'm so angry and pissed off and"—tears well in my eyes—"*hurt.*" I agree with Abbi's assessment. "I don't know what to do with all these dumb feelings." I swipe the tears away with the backs of my knuckles. "I wish I never intertwined so much of my life with Steve's. I hate that we have the same friends. I hate that I put my career on hold to support his. And I really hate that *he and Brittney* are living their best lives in *my* home while I've been banished to Boston."

Abbi clucks at my dramatics and I know she's gearing up to give me some tough love. I bang my heels against the bedroom wall. I'm in desperate need of tough love but that doesn't mean I want to hear it.

"Chloe," Abbi says patiently and in this moment, I love my best friend for helping me navigate these murky waters over the past few months, "you're not banished anywhere. You're taking a break from your life to sort out your next moves. You love Boston. Now, you get to spend the summer with your family in your old stomping grounds. You can visit your mimi and take her out to brunch. And when I come visit, we'll go clubbing and do a bunch of touristy shit."

"You'll really come?" My voice is small and that's another thing I hate. Since I learned the truth about Steve and Brittney, everything I thought I knew shifted. My perspective changed and in a matter of minutes, I lost some of my confidence. Instead, I feel shaky, like the ground beneath my feet is constantly moving. In short, I've become a less-than-independent, needier version of myself who I simultaneously despise and cling to. I'm blaming that on Steve too.

"Of course I'll come. You're not in Timbuktu, you're four hours away. I wish I could make the engagement party next weekend but I'll see you at Marissa's bachelorette in July. I'll extend my Boston visit then."

"Shit." My breath lodges in my throat at the reminder. How did I forget that Marissa Swanson, one of Brittney's and Abbi's and my friends, is marrying Adam Wilson, one of Steve's closest friends, in August? "Shit, shit, shit." I bang my heels again.

"You forgot about Marissa's bachelorette? Don't worry, I'll—"

"I forgot about the engagement party!" It's next weekend in Martha's Vineyard. After my relationship imploded, Marissa begged me to stay on as a bridesmaid, despite the hostility and tension between Brittney and me. Not wanting to sacrifice another friend, I agreed and now I am majorly regretting that decision. "I need a date."

"You do. You need a hot, hulking, sexy—"

"Where do I find one of those?" I cut Abbi off, panic edging my tone. How did I forget about Marissa's engagement party? My entire summer pretty much revolves around her wedding festivities.

When the daughter of a hotel tycoon and the son of a New York City hedge fund CEO decide they don't want to wait for their marital bliss, people spring into action. In a mere week, venues magically became available and designers personally called Marissa about her wedding dress. At first, when I was still engaged to Steve, I found my friend's ability to cram an engagement party, a bachelorette bash, and a high-profile wedding into ten weeks, exciting and romantic.

Now that I'm painfully single, I'm furious with Marissa for forcing me to find a date to two separate events—her engagement party next week and her wedding in August. How am I going to face *Steve and Brittney* not once, but twice?

"We can rent one," Abbi tosses out.

I roll my eyes. "I doubt that. Besides, I'd need to rent the same one twice if I want people to think I have a real relationship and not a pity date."

"Do you want people to think you're in a real relationship?"

"More than I want them to think it's a pity date," I say, exasperated.

"Fair enough." Abbi is silent for a long moment. "Drew?"

"I'm not taking my *brother* to a wedding."

"He's hot."

"You're making this worse, not better."

"Too bad he lives in Texas," Abbi continues as if I haven't spoken at all. If she keeps up, I'll need bleach for my eyes *and* ears.

A knock at my bedroom door draws my attention as Dad pops his head in. His smile is gentle, his eyes warm and I have the sudden urge to hug my dad tightly and cry into his strong chest the same way I did as a little girl. The same way I did two months ago after chucking my engagement ring at Steve's head.

"We're heading to the Merricks' in an hour," Dad reminds me.

I nod, pointing to the phone.

He nods and dips out of my room.

"Abbi, I gotta go. We're heading to a family friend's house for dinner tonight."

"Oh, see! You have a social life," she says way too excitedly.

I snort. Dinner at the Merricks is hardly a social event but considering I've barely interacted with the human species in the past two months, I'm not an accurate judge. "I'll call you tomorrow."

"Have fun tonight."

"'Bye, Abs."

"'Bye."

I disconnect the call and drag myself to my closet. Sliding open the door, I glance at my meager selection of clothing. I really need to unpack my shit but doing so would mean I'm staying in Boston and my life in Hoboken, everything Steve and I built over the past five years, is really over. I heave a sigh.

Flipping through my hangers, I wonder what to wear. Mary and Joe Merrick were my parents' closest friends, and our next-door neighbors, when we lived in Boston. Drew and their eldest daughter, Savannah, were in the same grade at school, just like me and their son Austin. As kids, Austin and his sisters, Savannah and Claire, were more like Drew's and my cousins. We pretty much grew up around their kitchen island and in their backyard. Summer nights catching fireflies with Claire and her cousin Indy, winter mornings sledding with Austin and Drew, and a very memorable shopping experience with Savannah, round out some of my favorite childhood memories.

Austin Merrick was once my closest friend but always in the-boy-next-door kind of way. If something was truly wrong, I could count on him for advice. But in our daily interactions, he was often more annoying than Drew. He hid my rock collection for an entire weekend, cut the colorful, glitter tassels off the handlebars of my bike, and teased me relent-lessly the first time I shaved my legs.

As we grew older and Austin became a hockey star, we drifted apart. In high school, he ran with the cool kid crowd while I was more of the bookish, geeky set. Even though he was crazy popular, with girls flocking to hang off his shoulders, I still looked at him and saw the boy who pantsed me at a family vacation in Martha's Vineyard.

Despite the vast difference in our social stratas, Austin *was* always nice to me at school. It was me who added the final distance to our friendship. Halfway through our sophomore year, I stopped walking home from school with him because it drew too much ire from his fan club. After that, I rarely saw Austin close-up unless it was a family gathering and he often missed those due to hockey. By the time my family relocated to New York at the end of my sophomore year, Austin and I were acquaintances at best. Afterwards, we lost touch completely, and my only updates about his life came via my mom or Savannah when our paths crossed in New York.

Now, he's the captain of the NHL Boston Hawks, something my dad shares with every single hockey fan he encounters. My parents' pride for Austin knows no bounds.

Will he be at dinner tonight?

Probably not. He must be way too busy with his career—his team just won the Stanley Cup—to have dinner with me and my parents.

I finger a simple, summer dress.

Does it matter if he's there?

For a blink, Austin's deep blue eyes, the color of the Atlantic in October, when winter's creeping in, flare in my mind. Even though my feelings are still raw from Steve, I can objectively admit that Austin was always devilishly handsome, with quick eyes and a sly smirk. He was a notorious rule breaker although he was too charismatic to ever face discipline for the trouble he stirred up. He was popular, likable, and infuriatingly immature, always hiding his smelly gym socks in my backpack or sneaking a bite out of the sandwich Mom packed me for lunch. Way back when, he used to wear spicy cologne and oversized hoodies. He asked me to dance the first slow song at the Valentine's Day dance my freshman year after my date kissed another girl.

I pull the summer dress off the hanger. Where did that thought even come from? This isn't some trip down memory lane. I'm tagging along with my parents while they visit their friends. I'm not rekindling a friendship with Austin, a guy who is now larger than life. I probably don't even register on his radar, save for a handful of childhood memories.

Man, Steve did a number on my head if I'm even thinking about Austin at all.

I shimmy into the summer dress. I slip into simple, strappy sandals and find a pair of earrings in my purse.

Austin's not going to be at dinner tonight. Neither is Savannah, since she lives in New York City. We'd occasionally meet for lunch before my life turned upside down and I was too embarrassed to see friends, save for Abbi.

If anything, I should hope Claire or Indy make an appearance so I can reconnect with girlfriends. At least they'll invite me out with them and sprinkle my summer with social outings that don't include bingo and rummikube with Mom and Mimi.

My phone buzzes with an incoming message and I swipe it up, assuming it's Abbi.

MIMI

I hope your heart's not too broken to notice Austin Merrick.

I snort. I swear, Mimi is more of a troublemaker than Austin. At eighty-four, she's sharper than a whip and more meddlesome than Mom.

CHLOE

I doubt he'll even be there.

MIMI

He's a good boy. Sees his Mom and Dad
once a week for dinner. He'll be there.

Eye roll.

CHLOE

Even if he is, he won't remember me.

My phone rings.

"Mimi, I regret ever teaching you to text," I answer.

She chuckles, her warm laughter spreading through the line and right through me. As much as the reason *why* I'm back in Boston pains me, spending time with Mimi is a definite plus. "I would have learned without you."

"I don't doubt it."

"Why don't you think Austin will remember you? You used to *bathe* together for crying out loud."

I wince at the visual because imagining a man like Austin *bathing* now…well, I shouldn't imagine that while on the phone with my octogenarian grandmother.

"I haven't seen him in fifteen years," I point out.

"He was at your parents' Christmas party a few years ago."

I squint, as if that will somehow help me recall the evening in question. It comes back slowly, the clink of glasses, sparkle of tinsel on the tree, and I vaguely recall seeing the Merrick family, Austin included. But that Christmas, I only had eyes for Steve. I barely remember anything other than my intense feelings for him.

"Hmph. He'll more than remember you, Chloe Ann. What I don't like is you needing me to remind you of this. Steve deserves a good talking-to after the way that boy treated you. In my day—"

"Mimi."

She sighs. "I know, I know. It's none of my concern how you squander your twenties."

I wince at her honesty, feeling very much like I wasted the second half of the decade wrapped up in Steve's life instead of cultivating my own.

"What are you wearing to dinner?" She changes the subject.

I describe my sundress and she hums appreciatively, making me laugh. "Get any ideas of playing matchmaker right out of your mind," I say. "If Austin is there, he'll be polite and charming, the way he always is."

"I'll say. That boy could charm the pants off of—"

"Good night, Mimi."

"Bring me doughnuts tomorrow morning. I want to know how big his biceps are now. And how he's handling all the pressure now that he's *won* the Stanley Cup. Won it, Chloe! He always did carry the weight of the world on his shoulders."

I roll my eyes because that's a stretch if I've ever heard one. But Mimi always had a soft spot for the reckless athlete.

She's still muttering when I gently remind her that I need to get ready.

"Oh, yes. Don't forget about your eyebrows. If you pencil them in neatly, you won't have to do that micro-blading thing that's all the rage these days. Although, in my day we did tattooing too you know. I can still teach you—"

"Mimi."

"Love you, Chloe girl. Have fun tonight. Real fun. With Aus—"

I disconnect the call, muttering to myself. Even though Mimi has an uncanny ability to predict my life, she's wrong about this one.

I haven't thought of Austin Merrick since high school. Dinner at his parents' house isn't going to change that.

I EAT MY WORDS.

I eat them all so quickly I choke on them.

Because when the door to the Merricks' home swings open, I'm greeted by the same intense blue eyes of my teenage years. My mouth drops open and the irrational thought of how the hell I ever forgot about Austin zips through my mind.

How does anyone forget a man who looks like, well, *him*?

"Chloe Crawford," Austin murmurs, giving me a sly smirk before greeting my parents.

I can hardly process the fact that he's here, looking like a sex god mated with a Roman one, as Mary and Joe pull me into their embraces and welcome me back to Boston. A whirlwind of exclaimed greetings and hugs unfolds in the foyer.

"You didn't have to bring anything," Mary says, her eyes shining as she kisses Mom hello and thanks Dad for the two decorative wine sleeves he hands her.

"We're so happy you're back," Joe chimes in, wrapping an arm around my shoulders.

I grin up at him, remembering the pep talks he used to give Savannah, Claire, and me when the neighborhood boys would exclude us from their hockey and basketball games.

Mary leads the adults into the kitchen but I hang back, my gaze finding Austin's. He's leaning against the closet door, his hands stuffed into the pockets of his jeans, a thoughtful expression on his face.

"You look different," I blurt out, feeling my cheeks blaze.

He snickers. "It's been a minute."

"I didn't think you'd be here."

He winks. "But you're happy to see me, right?"

I roll my eyes and he grins. He's taller than I imagined

and I have to crane my neck to look into his face. His smirk isn't as sly as it once was but his eyes are sharper, bolder, scanning mine with an intensity I feel down to my toes.

Strong shoulders, a broad chest, a tapered waist. *Stop checking him out!* I drag my eyes back to Austin's face, not missing the knowing glint in his eyes.

"It's good to see you again, Chlo." He straightens and holds his arms out for a hug like we're old friends. I guess, technically, we are.

But this feels different. Awareness unfurls throughout my limbs, my heart rate ticks up, and my skin tingles under Austin's gaze. I feel like a hesitant teenager again, like my skin is too tight for all of the emotions trying to break free.

I step into Austin's embrace, my eyes closing of their own accord when he holds me close. His cologne wraps around me the way it always did but now, even that's different. His chest is hard and warm under my ear, just like I remember. But the arms holding me now are the arms of a man and I want to sink into their strength more than I should.

A hell of a lot more than a woman with a broken heart and an uncertain future should consider.

CHAPTER 2
AUSTIN

Chloe Crawford's presence hits me as both a memory and a vision when I hug her hello.

Just seeing her jogs a million childhood moments I haven't thought about in years. Chloe and I grew up together. She was my first friend, thanks to our moms throwing us together at every opportunity. Back in the day, we took baths together, joined the same T-ball team, and had sleepovers. Our childhood bond morphed into more of a sibling rivalry during our middle school years, when Chloe irritated me just as much as Savannah and Claire. By the time we entered high school, our paths diverged as I threw myself into hockey and she was swept up by the dedicated, honors class crew whose intelligence was way out of my league. At first, I didn't think much of it, considering she lived just next door. But when the Crawfords moved to New York at the end of our sophomore year of high school, I felt her absence a lot more than I let on.

She showed up to nearly all of my hockey games, sporting my number and banging on the glass when the ref made a poor call. Every year, she met me at the end of her driveway on the morning of the season's first snowfall for a snowball fight. She was a permanent fixture in my life until she wasn't and by the time I realized how much distance existed between us, it seemed too late to do anything about it. Especially for a fifteen-year-old smartass who showed affection through pranks instead of meaningful conversation.

Right now, with her light brown hair skimming the tops of her shoulders and her arms wrapped around my waist in a hug, it seems like an entire decade hasn't passed us by. Instead, I recall my entire childhood with perfect clarity.

"Good to see you, too." She pulls back, tossing me an easy smile.

It hits me harder than it's supposed to because it shouldn't hit me at all. But God, she's gorgeous. I remember her freshman year of high school, confident and brazen, leveling the giggly girls who used to wait in front of my locker with a vicious side-eye. While the rest of us always seemed to be struggling to figure it out, Chloe always had her shit together. She dips her head and tucks her hair behind her ear, uncertain. Changed. The woman standing before me now is just that, a woman. Soft curves, smooth skin, and delicate features. But there's something else too, something I can't put my finger on but it causes a ribbon of unease to unspool in the pit of my stomach.

"When'd you get into town?" I ask, slinging an arm around her shoulders and guiding her to the kitchen. As usual, I'm the first of my family members to make it to Mom and Dad's house on time.

Claire and Easton are notorious for being late. My cousin Indy, always punctual, messaged that she was waiting for Noah to come home so she didn't have to drive over alone. Savannah and Mike live in New York now and no longer make weekly dinners. And Indy's parents, Aunt Leanne and Uncle Jemmy, are in Aruba. Aunt Lee is calling it their last hurrah before Indy's baby arrives.

Right now, not counting our parents who are already clinking wine glasses and talking a thousand miles a minute, it's just Chloe and me.

"About a week ago," she answers, her eyes darting around the kitchen. I wonder if she's seeing the same half-forgotten memories I am.

"Chloe, dear, we're so happy you could join us." Mom kisses her head for the second time in ten minutes and places a wine glass in her hand.

"Me too, Mary. Thanks." Chloe takes a sip of her wine.

Mom tsks, hugging Chloe close. "I wish the circumstances were different, honey. But your mom and dad are thrilled you're here and I'm certain your presence will brighten Mimi's summer."

Chloe flushes, dropping her head again to hide behind her wine glass.

Circumstances? What circumstances?

My unease heightens into concern.

"What happened?" I ask as soon as Mom scurries over to the oven to check on the appetizers.

Chloe shifts her weight and bites her bottom lip. Emotion swells in her eyes and my stomach sinks, a hundred awful scenarios flipping through my mind. Is Mimi sick? Are Greg or Diane, Chloe's parents, unwell? Why wouldn't Mom tell me?

An image flares in my mind. Three years ago, a Christmas party, a radiant Chloe with bright eyes and a wide smile. And an oily banker who's hand kept migrating to her ass. His shoes were too damn shiny and I didn't like him on sight. Seeing him and Chlo together filled me with a strange sense of nostalgia and melancholy that confused me almost as much as Chloe's indifference to everyone who wasn't him. What the hell is his name? Didn't he propose?

My gaze drops to her ring finger. No ring.

She flinches when she catches me looking and I blow out a sigh, putting it all together.

"What the fuck did he do?" I growl, hating that some clown hitting way above his average would hurt my friend. Three years ago, I didn't like the guy —what the hell is his name?—and right now, seeing the devastation in Chlo's eyes, I can't fucking stand him.

Chloe shrugs and clears her throat. She offers me a tiny smile that quickly falls flat. "It's not worth getting into." She sighs and raises her wine glass, a familiar spark zipping through her gaze. "Oh, who am I kidding? A few more of these and I'll be blabbering the whole sob story to anyone who will listen."

I snicker, knowing she's aiming for levity. Looking her over, it strikes me just how many years have slipped by without my checking in with my first friend. How now, I know absolutely nothing about her life. "You know I'll listen, Chlo. You okay?"

She exhales slowly. "I will be. It's still fresh."

I nod, even though I have no idea what the hell that must feel like. I don't do serious commitments, just easy understandings. In the past two weeks since my hockey team, the Boston Hawks, won the Stanley Cup, the subtle and not-so-subtle offers of simple, no-strings-attached sex have been in overwhelming abundance.

"You back in Boston for good?"

She shuffles from one foot to the next. "I'm not sure yet. Honestly, everything happened so suddenly and I just wanted…space. So, I'm here for the summer and then, I'll see what comes next."

"What about work?" I lean back against the kitchen island, crossing my ankles.

"I'm lucky my job allows for location mobility."

I run my palm over the back of my head. What the hell does

she do for a living again? Why can't I remember? I'm about to ask her when the doorbell rings. I glance over my shoulder but Mom and Dad are way too occupied with Greg and Diane to answer it. I gesture to the door with my head. Chloe falls in step beside me.

"Since you're here for the summer," I continue, "you need to come out with us. We're not nearly as sophisticated as your friends in New York but we're not awful either."

"We?" Her brow furrows.

I reach for the front door just as Claire pushes it open. It swings hard, bouncing against the doorstopper and Chloe jumps, chuckling.

"Ahh! You're here!" my sister announces, pulling Chloe into a hug.

My best friend and Claire's boyfriend, Easton, is close behind, followed up by my cousin Indy and her man, another one of my friends and teammates, Noah.

"Gang's all here," Noah announces, his eyes widening when he spots Chloe. "Chloe Crawford, is that you?"

Easton smacks my shoulder hello.

"I love when the kids outnumber the parents," Claire says.

Noah pulls Chloe into a hug, muttering how many years it's been since he's seen her. When I was thirteen, I met Easton and Noah Scotch at a hockey camp in Canada. For the following summers and all through high school, they would spend weeks at my house. Those first few summers, before the Crawfords moved to New York, their paths crossed with Chloe's. Another thing I forgot all about.

"We're both back!" Indy exclaims, greeting Chloe hello.

"Wait a second," Chloe chuckles, her finger wagging between Easton and Claire and then Noah and Indy. "You guys are together? Like, all hooked up?"

Indy beams and links her arm with Noah's. "We're having a baby!"

"I can see that." Chloe smiles and squeezes Indy's hand,

her gaze darting between Indy and Noah. "Congratulations. You guys, this is, wow. It's kind of a lot."

"Tell me about it," I mutter.

Claire laughs. "Good thing you got out of here, Chlo, or you might be dating Austin now."

Chloe chuckles as I flip my sister the middle finger.

I close the door and take Indy's shoulder bag, weighted down with her laptop, as Claire leads the group into the kitchen for drinks. The greetings and laughter float into the foyer.

How has it been nearly fifteen years since Chloe was a permanent fixture in this house? How have I gone this long without checking in with my oldest, childhood friend? And why the hell is the distance between us bothering me now when I haven't even thought about it in years?

"KINGS!" Claire claps her hands excitedly.

"No, no." Easton shakes his head. "Never Have I Ever?"

"Meh." Indy wrinkles her nose.

"Good to know we're not too old for drinking games," Noah murmurs.

Chloe grins and leans back in her Adirondack-style chair. "Never too old for those, Scotch."

We're seated around the firepit in my parents' backyard. The adults are inside, munching on a charcuterie board and drinking wine and craft beer. But the kids, the kids have banded together just the way we did in high school, coming out to the backyard to drink and play games.

The fire flickers, a nod to our old high school days, even though it's too warm to really use. It reminds me of the bonfires we used to have in an old field, about five miles outside of town, in high school. Seeing Chloe now, with her hair pulled away from her face, her eyes dancing, brings me back to freshman year. A bonfire. The night Mason Kinner kissed her and my chest pulled uncomfortably tight. I hated the way Mason touched her face, her hair, as if he knew her body a hell of a lot more intimately. More than that, I hated that she leaned into his touch.

I couldn't look away and for the first time, I felt true jealousy. Which was ridiculous. Chloe and I had been friends my entire life. She pissed me off more often than not.

"Cheers to the Governor?" Chloe suggests, pulling me back to the game.

"Cheers to the Governor," Claire agrees.

Easton sighs and leans back in his chair, bringing a club soda to his lips. I study him to make sure he's fine with this. East has been in recovery for a handful of months and has been doing an awesome job with his sobriety. Sometimes, I worry that stupid nights like these will trigger something for him. But he seems fine. Same with Indy, now in her third trimester and sipping on a ginger ale.

"Okay," Claire springs into action. She swiped a bottle of wine from the kitchen and adds some to her and Chloe's cups.

Noah and I sip our beers and wait for Claire to decide the starting rule.

"A quick recap," Claire says as she settles back into her chair. "We go around the circle and count to twenty-one, then we cheers the governor. Whoever says number twenty-one, gets to make a new rule that will be incorporated into the next round. And we keep going. Our starting rule is to swap number three with eleven."

"All right," Chloe says, kicking it off by saying one.

Our first round is easy and we all cheers and drink as Indy declares the new rule. "Instead of saying seven, you have to share an embarrassing truth."

"That'll be easy for me," East mutters. Claire leans over and gives him a quick peck on the lips.

I catch Chloe take in their interaction, longing flashing across her expression before she clears it. Over the course of dinner, as the wine flowed and the conversation naturally picked up as if we haven't seen Chloe in a few weeks instead of more than a decade, she relaxed substantially.

I tip my head toward hers. "Don't worry, you get used to it. They're pretty much always disgusting."

"Hey!" Claire says, pointing at Indy. "We're not nearly as bad as them."

I raise an eyebrow. "Depends on the day."

Chloe chuckles and opens her mouth but before she says anything, Noah begins the next round. When we make it to twenty-one, we cheers and drink.

"Next rule," Claire announces, "instead of saying number four, you have to sing the chorus of Madonna's 'Like a Virgin.'"

Easton belts out the lyrics like a pro, surprising the girls. Chloe cracks up as Indy claps and Claire whistles.

"Didn't think I knew that, did you?" East asks when he's done.

"I'm impressed!" Chloe cheers for him.

We make it to twenty-one three more times, before the rules segue into memories and old stories. Soon, we're chatting high school and hockey and it's so familiar that a wave of nostalgia crashes over me, pulling my thoughts in different directions.

Back then, things seemed complicated and uncertain. I would talk with Chloe, who had her whole future mapped out. She wanted to attend Columbia University, major in journalism, and become an investigative journalist.

Her confidence, something I admired, always left me feeling worried about my future. Would I get a hockey scholarship to college? Would I make it to the NHL? Would I still be friends with the guys on my team? If only I knew then how much the pressure would swell, how difficult it would become to balance hockey and life.

In hindsight, I knew nothing about managing stress and shouldering responsibility. Since becoming team captain, the anxiety I've always been prone to has swelled to epic proportions. The past few weeks, since we've won the Cup, it's been almost unbearable. Because we won the fucking Cup.

I suck in an inhale, my gaze trained on the low lick of flames in the firepit. My knee begins to bounce up and down as my thoughts spiral.

Now what? How are we going to beat that this season? How do we compete with ourselves now that Torsten Hansen retired? How do we hang onto a victory that was nearly impossible to secure in the first place? Will the team question my leadership if we don't make it? Will I?

"Our summers here were always the best. Probably the only thing East and I looked forward to all school year," Noah says in response to something Claire mentioned.

I lean back in my chair and take a pull of my beer. I focus on quieting the thoughts in my mind so I can pay attention to the conversation. To the present.

East nods in agreement, lifting his chin to Chloe. "When did you move again? End of our freshman year?"

"Sophomore," Chloe supplies, taking a sip of her wine. Her cheeks are ruddier than they were an hour ago and she eases back into her chair.

"Was it hard, starting over at a new high school?" Indy asks.

Chloe tilts her head, considering the question. "It was okay. The first few months were tough because I was trying to find my place again, you know? Here, I took pride in being the nerdy girl—"

"You weren't the—" I start but Chloe gives me a look.

"Amen to being the nerdy girl." Indy raises her ginger ale.

Chloe and Indy grin at each other and each take a drink.

"But then I made friends. Abbi and Brittney." She visibly winces when she says the second girl's name and I narrow my gaze. "We were tight through high school and college. I mean, Abbi and I are still really close. She's like a sister to me."

"But Brittney?" Indy asks slowly.

Chloe lets out a long sigh and glances around the group.

"We don't like her, do we?" Claire asks.

One side of Chloe's mouth tugs upward but her eyes fill with tears and my sister swears, leaning forward in her seat. "Oh God, did something happen to Brittney?" Claire asks, panic in her wide eyes.

Chloe shakes her head and wipes her eyes, snorting. "Brittney and Steve were having an affair. I, I caught them and—"

"*Your* Steve?" Claire asks, her mouth dropping open. "With *your* friend?"

Indy gasps.

A blaze of anger shoots through me at the anguish twisting Chloe's expression. My hand not gripping a beer bottle clenches into a fist and my teeth click as I grind them together. Next to me, Noah tenses and across, East swears. It's worse than I thought. Not only did the douchebag step out on her but he did so with one of her best friends? What a piece of shit. And what a crappy friend.

Noah shakes his head, muttering under his breath.

"The wedding's off, right?" East asks.

"Of course," Chloe sniffles. "I just, God, I feel so stupid."

"Don't." Claire jabs her finger at Chloe. "You're one of the smartest women I know, Chloe. And I'm related to this one." Claire hooks her thumb toward Indy, the only person in our family to have a PhD, and Indy blushes. "How long ago?"

"Two months," Chloe admits. "I moved back in with my parents right afterwards but they already sold our family home and were transitioning back here. So, here I am, back in Boston. For the summer at least."

Indy's face falls as she watches Chloe. "I'm really sorry, Chlo. I'm sure you've heard this a thousand times but really, you dodged a bullet."

"Hell yeah," Claire adds. "It's definitely better to know what an asshole he is before you were legally bound to him."

"And what a bad friend *she* is," Indy adds.

Chloe nods slowly, her eyes glazed over. She's probably had this conversation several times and still, knowing she's better off isn't making her *feel* better off.

Chloe drains her wine glass. Indy shifts to refill it and Chloe sighs. "Guys, I don't know what I'm going to do. I'm here for the summer, maybe longer. I moved out of our condo and Brittney moved right in."

Indy gasps again.

"But two of Steve's and my mutual friends are getting married this summer. Their engagement party is next weekend and we're all in the wedding party—me, Brittney, and Steve."

"Jesus," Easton mutters.

"I know," Chloe agrees. "I can't just bail because I don't want to face Steve and Brittney together. Can I? I mean, should I?" She winces. "The thought of seeing them together, of having everyone stare at me and whisper 'oh poor little Chloe, look at her all alone.'" She shivers as if the thought turns her stomach. "It's going to be awful. I can't even think about the wedding in August."

"Screw him," Claire says.

"You need a date to the engagement party," Indy decides.

Claire nods. "A super sexy, chiseled—"

"I'm sitting right here," East reminds her and she swats at him.

"You need man candy," Indy agrees.

Chloe closes her eyes. "You sound like Abbi. I'm practically a hermit these days. Where the hell am I going to find man candy?"

Indy's eyes swing to mine and a small smile forms on her face.

Oh no. I know that look. That's scheming Indy who thinks she's about to announce something brilliant when in reality, she's meddling. I raise my hand, my mouth opening to stop her when—

"Austin can take you!" Indy squeals.

CHAPTER 3
CHLOE

At Indy's insane suggestion, my gaze darts to Austin.

He's seated beside me around the firepit, his hands clenched and his jawline tight. Oh shit. He definitely does not like this idea and now he's going to feel obligated to agree.

"Oh, I'm sure Austin has a million more important things to—"

"I'll take you," Austin says, surprising the hell out of me and everyone else in our circle.

"Wh-what?" I sputter, my limbs locking down. Austin Merrick, Captain of the Boston Hawks, is going to escort *me* to an engagement party? "You don't have to do that."

"I want to," he says simply.

Claire's eyes dart between her brother and me, while Indy sits back with a satisfied smirk on her face.

"I mean, I don't know about man candy," Easton jokes, tilting his head as if studying Austin's appearance.

Austin flips him off and East and Noah laugh.

"I love summer weddings," Claire sighs dreamily. She glances at me. "They're having an engagement party and wedding in the same summer? Is she, you know…" She clicks her tongue and points to Indy's baby bump.

I snort and shake my head. "No, no it's not a shotgun wedding. Marissa's a hotel heiress and Adam's dad is a hedge fund CEO. They decided they wanted to do it all in one summer and voila—"

"It's done," Claire finishes my sentence. She shakes her head and tosses me a smile. "All right. You show up all sexified on the arm of a professional athlete, even one as ugly as my brother, and Steve is going to regret ever stepping out on you. Plus, Brittney will have to console herself knowing she's only good enough for sloppy seconds."

Indy holds up her palm and Claire high-fives her.

I giggle, glancing between my old friends. "You really think, I mean"—I look at Austin again—"are you sure?"

"Yeah." He clears his throat.

"Where's the party again?" Noah asks.

"Martha's Vineyard."

"Ooh," Indy's eyes glitter. "Good thing Aus just led the team to the Stanley Cup. He has some downtime and he *is* a Massachusetts hero."

"You should throw his name around," Noah agrees, getting into the planning of this insane shenanigan.

Austin winces, turning away from the firepit and taking a swig of his beer. I worry my bottom lip between my teeth. Is he sure about this?

"And wear your hair up," Noah continues, pulling my attention back to the group.

"What?" I ask, unsure if I heard him correctly.

Indy nods. "That way, when Austin kisses your neck—"

"Hold up," Easton cuts in, glancing between Austin and me. "Are you guys going as friends or as—"

"You have to go as real dates," Indy argues. "To the engagement party and then, to the wedding. Otherwise, it looks like a pity date." She winces, giving me an apologetic look. "Sorry."

I shake my head. "No offense taken." Didn't I voice the

exact same concern to Abbi a few hours ago? The wine is definitely kicking in now because instead of protesting this ridiculous idea, I'm turning it over in my mind. If Abbi was in my predicament right now, what Claire and Indy are suggesting is exactly what I would be telling her.

Besides, Austin is my childhood friend so he really is the perfect candidate. He's not going to see me as more than the girl he used to irritate and he's not going to get any kind of weird ideas about sharing a hotel room or slow dancing together. We can do this as friends, right? There will definitely not be any kissing of necks or canoodling because, who the hell would want to canoodle with me? A man like Austin—successful, charming, and ridiculously hot—wouldn't want to touch my current state of damaged goods with a ten-foot pole.

Still, I don't want to put him on the spot. Correction: I don't want to seem too eager to put him on the spot. I glance at him again. "We can do whatever you want. You really don't even have to do this."

A muscle in his jaw ticks as he stares at me. His blue eyes swirl, brimming with thoughts I don't understand. "You want to make him jealous?"

My cheeks burn under the scrutiny of his gaze. His stare is so intense, it's like he can see beneath my skin, to the insecurities I try to hide. Slowly, I nod, hating how pathetic it makes me look. Especially to a man like him who, according to information gleaned from my last lunch date with Savannah, dates models and successful girl boss women.

"Regardless, Steve's getting off easy," Austin murmurs, so quietly I almost miss the words. "It'll be years before he realizes what he lost."

I pull back, surprised. Where is this intensity coming from? Is he drunk?

"But..." He grins, his expression smoothing back out. My eyebrows dip together from the sudden change in his mood.

Hell, am I drunk? "You don't know this about me, Chlo: I'm one hell of a dancer."

Easton snorts as Indy laughs.

But I remember the Valentine's Day dance freshman year and how it felt to be held by Austin. The slide of his hands, rough and large, over my hips. The strength of his body when it pressed into mine. The natural rhythm he didn't even have to try for as he guided me across the high school's gym floor.

"I remember," I say.

His expression softens. "I'm free for the weekend. And for the wedding in August."

"I didn't even tell you the date," I laugh.

He grins. "It doesn't matter. I'll make it work. No pity dates for you, Chlo."

I scrunch my nose at him, feeling all warm and gooey inside. "Thank you, Austin. Truly. But if you're serious, you should know what you're getting into. There's an entire weekend itinerary planned. For the engagement party *and* for the wedding."

He smirks. "Book us in. Steve's going to beg for you back and I'm going to take great pleasure in watching you kick him down. A man who would pull that shit with you doesn't deserve an ounce of your energy. Not a goddamn ounce." His tone holds a severity that surprises me and I nod slowly.

"Amen to that." Claire holds up her drink.

Noah gives me a searching look before flashing a quick grin. "You guys will have fun."

"Fun," I repeat, trying to remember the last time I felt even a flicker of hope for the future. This moment, I realize. I'm still dreading Marissa's engagement party but now, my dread is mingling with a thrill of excitement.

OVER THE NEXT HOUR, Indy grows tired and Noah decides they should head home. Easton and Claire aren't far behind them.

"Listen to that laughter," Austin comments when it's just the two of us by the firepit.

I glance in the direction of the house, where Mom's loud laughter followed by Joe's booming voice, floats out through the open windows.

"They're reminiscing," I realize, smiling at the happiness threaded through our parents' voices.

"Mom and Dad really missed your parents," Austin says.

"Same," I agree, recalling how hard it was for Mom to find her social footing without her bestie when we first moved to New York. "It's nice to be back. Even if it's just for the summer."

Austin nods, his eyes searching mine for a moment.

I take a small sip of my wine, positively tipsy now. I've drunk more tonight than I have in the past year. Not counting the night I walked in on Steve and Brittney and encouraged Abbi to feed me whiskey until I vomited in a parking lot facing the Manhattan skyline. It was a low point in my life for sure. An entire expanse of dreams just across the river that I distanced myself from in order to support Steve. My early years in the city, living in my tiny walkup in Brooklyn, drinking my morning tea in a park filled with sunshine and open space and a community flower bed, seemed like another life but one I gave up on way too quickly when I met Steve.

Was I just as happy in the beautiful condo in Hoboken? The one with the pot-filler faucet and wide-planked hardwood floors that Steve was too worried about scratching to properly enjoy?

I squint at the flames, my memories hazy. I think I was happier alone, in Brooklyn, with no financial security, than dealing with the heartache of Steve's betrayal in a luxury condo.

Austin clears his throat and I turn back toward him.

"You don't have to stay," I say, tilting my head toward his house. "I'm sure you have a lot to do tomorrow."

"They're going to be a while," Austin comments as another peal of laughter wraps around us.

"It's fine," I murmur, tipping my head back to look up at the stars.

The balmy night air wraps around me, transporting me to freshman year of high school and old thoughts, memories of before. Silence ensues but I feel Austin's eyes studying me.

"Want to play a board game?"

A slow smile spreads across my lips. "A game?" I don't know why the idea strikes me as funny. It's something Austin and I did a hundred times as kids. It's familiar and comfortable and…so not what I expected from him tonight. "Sure," I agree easily.

"Scrabble?"

"It's one of my favorites."

"I remember," he murmurs and my heart rate ticks up the tiniest bit. "Come on, we'll play in the den." Austin stands and pinches the rims of his beer and my wine glass together to hold them in one hand. He extends his other hand to me.

I place my hand in his, my heart rate beating even faster, when his fingers encircle mine. His grip is gentle but the heat of his palm seeps into mine and a shiver rushes through me.

"You cold?" He frowns.

"No, no, I'm fine," I rush to explain, feeling the heat in my cheeks. I drop my head, letting my hair fall forward.

But Austin wraps his arm over my shoulder and hugs me into his side as we make our way back to his parents' house.

I breathe in deep, holding in the scent of a new, even spicier cologne in my lungs. Austin Merrick is all man. For a second, Mimi flickers in my mind and I snort, hating that even this time, she might be right. I'm definitely not too heartbroken to notice Austin Merrick. I don't know if it's possible to *not* notice him.

"What are you laughing at?" he asks.

I shake my head. "Just thinking of Mimi."

"What about her?"

"I owe her a doughnut," I explain as we step inside. "You sure you want to play Scrabble?"

"Don't you?"

I nod. "It's just…"

"What?" He heads over to the built-in shelving unit next to the fireplace and reaches into a cabinet.

"I write crossword puzzles," I explain as I plop down next to the coffee table.

Austin turns, the Scrabble box in his hand. His brows are furrowed and his lips are pressed together like he's trying not to laugh. "What?"

"For a living," I say, peering up at him.

"Wait." He drops the box in the center of the table and sits down on the floor across from me. "Your job is to write crossword puzzles?"

I nod.

Austin bursts out laughing, tipping his head back. The sound is deep and genuine, rumbling from his chest and erupting into the air like confetti. Tiny sounds of pure amusement and delight.

I smile at his response. "Why is that so funny?"

"Jesus." He wipes the back of his hand over his eyes, as if wicking away a tear. "I missed you, Chloe. I missed you more than I ever realized." He chuckles again, his eyes dancing when they find mine. Slowly, his laughter dies down and he shakes his head. "I think you're the only person I know who could have that job and I'd believe them."

"I know." I wrinkle my nose, pleased that I managed to surprise him in some way. "It also means that I'm going to kick your ass at Scrabble."

Austin opens the box. I place errant tiles back in the bag as Austin unfolds the board.

"I have no doubt," he agrees. "How the hell did you find that job? Who do you write for?"

"*The Brooklyn Gazette.*"

"The newspaper?" He looks impressed.

"Yes. It sort of happened by accident." I hold out the bag and Austin chooses seven tiles. "One of my college professors recommended me for a contest and one thing led to another…"

"Wow."

"Funny how life happens, isn't it?" I shake out seven tiles and place them on my stand, rearranging the letters. "I never thought I'd still be writing crosswords. By now, I figured I'd be doing more investigative journalism but…" I shrug, not wanting to tell him that nearly two years ago, I turned down an opportunity to spend time in Nigeria to follow and report on Boko Haram attacks and expansion.

It was the type of opportunity I would have eagerly jumped on several years before but when Steve pleaded with me to stand by his side as he angled for a promotion, I chose to support his career over mine. It's a decision that still leaves a bitter taste in my mouth.

Austin looks up, studying me for a long beat. His eyes hold mine, as if trying to uncover all the words I didn't say. "Do you still want to? Do investigative journalism?"

I nod slowly. Since Steve's betrayal, the thought has crossed my mind several times. But what do I even say to my boss, Janie, when I turned down an amazing opportunity two years ago? Back then, I saw the flash of disappointment in her expression and it's bothered me ever since. I lick my lips and force a smile. "Two summers ago, I had the opportunity to travel to Nigeria, to write a piece for the paper on Boko Haram."

Austin's eyebrows bend together. "You didn't go?"

I shake my head, embarrassment flooding me. "Steve was up for a promotion and had a series of functions he wanted me to attend..."

An awkward silence settles between us as we both acknowledge how much I allowed Steve's life to outshine my own.

"It's not too late," Austin says finally. "If you still want to write articles, it's not too late. But seriously, I never met anyone who writes crossword puzzles."

I tip my head in his direction, appreciating the kind words and encouragement. "Yeah, well, you're the only NHL captain I know."

"You know other NHL players?" He narrows his eyes.

I snort. "The Scotch brothers. Your brother-in-law Mike."

Austin smirks. "Not counting them."

"No, there's no need to rub it in."

He chuckles.

"I was so happy when you guys won the Stanley Cup. Congratulations."

"Thanks," he says, glancing at the board. His eyes lose some of their light and his lips pinch together.

"What is it?" I ask.

Austin shakes his head and glances up. "Honestly? Now that we won, I'm worried for next season. How the hell do we measure up when..."

"When you've already attained the goal?"

He nods. "It seems harder now. Maintaining a winning streak is a whole different level than trying to prove ourselves, to claim the win." His eyes cloud over and for the second time, one of Mimi's observations flickers through my mind. *He always did carry the weight of the world on his shoulders.* I laughed it off then but maybe...maybe Mimi was right.

"I can't imagine the pressure you feel," I say, reaching across the coffee table to place my hand on his wrist. "But your winning the Cup wasn't a fluke, Austin. You led the team to a Cup win and you have all of them—Noah, Easton, your other teammates—behind you. You don't have to shoulder all of this alone."

His eyes snap up at my touch, boring into mine with a hint of vulnerability that causes my chest to tighten. He looks so lost, so concerned, that I want to reach across the table and hug him. The Austin I remember was pranks, good times, and flippant remarks. But the version he's showing me now is so much deeper than I ever gave him credit for. Shame fills the pit of my stomach and I tighten my hold on his wrist, wanting to press my apology, my understanding, into his skin.

"What if we lose?" he whispers. "What if I let everyone down?"

"Impossible."

He shakes his head. "It's not."

"It is," I counter. "You've already made so many people so proud, Aus. Hell, you've got the whole state of Massachusetts rooting for you. Don't hold yourself back for fear of failing but let all of the support propel you forward. Trust yourself. You've already proved you can do the impossible." I glance at the board before picking up my first tile. I feel Austin's gaze, intent, as I spell out my word.

Hurdle.

"The Austin Merrick I know never backs down from a challenge," I remind him.

"This seems like a hell of a lot more than a hurdle," he responds but some of the severity leaves his face.

"Yeah," I agree, liking the way he watches me, as if what I have to offer to this conversation matters. Maybe it does? "Because you haven't taken the first step yet. You still need to enjoy the win, savor the end of the season. Give yourself time to let loose and enjoy a few weeks before you start gearing up for next season. Austin, it's only been two weeks since you guys won."

"I know. It just feels like…"

"The pressure is already building?"

He nods, his expression wary, his eyes flaring.

"You need a vacation," I joke.

"Good thing I'm going to Martha's Vineyard with a beautiful girl next weekend," he shoots back.

I blush, rolling my eyes. "You really want to go?"

"Sure."

"As my date?" I press, feeling more out of my element now that Austin and I are alone, without Indy's observations and Claire's outrage.

Austin must hear something in my tone because he grips the letter he was about to place on the board and sits back instead. He studies me again, his gaze like a poke, trying to dig deeper.

"Yes," he says finally. Then, he spells out his word, using the u in *hurdle* to make *rule*.

I stare at his word. "Rule."

"Rule."

"We should make some."

"Huh?" He glances up.

"We need some ground rules," I elaborate.

He lifts an eyebrow, a wry smile twisting his lips. "Such as…"

"No kissing on the mouth," I blurt out. Immediately, my skin heats and flushes because—

"Who said there would be kissing?" His eyes are narrowed but I note the laughter in them. At least I amuse someone.

"I, well, you—" I sputter, at an absolute loss. Why the hell would I suggest something so asinine? Of course Austin isn't going to *kiss* me! Mimi's going to have a field day with this.

"Relax." He touches the back of my hand. "I'm messing with you. In order to make this believable, we'll definitely have to touch. I'll have to hold you. Occasionally kiss your cheek, or the top of your head, your shoulder. You know, we'll need to act…couple-y."

My throat tightens at his words. Kiss my shoulder? Austin is more romantic as a fake date than Steve was as a real fiancé. I clear my throat. "Couple-y?"

"I don't write crossword puzzles for a living."

I grin, feeling some of my embarrassment fade. "Fair enough."

"So, no kissing on the mouth. Anything else?"

"We dance at least three slow dances," I decide, knowing Steve will only dance one with Brittney. At least, he only ever used to dance one with me…

"No."

"What?" I look up sharply. "I thought you liked dancing. Two?"

Austin shakes his head. "No way. We dance every single dance we want to dance and everything by Ed Sheeran."

I laugh, the sound surprising me as it's loud and uninhibited. Sincere. The more time I spend at the Merricks', the more my past seeps back in. The more I feel like *myself* again. "Really?"

"Really."

"Okay," I agree.

"Anything else?"

I glance at the board before building off of hurdle's "e" to spell out *yes*.

"Yes?" Austin reads. "Are you answering my question with a Scrabble turn?"

I smile. "We say yes. When we want to say no, we say—"

"Yes." He grins. "To all the things?"

"To all the things."

Austin picks up his beer and I clink my wine glass against it.

"To Martha's Vineyard," I toast.

"Cheers, Chlo."

CHAPTER 4
CHLOE

"He's your date!" Mimi's eyes glitter like gemstones as she claps her hands together under her chin. For a whole breath, her doughnut, jelly-filled with powdered sugar, is forgotten.

"Is that insane?" I wrinkle my nose. My mom and Abbi thought the plan fabulous but they're also not as blunt as Mimi. I know she'll be straight with me.

"Insane?" She scoffs. "It's a lot less ridiculous than agreeing to Steve's marriage proposal."

Ouch. "Thanks, Mim."

She nods, my sarcasm flying over her sixties-style bouffant. "Now, what are you wearing?"

I grin at my fashion-loving grandma. "I don't know yet. Claire and Indy are taking me shopping."

"Wonderful!" She claps her hands. "They'll help you pick out something alluring, something daring."

"Daring?"

"You gotta show off the goods a bit, dear. Everyone knows that."

I laugh and shake my head. "You're too much, Mimi."

"Don't I know it," she agrees with gusto, picking her

doughnut back up. "Thank you for these, Chloe. I haven't had one since—"

"Dr. Stern advised you to cut back on sugar?"

"Your father takes everything that man says as Gospel."

"He's your doctor."

"Ach." She flicks a hand dismissively.

"Don't think this is going to become a habit." I point at her doughnut as I lift my coffee to my lips.

"If you're that serious, you shouldn't have brought a whole box," she accuses, peering inside said box.

"They're for company."

"Company? You're my favorite visitor."

I smile for real at the truth underlining her words.

"At least have one," she encourages, nudging the box closer.

I sigh and shake my head. "It's an engagement party on Martha's Vineyard."

"I'm familiar with the place."

"I'll be in a bathing suit."

"The beachgoers are going to be delighted when they see your curves instead of the emaciated look of recent years."

I roll my eyes. "Mimi."

"Eat a doughnut, Chloe. You need to start saying yes more."

I pause, the rule Austin and I made the other night blaring in my mind. While playing Scrabble (I won 427 to 280), we discussed how long it's been since we said yes to things just for the hell of it. Just because we wanted to.

When was the last time I ate a doughnut? With Steve, I always watched what I ate because I was always watching my figure. Those five, ahem ten, or more like fifteen pounds Steve used to criticize, melted away some through my recent heartache. But I've still got plenty of curves and dips, nothing that can be properly nipped and tucked in a bathing suit.

When did I start caring about that? When did I even start

noticing? Before Steve, I never had any qualms about my body. And when Austin looked at me the other night, I swear there was heat in his gaze. He clearly liked what he saw.

I drop my chin, letting my hair conceal my face as I blush. I squirm in my chair, recalling the flicker of desire in Austin's eyes. When he looked at me, I felt confident again. Strong. Maybe even a little bit sexy?

"Chloe?" Mimi asks, concerned.

"You know what, Mim? You're right."

"I usually am, dear."

I snag a doughnut, sinking my teeth into the frosting, decorated with colorful sprinkles. Oh shit, this is good. I groan. "This is delicious."

"That's the spirit!"

"Sprinkles are magical."

"Like unicorns." Mimi pats my hand.

"Missed you, Mim."

"You have no idea, Chlo. Now, a daring dress?" She lifts an eyebrow.

"And swimsuit," I declare.

Mimi claps again, her entire face transforming like I just informed her she got the last random item on the Home Shopping Network sale. "A two-piece?"

"A two-piece."

Mimi holds out her doughnut and I bump mine against it before taking another bite.

"I'm just so proud," Mimi murmurs and I grin.

Because so am I.

"THIS IS THE DRESS." Claire clasps her hands together

under her chin, her blue eyes, lighter than her brother's, sparkling.

"Yes! Definitely the winner," Indy agrees, sampling a macaron from the boutique we're shopping at on Newbury Street.

"Are you sure it's not too much?" I skim my palms along the emerald green lace. I know I told Mimi I was ready but right now, in front of the three-way mirror, some of my confidence slips. The nude sheath below the lace peeks through, giving the dress a hint of sexiness I'd usually shy away from. It's certainly *daring*.

"Not at all." Claire hands me a pair of strappy, nude heels, about two inches taller than anything I own.

"I'll break my neck in these."

Indy snorts and shakes her head. "You won't. Aus will hold you up."

"It's just for your entrance," Claire explains. "At some point, you can slip into sandals. Especially since the party is beach-y. But you need to pull out the big guns at the beginning."

"Which means, we need to bikini shop next," Indy says.

I stumble and Claire's hand darts out to steady me. "You literally look like you've seen a ghost," she murmurs.

"We need to discuss this…two-piece," I say slowly, mentally hung up on the word *bikini* which looks nothing like the safe, sensible, high-waisted two-piece I've come to terms with.

"Bikini," Claire corrects.

I cringe. Why the hell did I agree to saying yes and being daring and doing all of the things out of my comfort zone? Telling Mimi I'm ready is an entirely different thing than buying a *bikini*. It's so far out of my realm, it's not even in the Milky Way. My thoughts race and I press my fingers into my temples to slow them down.

What will Austin think when he sees *me*, curvy, soft,

nothing like the models he's often photographed with, in a bathing suit? My skin is pasty from winter and years of avoiding any type of beach, pool, or even here-are-some-shorts social settings.

I freeze, staring at myself in the reflection of the mirror. It dawns on me that my first thought was of Austin's reaction and *not* Steve's. I smile. That's progress, right?

"You can opt for a one-piece," Indy says reassuringly. "Although with your curves, I'd rock a bikini. Even with my massive belly. Cause no one would even get that low if I had a chest like yours."

My hands automatically slap over my breasts and Claire cracks up.

"Guys, wait," I murmur. "This is…a lot. I don't wear dresses like this and buy *two-pieces* and, and socialize with… with men who look like Austin."

Claire wrinkles her nose before pushing me down onto the couch placed in front of the dressing rooms.

Indy passes me a macaron, as if sensing my need to emotionally eat. I bite into it and moan as the strawberry filling bursts in my mouth.

"They're good, right?" Indy grins. "No one will even chastise us if we eat them all because I'm pregnant."

"Okay, tell us what's really going on," Claire demands. "You are a hot, intelligent, badass woman who can outsmart any man in any room you enter. Why are you tripping over wearing a dress that makes you look sexy as hell and buying a bathing suit when curves like yours are meant to be highlighted? They're like a homing beacon for men and a reminder to women everywhere just how hot a natural body is."

I blush at her praise. Indy nods encouragingly.

"Steve always said I needed to lose five," I flush, "ten," I cough, "fifteen pounds. And I have lost a few pounds since we broke up. But…I haven't been in a bathing suit since my senior year of college."

Claire balks and Indy's mouth drops open.

Claire's fuming. "That piece of—"

"Are you ladies doing okay?" the saleswoman interjects.

Claire turns and nods. "We're great, thanks. Do you have any swimwear?"

"Oh yes." The woman's eyes light up, knowing she's in for some serious commission.

"Can you please pull some options for our friend?" Indy places a hand on my shoulder.

"Toss in a bikini or two," Claire advises.

When the saleswoman disappears, Claire faces me again. Her eyes are brimming with indignation. "Chloe Crawford, I spent my childhood wanting to be you."

I gasp.

"Not me?" Indy asks.

Claire rolls her eyes. "You only made an appearance in summertime so your impression faded by winter."

"Gee, thanks," Indy snorts.

I smile at my old friends, enjoying their company. Being with them is natural, like picking back up where we left off even though it's been fifteen years and what feels like, a lifetime of milestones.

"This weekend, you're going to be the talk of the engagement party," Claire explains.

"But take care not to outshine the bride. No one likes that," Indy adds.

"True," Claire agrees. "I promise you, Chloe, Indy and I have your back. We aren't going to steer you wrong. And when Steve gets a look at you in that dress, he's not going to be able to tear his eyes away long enough to kick Brittney to the curb."

"Yes!" Indy claps her hands.

I grin and dip my chin, feeling a little less self-conscious now that I've admitted some of my insecurities aloud. Confiding in Mimi is one thing but chatting with peers about my body image concerns is something else entirely.

I know we're here to make sure Steve regrets his choices. For over two months, Steve's betrayal has been the one, consistent, thought in my mind. But when the saleswoman reappears with a handful of bathing suits, a new thought replaces Steve.

Austin.

What will Austin think when he sees me in this dress? In one of those bathing suits? Will his eyes gleam appreciatively? Will he look past the dimples on my thighs and the stretch marks on the backs of my arms?

Will he see past all the things Steve fixated on?

And why is his response so important to me?

When did this become more about Austin and less about Steve?

And when the hell did it stop being about *me*?

I stand up and give myself a long once-over in the mirror. The dress has a deep V in both the front and back, hugging my curves in all the right places. The color makes my eyes pop. I turn, checking out my backside. The dress dips low, showing off the expanse of my back and Claire's right, it looks great.

"I'll take this," I say to the saleswoman.

Indy beams as Claire passes her the nude heels. "And these."

Indy flips through the bathing suits and presses a few into my hands. "We'll get back to you about these," she adds.

The saleswoman smiles graciously and scurries away as my friends push me back into the dressing room.

For the first time in what feels like months, I laugh as I shimmy out of a beautiful dress. I hold up a bright, fire-engine red swimsuit with a plunging neckline and ruffles that will definitely draw attention to my breasts. Taking a deep breath I step into it and work it up my legs, over my hips, until I can slip my arms through the straps and straighten it.

And damn. My mouth pops open. Because I look good. Better than good. Turning in the mirror, I note that I've lost more than a few pounds since Steve and I broke up, but it's more than that. I look healthy and…happy.

"Girls." I push open the curtain and step out. "What do you think?"

Indy's eyes widen as Claire shoots up from her seat. "We'll take this one too!"

The three of us burst into laughter and it feels good, to be surrounded by true friends, to push Steve's negative comments out of my head, and to admit that I'm looking forward to this weekend much more than I thought I would.

CHAPTER 5
AUSTIN

"You sure about this, man?" Easton asks over my Bluetooth as I pull onto the highway, in the direction of Chloe's house.

"Yeah, what do you mean?"

"You're going to an engagement party, with a woman you have a past with, to piss off her ex-fiancé." Easton spells it out slowly.

I glance in my side mirror before switching lanes. "East, Chlo's one of my oldest friends. She's not 'a woman I have a past with.' She's just…Chloe."

Easton chuckles. "Whatever you say, Aus. Call me if you need to be bailed out of jail."

I laugh, shaking my head. "I'm not going to fight Steve."

"You may if he puts his hands on her."

My grip on the steering wheel tightens and my teeth click together. I take a moment to consider my words and Easton's irritating chuckle irks me. "Stop. That's not going to happen." I sound more like I'm trying to convince myself.

"I don't know, Aus. I still remember you from high school. So does Chloe. And in high school, you were a hell of a lot more hot-tempered. Back then, we were troublemakers."

"I've grown up," I remind him, recalling all the stupid stunts I pulled in high school. There was the time I convinced the hockey team to cover all the hallway floors in bubble wrap, creating chaos as several hundred students swarmed the corridors after homeroom. And another incident involving tinfoil, confetti, balloons, and the coach's office. I snort, recalling my high school coach's surprised expression before he cracked and laughed. But there were also a handful of locker room pranks that went awry and ended with me coming to blows with hockey players from rival teams.

In hindsight, I'm lucky I never got slapped with so much as a detention for some of the pranks I pulled off, even though they were mostly harmless. But I don't do stupid shit like that anymore. Not as team captain and certainly not when I'm looking out for one of my childhood friends. "Look, Chloe's a great girl. I've known her my entire life. Of course I stepped in to help her out, but things aren't like that between us. Wouldn't you do the same if my sister had asked you a few years ago?"

Now Easton's laughter is full blown and I frown at the speakers.

"Yeah, man," he finally guffaws. "That's what I'm saying. I would have jumped at the chance to be alone for the weekend with Claire, my best friend's little sister, while swearing to everyone that it meant nothing. Now look, we're living together and I gotta go because your sister is baking brownies."

I groan at Easton's point and disconnect the call, but not quickly enough because his laughter rings through. Blowing out a sigh, I take the exit ramp. Ever since last weekend, my entire family has been giving me knowing glances whenever Chloe's name is brought up. Even Savannah asked about her when she called Mom and Dad's and I picked up the phone. They're all driving me nuts, acting like I'm doing something so out of character by agreeing to be Chloe's date. Which is crazy, and frankly, insulting, because I'm a nice guy who would help out any of my friends if they needed me. Right?

I helped get East into rehab. I helped Indy move into her tenement apartment. I helped Noah sell his house when he didn't marry his ex-fiancée, Courtney. I helped James after Layla passed…

I frown. Other than my cousin and sisters, do I hang out with any women I'm not hooking up with? The realization slams into me as I stop at a red light. I have no female friends.

None.

There're only four categories. Women I've hooked up with. Women I want to hook up with. Women who don't register on my radar. And the women in my family who I'd do anything for.

And Chloe. Chloe is the fifth category because she doesn't fit into any of the others. I mean, she kind of fits into women I want to hook up with because how could any red-blooded male look at Chloe and not want to hook up with her? And she kind of fits into the women of my family because I'd do anything for her. But I still want to kiss her and…

I shake my head. I'm going to junk punch Easton for filling my mind with these dumb thoughts and ideas moments before I see Chloe. There's nothing between us. We're childhood friends. That's it. And isn't it nice that I have one childhood, female friend? That after all these years, I didn't fuck everything up between us by pranking her or sleeping with her and never calling?

I turn onto the Crawfords' street.

This weekend is going to be fun. Chloe and I will reminisce about old times. We'll hang out and piss off her short-sighted ex-fiancé. But I'm not taking her to a party to cause trouble, or start something between us, or do anything other than what she needs in this moment. To help her save face.

I pull up to the Crawfords' house and all the thoughts swirling in my mind still. Because Chloe is already standing out front, lifting her hand in greeting, a smile stretching across her face, looking like the most breathtaking woman I've ever laid eyes on.

How does she do that? Look so effortless all the time while still looking perfect.

Does she always smile so brightly? At everyone?

I heave out a sigh. Easton sucks.

I step out of the car and wave to Chloe. "You that eager to get on the road?" I gesture to the small rolling suitcase beside her and the garment bag draped over her arm.

She glances over her shoulder and then bounds down the porch steps, her suitcase banging behind her. "We need to get out of here before Mom gets off the phone with Mimi."

"That so?" I ask, amused. The Crawfords and my family have been friends for a long time. So long, that I forgot they are the only family I know as batshit crazy as my own.

Chloe nods, turning to look at the house again. "Yes. Otherwise, Mom will make you come inside and insist on feeding us lunch. She will grill you for a solid hour about your dating life, maybe sprinkle one or two hockey questions in there to be polite—"

I laugh.

"And field several phone calls that will all be Mimi, adding her own questions to the list. By the time they're done, Dad will be coming in and then you'll go through the whole ordeal again, but this time it will be all hockey questions with one or two general wellness ones to appease Mom."

I grin at Chloe, noting the color in her cheeks, the amusement mixed with a dash of worry, in her eyes.

"So we make a run for it?" I surmise.

"We make a run for it."

I grab the handle of her suitcase and her garment bag, and pop the trunk of my SUV. While I stow her belongings next to mine, she slips into the passenger seat. The front curtains shift as I slide into the driver's seat.

"Quick! She's spotted us," Chloe orders, looking straight head.

I snort, glancing at the house. "Are you sure you—"

"Drive!" Chloe's hand darts out to cover mine on the steering wheel. "Go!"

The front door swings open just as I flip the ignition.

"Chloe!" Diane waves as we pull away.

I glance at her in my rearview mirror, grinning as Diane's expression collapses in laughter.

A second later, Chloe's phone rings and she groans.

"Mama?" she answers. "Yes, yes I know. No, it's not that. It's just, we want to beat the weekend traffic. Be on the road by two. Of course. I know." She giggles and glances at me. "Yes, I'll tell him. Okay. Love you too. 'Bye."

She hangs up and leans back in the seat.

"How's Diane?" I ask, biting my cheek to keep from cracking up. It's so silly, really. But sneaking away without saying goodbye to Diane is something Chloe and I did a thousand times, what feels like a thousand years ago. We were always taking off on our moms. Now, I'd never think to do something like that. Unless I'm with Chlo, apparently.

"She wants me to remind you that we only drink sophisticated cocktails this weekend, that I'm partial to lobster, not shrimp, and that if you pulverize Steve and need to be bailed out, Dad's happy to pay the fee."

I toss my head back and laugh as I pull back onto the highway. "Easton said the same thing. I don't know why everyone thinks I'm going to get in a fight."

"High school." Chloe shrugs.

"Did I really fight that much?" I glance at her. I remember being rowdy in high school, but not wild.

She bites her bottom lip and I can't help but notice the flush that works over her face. "No," she says finally. "You fought when you felt you needed to and I always thought your reasoning was sound."

"Thank you."

"But it was more often than anyone else on your team. Or in our entire school," she admits and we both laugh.

"So, your Mom really wants us to stick it to Steve, huh?"

"Ugh," Chloe groans, shifting in her seat. "Mom was never Steve's biggest fan and all of this, with the engagement and Brittney, really drove the point home. I know Mom's reacting the way she is because she hates to see me hurting… but she even called up his mother."

"No," I gasp, looking at Chloe who sinks down in her seat.

"Oh yeah."

"Damn. My respect for Diane just multiplied."

"Don't encourage her bad behavior when you see her."

"How'd that conversation go?" I ask, wondering how Chloe's been managing the fallout of her engagement.

She rolls her eyes and tucks her feet beneath her. "About as well as you'd expect. Mom went on about how careless and hurtful Steve treated me and Steve's mom lashed out, saying I clearly wasn't the right girl for her son." She scrubs her hand over her face and glances out the window. "I know her heart was in the right place but it made everything even more…humiliating."

"She's just looking out." I reach over to squeeze Chloe's arm. "It's what family does."

"Yeah, I know." She shifts again, toward me this time, her elbow landing on the center console. "And how's your family been looking out?" Chloe gives me a knowing glance.

I know she's reaching for a lighter topic of conversation so I play along and groan out, "Don't even get me started. It's like my whole family's mission is to set me up."

"Tell me about it."

"Mom *surprised* me for breakfast last month, right in the middle of Cup Finals, and pretended to be utterly shocked when she found a woman with me. Then, she invited her to breakfast with us so they could 'get to know each other.'"

"No!" Chloe's mouth drops open. "Oh my God, Aus." She laughs loudly.

I grin at her, loving how uninhibited her laughter is. She snorts, clapping a hand over her mouth and I chuckle.

"What did the girl say?" Chloe asks.

"It was the most uncomfortable morning-after breakfast ever. Mainly because there shouldn't have been a breakfast at all."

She shakes her head, the dimple in her left cheek making an appearance. "That's rough. If it makes you feel better, the week after Steve and I called it quits, Mom tried to set me up with her tennis coach."

"She was obvious about it, wasn't she?"

"She told him I like to wear short skirts, even when I'm not playing tennis."

"Oh shit. Diane may give Mary a run for her money." I slide my hand over the top of the steering wheel. "They're two peas in a pod."

"It's bound to get worse now that they're together again. They'll be encouraging each other's scheming ways."

"Shit," I say again, realizing Chloe's right. "We're in for it this summer then."

"I know." Chloe tucks her feet back up again and sighs. She plugs her phone into my USB cord and flips through it, looking for a playlist. "I have my cousin Sara's wedding next month too." She glances at me. "My family I can handle but I'm relieved you're coming to Marissa and Adam's wedding."

"Don't mention it. I have a gala in September that Mom's already started asking details about."

Chloe glances up at me. "What kind of gala?"

"It's for hockey. I'm…" I trail off, shooting her a sheepish grin.

She lifts her eyebrows, waiting for me to continue.

"I'm receiving an award," I admit, feeling silly.

Chloe's expression brightens and she squeezes my bicep. "Really? Congratulations, Aus. What's it for?"

"Some programs I sponsor for kids in the community. It's not a big deal."

Something shifts in Chloe's expression but I turn my eyes back to the road before I read into it. "Don't tell Mary that," she jokes.

"Exactly."

"Well, I think it's pretty incredible. Congrats."

I tip my head in thanks. We sit in silence for a few minutes and I can't help but turn some ideas over in my mind.

Here we are, Chloe and me. I've seen her once or twice in fifteen years and yet, right now, it's like no time has passed at all. Things are natural, easy between us. They always have been. What if she didn't have to find a date to her cousin's wedding? And what if I didn't have to ward off Mom's attempts at setting me up for the next few months? What if Chloe and I went to our summer events together? Our parents would be over the moon, our mothers would certainly rein in their matchmaking attempts. I'm certain I'd have a much better time with Chloe than I would forcing small talk with women I'm not interested in but obliged to see because my mom made some ridiculous promise to their mothers.

"Chlo?" I turn toward her.

"Hmm?" She glances up from her phone.

"What if we do each other's summer events? I'll go to the weddings with you and you come to the gala with me and—"

"Our moms stop setting us up with strangers?" She catches on fast.

"Exactly. We just…" I pause, meeting her eyes. "Keep it casual. Fun."

"Yes! Oh God, Austin, that would be ideal. Are you sure, though? Because I have a lot more events. Two weddings," she reminds me, holding up two fingers. "And Marissa's is in New York."

"That's fine." I wave a hand. "I love New York. I'll get to see Vanny and Mike."

"That's right! I wish I had seen Savannah more but we only managed a few lunches this past year."

"So, you're in?" I ask.

"I'm totally in," she agrees enthusiastically, relief rippling over her expression. "Now, how do you feel about this?" She presses a button on her phone and the opening of Chingy's "Right Thurr" floods the speakers.

"Oh shit." I shake my head, recalling our freshman Valentine's Day dance. "Do you remember when Frankie Morello tried to do the worm to this—"

"And chipped his front tooth?" Chloe laughs. "Yes. What about when Mason—"

"Kinner," I snarl.

"He wasn't that bad. He spiked the punch."

"He was always trying to get in your pants," I tell her, switching lanes.

She tosses her head back and laughs. "Right, because all of the girls following your every move had the purest of intentions."

"I never looked at anyone twice."

Chloe lifts an eyebrow.

"What? I was all about hockey in high school," I say, defensively.

"That's not what I heard."

"What'd you hear?" I glance over at her.

"Oh, so many things, Austin Merrick. You were the talk of the girls' bathroom."

I groan, imagining how many rumors were started in those stalls.

"None of it's true," I joke, holding up a hand.

"None of it?" Chloe raises an eyebrow in challenge, a smirk on her lips.

For a second, the air in the car intensifies and I desperately want to know the thoughts running in her mind to make her eyes darken like that. From sage to hunter green.

But then she laughs and I grin and the tension breaks over us like a wave. Chloe's laughter is infectious and I can't help but join in as we both start dancing to Chingy, Chloe the same way she did in high school.

Lamely. With absolutely zero rhythm.

It's more endearing than it should be.

CHAPTER 6
CHLOE

The summer breeze whips through the cracked windows as Austin and I drive to Martha's Vineyard. It's just after five when we pull into the hotel parking lot and I take a deep breath to settle my nerves.

"You okay?" Austin turns off his SUV.

I nod, biting my lip. The hotel is warm and inviting, with a wraparound porch and large windows. It's perched right on the beach and styled simply, in an understated manner that hints at old money. I glimpse the ocean and my childhood comes rushing back. The walks along the beach Mimi and I used to take, searching for seashells and sea glass and treasure.

I was so excited about Marissa's engagement party because I wanted to share this part of my childhood with Steve. I wanted to hold his hand and walk down the beach and point out parts of my past that I still cling to because memories made with Mimi are still my favorite. An ache throbs, deep in my chest, and I press my fingertips to the center of my breastbone. What was I even thinking? When has Steve ever shown the slightest interest in my family?

"Chloe?" Austin's voice is low beside me.

I turn toward him just as he clasps my wrist, his hand strong and steady. His skin is warm and his touch sends a zing up my arm.

I meet his gaze and pull in an inhale, trying to force my thoughts in a new direction. One that isn't centered on everything I think I lost but on the future. The one that is supposed to be brimming with new opportunities and endless possibilities.

My eyes fill with tears instead and I drop my head, mortified. Why am I acting like this? Steve and I are over. I wouldn't take him back now if he begged me and yet…

"Tell me what's wrong, Sunshine," Austin murmurs, tossing out my childhood nickname.

I half snort, half laugh, my emotions surging at the familiarity of it. "No one has called me that in years."

"No one has known you as long as I have."

I look up again, falling headfirst into Austin's blue eyes, as deep and dangerous as an iceberg.

"Tell me," he prods.

I release a shaky exhale. "Sometimes, I don't know if I'm mourning the end of Steve and me, or the death of the future I imagined for us. What's even worse is I think I'm having a harder time moving past the *idea* of him. The concept of having a person to share my past and future with and knowing, really *knowing*, that they'll be there for it all. Not just because they have to be but because they truly want to be. For *me*." My fingertips dig into my chest again, as if to alleviate some of the hurt building there. "Isn't that awful?" I whisper.

Compassion blazes across Austin's expression as a tenderness I've never witnessed him wear flares in his eyes. The corner of his mouth turns up in a wry grin and he leans closer, tucking my hair behind my ear. I hold his gaze as his fingers brush along my jaw, stopping to grasp my chin. He angles my face toward his and shakes his head. "It's not awful that you're human, Chlo. We all want to find that person, the one we can trust with everything, the one we can rely on, the one that we know has our backs. There's nothing bad about that."

"But I don't think Steve was that guy," I murmur, my chest squeezing painfully.

"Then isn't it good you didn't marry him?" Austin's brows bend and I know I'm confusing the hell out of him.

I'm confusing myself but—"This weekend, I was so excited to walk down the beach with him. To hold his hand. To just be with him and show him all the places Mimi used to take me."

"I forgot you used to spend a few weeks here every summer."

"Yeah. I thought Steve would understand more about me, about my wanting to see my family as much as I do, if he could experience some of my childhood." I wrinkle my nose. "It's so dumb that this is why I'm upset right now, isn't it? It's silly to be upset over something that never even happened."

"No," Austin says, his thumb swiping down the center of my chin. "It's not. You wanted to share your childhood with him and you wanted him to understand just how much this place means to you, how special your time with Mimi is to you."

I nod, relieved that he understands what I mean even though I'm having a difficult time explaining it.

"So show me," he continues and I rear back, surprised. But Austin's hand holding my wrist tugs me closer. "Who better to share your childhood memories with than the guy who was there for most of them? We'll visit all your old stomping grounds with Mimi this weekend. Hell, I can prob-ably even remember a few from that trip our families took together. I promise, Chlo, we're going to have fun. Not to hurt your feelings, but I can pretty much guarantee that you'll have a better time with me than you would have with Steve anyway."

I let out a small laugh, missing the earnestness with which Austin navigates life. Steve was always overly confident and sometimes, downright pompous. But Austin's always been so…genuine. Real. "Thank you for coming with me, Austin."

He moves closer and drops a quick kiss to my cheek. "Don't mention it again, Chlo." He pulls back and opens the driver's side door. Glancing at me over his shoulder he says, "Now, dry your eyes and let's get going before I blast some throwbacks and dance right here to make you cry from laughter."

I laugh and he smiles.

"You know I'll do it, Chlo."

"I know." That's the thing about Austin. He doesn't embarrass easily and he'll do pretty much anything to cheer someone else up. Between Savannah, Claire, Indy, and me, he's had a lot of practice pulling mopey, emotional girls back into reality.

I step out of the car, pausing as the breeze kicks up and wraps around me. I drink in the beautiful expanse of endless blue sky and breathe in the salty air of the sea.

Austin plops our suitcases at our feet, drapes my garment bag on top, and slips his arm around my shoulders. I look up at him, noting the amusement and understanding in his eyes.

"I'm ready for some fun, Aus," I say and this time, I mean it. I *need* it.

"Then let's kick this weekend off with some drinks, Sunshine." He holds me close for one blink before grabbing the handles of our suitcases and striding toward the hotel like a man on a mission.

I scurry beside him.

Right before we enter the hotel, Austin turns to me and winks. "I got your back, Chlo. Always. And I'm here because I want to be. For you."

A hotel staff pulls the door open for us and I step into the lobby beside Austin. My heart is still stuttering from his words, from the look in his eyes when he said them, but it pretty much stops as we enter the lobby and a silence falls.

I note members of the bridal party and wedding guests, family members of Marissa's, milling about and checking in. I spot the beautiful bride and the groom, Adam's mouth hanging open as he stares at Austin.

Whispers and gasps swarm through the lobby.

"Holy shit, is that Austin Merrick?"

"He's the captain of the Hawks."

"He just won the Cup."

Austin ducks his head, I snicker, and then we both burst into laughter.

"I'm tossing your name around alllllll weekend," I tell him.

Color works its way over his cheeks but he winks and this time, I think my heart skips a whole beat.

THE HOTEL BAR is filled with patrons, mostly wedding guests, grabbing a pre-dinner drink and catching up before this evening's festivities kick off. A man squeezes next to me, trying to grab the bartender's attention, and I shift closer to Austin, wishing we snagged barstools. I'm about to ask him if he sees any empty seats when the air shifts.

It tightens with a tension that causes the back of my neck to tingle. I draw in a breath and hold it, my limbs locking down. I don't want to turn around to confirm that Steve and Brittney just entered the bar but part of me is desperate to see if it's really them.

The looks in my direction, the whispers that ripple down the bar, teeming with wedding guests, is confirmation enough.

"He's here," Austin murmurs, lifting his Negroni to his lips and taking a sip. His eyes harden and narrow as he glares at the man I almost married. "Relax, Sunshine." Austin places his glass down on the bar and leans closer to me, his hand landing on my thigh. "Look at me."

I meet his gaze. His eyes are warm, filled with an understanding that settles my nerves. His touch on my leg comforts me, grounding me in this moment. I exhale slowly and Austin smirks, shooting me one of his knowing grins that affects me, the same way it did in high school.

"We got this," he declares before picking his glass back up and draining it. His fingertips brush back and forth over the material of my summer dress, little reassurances that I'm not doing this alone. We're going to face Steve as a team and then, the moment I've been dreading, will be over and I'll get to enjoy the rest of my weekend with Austin.

I can do this. I'm ready to—

"Chloe," Steve's voice interrupts my silent pep talk and I turn, glancing at him over my shoulder.

Brittney is at his side, her hand clutched in his. She gives me a tight, nervous smile, her eyes begging me not to make a scene.

As if that's ever been my style. I'm not the scene-making type of girl. I'm more of a hide-in-a-closet-and-sob kind of chick. But not today. Right now, I'm a confident, bold woman laughing at a bar with the sexy guy who took Boston to a Cup win. That girl doesn't slink away and cry. That girl smiles nonchalantly and says, "Oh, hi, Steve. Brittney."

Steve clears his throat, his gaze darting from mine to Austin and back again.

Brittney shamelessly stares at my date. I tamp down the swirl of anger building in my chest. She's not worth it. He's not worth it. Plus, it's Marissa's wedding weekend and our happiness for her and Adam needs to be stronger than my desire to smack those googly eyes off of Brittney's face.

Austin shifts his weight, angling closer to me, as he sticks out a hand. "How's it going, man?"

Steve's posture straightens as his gaze drops to Austin's hand. I can tell it's killing him to shake it but he does so, his mouth thinning into a line. "Austin, right?"

"That's right," Austin says easily. "Can we get you a round?"

"Oh," Brittney gasps, "I'll have—"

"We're fine, thanks." Steve cuts her off and I dip my head to hide the giggle that bubbles to my lips.

Instead, I pick up my old-fashioned and take a long drink.

"How are you?" Steve asks me, his hand lifting to my shoulder before he thinks better of it and lets it fall back to his side.

"Good, you?" I respond breezily. See, I can do this? I *am* doing this.

Steve dips his chin, lowering his voice. "I wasn't sure if you'd come on your own but..." He turns back toward Austin. "It was nice of you to step in this weekend so Chlo didn't have to come solo. I know this can be a lot," he says contritely, gesturing to the wedding guests aka, bar patrons, watching this showdown like prime-time TV.

Austin shakes his head, that winning smile that appeared on magazines across the country, flashing. "Nah, man. I didn't step in for anything. You did me a solid, dude. I should probably thank you." He chuckles, raising his glass to his lips.

I swivel toward Austin, not missing the open mouths of two of Marissa's bridesmaids. Her cousins, I think.

"Thank him?" I repeat, wondering what the hell is happening. I know Austin and I were going to make this look *couple-y*, but we never talked about the lengths we were willing to go to make things believable.

Austin's hand slides from my thigh to my hip. He pinches my side affectionately and I hear Steve grunt at the gesture.

"Yeah, Sunshine—" My childhood nickname, affectionately used by my dad before catching on with the Merricks, rolls off his tongue effortlessly. Except right now, it sounds like a sweet term of endearment and at Steve's pinched lips, I'm beyond grateful. "If Steve didn't fuck himself over, we never would have had the chance to reconnect."

"Reconnect?" Steve repeats, his tone irritated.

Austin calmly takes a swig of his fresh Negroni and nods. "Everyone who knows me knows I've always had a thing for Chlo. Stars finally aligned. I'm in Boston all summer, she came back to the city with her family, and we were able to catch up. The second I heard about the party this weekend, in Martha's Vineyard, where Chlo used to spend her summers with Mimi"—Austin whistles—"no way was I missing the opportunity to spend a weekend with my girl in one of her favorite places." His eyes hold mine as he tucks a piece of hair behind my ear. He grins, slow and lazy, letting it spread across his face like he can't help himself.

I smile back, loving that he's playing this role so well. Loving that he's helping me find my footing in Steve's presence when the thought of seeing him again filled me with such anguish.

I wrinkle my nose. *What are you doing?*

Austin's grin grows larger. *Go with it.*

We have an entire conversation through our eyes and after a moment, I chuckle and pick my drink back up.

"Um, we should say hi to Marissa and Adam," Brittney says awkwardly, shifting her weight from one foot to the other. She looks between the little huddle with confusion etched into the lines of her face. But Steve, Steve looks furious. Patches of red crawl up his neck and his hands curl into fists and I have the sudden image of a toddler about to stomp his foot and throw a hissy fit because he didn't get his way.

"Steve," Brittney repeats.

Steve nods but doesn't tear his eyes away from where Austin's hand is resting on my hip. Austin slips his hand higher and Steve flinches. I inch closer to Austin, who has touched me throughout this entire exchange. Regardless of the motivation behind his hand on me, I don't want him to remove it. I like his touch, his warmth, the ease that washes over me in his presence.

Brittney tugs Steve toward the bride and groom.

"We'll see you around," I say, keeping my gaze focused on Austin.

Austin rolls his lips together to hold back his laughter.

Steve and Brittney relocate to a small high-top table where one of Adam's friends welcomes them. But I don't turn to look because right now, I don't care. Austin's grin, the glint in his eyes, the focus with which his gaze scans my face, is a stronger pull.

With Austin's eyes on me, I feel *it* again. The spark, the zing, the understated confidence of being desired. Desirable. It fills me up with a self-assuredness I've been lacking for too long. I'm not a role in Steve's life but the star of my own. I smile back at Austin, realizing that I'm ready to start *living* it.

CHAPTER 7
AUSTIN

"**F**orget hockey. You should have gone into acting," Chloe mutters, her green eyes slamming into mine, hijacking my thoughts.

Because a second ago, I was cursing myself out for being so reckless. For spinning a lie that has the potential to get out and spread, grow into a rumor. I was wondering if I pushed too hard and if Chloe was frustrated with me for insinuating that we always had a thing between us.

But now, right now, with her eyes shimmering with gratitude and the apples of her cheeks coated in the softest pink, I can only think about what a douchebag Steve is.

"I'm happy you didn't marry him," I say instead, meaning it.

"Thank you for that. You were...you didn't have to do that."

"He never deserved you," I say instead.

Chloe wrinkles her nose and nudges one of the shot glasses she ordered closer to me.

I pick it up and hold it toward her. "What are we drinking to, Chlo?"

"To saying yes."

I clink my glass against hers and toss back the chilled vodka. "Lemon drop?"

She shrugs. "It's a good starter."

"Starter? How many shots are we taking tonight?"

Chloe shrugs again, twirling a strand of hair around her finger. "Night's young, Aus. We haven't even started the evening itinerary."

I snicker. "You're a troublemaker, Chloe Crawford."

Her mouth drops open in protest. "Me? I create crossword puzzles, Austin. I'm a rule follower. You're the one icing perfectly pleasant players and—"

"Perfectly pleasant?"

She smirks. "The Charles Crows."

This time, my mouth falls open. "Are you kidding me?" I snort, amazed she remembered who our high school played in the finals my freshman year. And impressed. More impressed than I want to be. "How do you even remember that?"

"You practically took out their center!" she accuses, gesturing toward me. "How could I forget it?"

There's laughter in her tone but at the reminder of how damn reckless I used to be, I still. She's right, of course. I did almost take out their center. Why? Over some cheap shot and smack talk? Another memory, one with a hell of a lot worse consequences, rolls over me and I shudder.

"Hey." Chloe's laughter dies and she reaches out, touching my forearm. "I'm just messing with you, Austin." She frowns, her brows pulling together in a line I want to smooth out. Because she shouldn't feel bad about bringing up all my past stupid mistakes.

Is it better to be with someone who already knows all your fuckups but also the challenges you overcame? Or is it better to start fresh, to have a clean slate to keep pristine or fuck up whatever way you see fit?

I shake the thoughts away. Who the hell even cares? This

thing, this summer, between Chloe and me, is just that. A fun summer to keep our scheming mothers at bay while having a few laughs at our social obligations.

"Austin?"

I force a grin. "I know."

"Nope." She shakes her head.

"Nope what?"

"You're not getting off that easy. There's no way in hell you would react like, like that"—she gestures at me—"over some high school hockey game when you were a *freshman*."

I gesture to the bartender that we'll take another round.

"That bad, huh?" Chloe comments, pursing her lips.

"What are you talking about?" I chuckle, shifting my weight toward the bar.

She shakes her head again, her touch on my arm morphing into a grasp.

I glance down at where she's holding me. Her fingernails are manicured, short, neat, and polished a neutral beige. She squeezes my arm and I meet her gaze again.

"What happened?" she murmurs, her voice softer this time. There's empathy in her eyes that lures me closer.

Because it's genuine.

A lot of women have looked at me with bedroom eyes. Irises colored with hope, edged out with just a glint of ruthlessness. It's the glint that's always held me back. The knowledge that deep down, they want me for the status, for the title, for what I am more than *who* I am.

Most women would sell my secret to the highest bidder for a payday. Not that my secret is a secret. The game that landed Sammy Snell in the hospital is public knowledge. Worse, it wasn't by my hands but by my goddamn stupidity.

Chloe angles her head, waiting for me to respond. Her gaze is patient, caring. Not urgent and curious.

"It's not worth getting into right now. Honest," I say, dipping my head. I don't want to talk about that night, about college, about letting so many people down. Not when my thoughts are already twisted up about this season. Not when I'm sitting next to Chloe, enjoying being with her. "Besides, we're on our trial run."

"Trial run?"

I nod. "Gotta practice for all our social events. Especially if we're to be the talk of the season."

Chloe snickers. "Talk of the season? You watched *Bridgerton*, didn't you?"

I groan, hating that she already called me out. "I have two sisters and a cousin who might as well be my third."

"You live alone!"

I snort and hold my hands up in surrender. "Fine. I watched *Bridgerton*. But so did Easton and Noah."

Chloe laughs harder, shaking her head at me. "That's even worse. You're not supposed to give your friends up like that."

"Hey! I thought I can trust you."

She nods, her cheeks ruddy. "You can," she swears, crossing her heart like the nine-year-old girl with pigtails and gap teeth I still remember.

I grasp her finger and tug her flush against my chest. She comes easily, falling into my arms like it's something she does every day. Any lingering doubts or awkwardness between us has dissipated. Chloe and I have fallen into old habits effortlessly, like no time has passed at all.

And I like it. I like being with her, laughing and joking.

I like how easily she pulls me into the now, keeps me rooted in the present, when I have a habit of getting hung up on the past or worrying about the future.

I notice the glances in our direction. I spot the narrowed eyes on our embrace, the whispers behind cupped hands. The attention we're garnering speaks to the white lie I created.

I should shut it down. Right now, I should back away, create some distance between Chloe and me. Let people suspect things between us without really *knowing*. But I don't want to. For the first time in years, I don't do the right thing. The noble thing.

Instead, I tip my head in the direction of the nosy, desperate-for-gossip bar patrons. "Want to make this real?"

She shakes her head, confused. "Make what real?"

"Our blossoming relationship, of course."

Her eyes widen and she gasps.

I drop my head the tiniest bit, lifting my hand to cup her cheek. The couple on the other side of Chloe abruptly end their conversation. Necks swing in our directions, eyes wide and waiting.

Chloe blushes furiously, her tongue darting out, swiping across her lower lip. And Christ if I don't want to lean down and pull it in between my teeth, nip once before kissing the sting away.

"What do you have in mind?" she whispers, her voice throaty.

Sexy.

So different than the Chloe I know and yet, so fitting.

My other hand settles on her hip, resting there. I like the feel of her curves under my palm. I like the heat of her skin. I especially like the uptick in her breathing. I affect Chloe Crawford which is somewhat of a relief considering she sure as hell affects me. Not that it will ever come to anything but right now, I cling to the trust in Chloe's eyes, knowing mine mirror the sentiment. Yeah, we can do this for a summer. We're already doing it.

"Take a walk on the beach with me, Sunshine?"

She blinks once, a little dazed. Slowly, she nods and I grin. I pull out my wallet to toss down some bills. Chloe threads her fingers with mine as I lead her toward the side entrance, where the salty air and whispering waves beckon.

I feel eyes in between my shoulder blades, attention prickling the back of my neck. I squeeze Chloe's hand and she smiles up at me, sweet and knowing and beautiful.

We push outside and her smile turns into uninhibited laughter.

"Oh my God, Austin Merrick." She twirls toward me, dropping my hand and walking backwards toward the stretch of sea. "You are a natural."

"A natural?" I repeat, trying to hold back my grin. Why the hell am I smiling so much anyway?

She nods. "You sold that better than I could have hoped." She gestures toward the hotel.

"You did pretty good yourself, Ms. Crawford."

She grins, her dimple flashing. "What do you want to do? We have…" She pauses to check her watch. "About an hour before dinner starts."

I shrug, toeing off my shoes. The cool sand rises between my toes. I breathe in the heavy air and slowly exhale. "I can't remember the last time I was at the beach."

"Seriously?"

"Not like this. I may have driven past beaches during away games but not just on my own. Not when it's been quiet and dark and just…"

"A place for reflection?" Chloe guesses, reading my mind.
I nod.

She steps closer, her fingers threading with mine again. "You got a lot going on up there, Austin."

"Thought I was just some dumb jock?" I tease.

She snorts. "Please. I've always known you've been more than just hockey."

"What do you mean?" I'm curious to know what she thinks about me. Especially now. After all these years. How have I changed? For the better? Worse?

"You've always cared so much about your team, way beyond how team dynamics affect a game or a season. You've always cared about them like they're your brothers. Right now, it seems like you've got a lot on your mind. Like you're working through things."

I sigh, glancing over her head at the rolling waves. "Feels that way too," I admit.

She squeezes my hand. "Want to talk about it? You know I'll listen."

I stare at her for a beat, knowing she really will listen. She'll probably even understand. I shake my head. "It was a long time ago, Chlo. A teammate got injured and it was on me, but I don't want to get into all the details tonight. Tonight, I just want to enjoy the moment."

She tips her head in understanding, a blaze of compassion crossing her face. "If you change your mind and want to talk…"

I nod at her offer.

"Well, I have something that will cheer you up."

"Really?" I waggle my eyebrows. "How far are we taking things between us, Crawford?"

She rolls her eyes. "Get your head out of the gutter. Besides, Maebelle's ice cream is better than sexy times."

"Not if you're doing it right," I mutter.

Chloe gasps and I grin, enjoying her reactions to silly things I say. Just like she did when we were kids. Oh, how I used to drive her nuts with my creepy crawlers and pretend snakes. She fell for my tricks every damn time, too.

She wrinkles her nose. "You're probably right."

Hold up.

I slow my gait, my gaze sharpening on her. "What?"

She sighs, glancing away. But I catch the blush on her cheeks in the shifting light of dusk. "Steve used to say, jeez, this is embarrassing. Clearly, I drink too much around you and forget myself. It's nothing."

"Tell me," I demand.

She lifts an eyebrow. "Like you've been so forthcoming with all of your secrets?"

I shake my head. "That's different."

"How?"

"It didn't involve dipshit Steve. Or sex."

"It's the vodka talking." She backpedals. "I didn't mean anything by it."

I narrow my eyes at her, waiting her out. Chloe always cracks under the silence.

After three seconds she heaves out a sigh and I bite back my grin.

"Steve used to say if I was thinner, you know, sexier, that he'd want to, that we'd have done, Jesus." She blushes furiously and even though she's embarrassed, I wait for her to finish her sentence.

Because anger is swirling dangerously in my bloodstream. It burns through me like a wildfire and I have to work not to crush Chloe's fingers in mine. "You'd what?"

"Have better sex. More…sex. That it would have been… better."

"He's a fucking liar." I stop walking.

Chloe freezes beside me. I grasp her shoulders and turn her so I can stare directly into her eyes.

"He's a fucking liar, Chloe. If you believe anything I say, trust this. It was good for Steve. Fucking great for Steve. But men like Steve suck in bed. Let me guess, he never got you off?"

She lowers her gaze, her cheeks painfully red.

Fuck. I hook my finger under her chin and lift her face to mine again. "Did he?" I whisper, burning from the inside out with curiosity. I don't know what the hell I even want her to say. If she says yes, I'll be pissed. And if she says no, I'll also be pissed because what the fuck has he been doing with her for five goddamn years?

"No." It's a whisper on the ocean breeze and yet, it bangs in my head like a firecracker.

"Because he sucks," I explain. "And he has to make excuses for himself. In order to make him feel more like a man, he has to tear you down. But he's so fucking wrong,

Chlo. Being with you, *intimately*, would be hitting the goddamn lottery for *any* man." My voice practically trembles with anger and…and what? I can't even name the emotions rocking through me but they're there. Intense, powerful, and very present. "But especially for a piece of shit like him."

She works a swallow, her eyes wider than I've ever seen them. Her mouth parts and she's so trusting, so goddamn vulnerable, that a part of me wants to dip my head, capture her lips, and kiss her hard. Hard enough to prove that she's worthy of a relationship a million times better than what she had with Steve, and hard enough to erase any lingering thoughts of him from her mind entirely.

Instead, I curl my fingers into my palms and step back, adding space between us so I can get my head on straight before it rolls all the way off.

Shit. I drag in a deep breath.

"There's no ice cream on the planet better than sex with the right person," I mutter, shaking my head. "But right now, I could fucking use it. So, lead us to Maebelle's."

She nods and begins walking, her back straight.

After a few paces, I reach back out and grab her hand.

And when she lets me, I know she's not angry with me. But maybe with Steve. Or maybe with herself.

And I know firsthand, that that's the worst kind of anger there is. Because it festers, like an open wound, infecting all your good thoughts, all your warm feelings.

Sunshine's always been all good, all warmth, all soul. Always.

CHAPTER 8

CHLOE

"Butter pecan. With rainbow sprinkles, please," I order my ice cream cone.

"Rainbow sprinkles?" Austin hip checks me next to the counter.

I nod, unable to look at him. After that showdown on the beach, I feel completely out of sorts. Like I'm drowning from the inside out but also burning up.

Because, wow. The heat in Austin's gaze was scorching. But the conviction in his tone was…real.

I shake my head to clear it from all the thoughts I shouldn't be having. Especially when Austin's eyes are on mine. "Yep. Rainbow sprinkles are magical."

"Magical?" He lifts an eyebrow, his tone conversational.

I nod, grinning my thanks at the guy behind the counter as he passes me my cone. I take a taste of the ice cream and moan. God, I forgot how good it is. "Sprinkles make everything better," I explain. "And I can't remember the last time I had ice cream."

Austin's eyes narrow but his attention is pulled away as it's his turn to order.

"Cookies and cream," he asks and I wrinkle my nose. "What?"

"Cookies and cream?"

He snorts. "What's wrong with cookies and cream?"

I shrug. "Nothing. It's just, kind of outdated, you know?"

"Outdated?" He points at me. "You're eating rainbow sprinkles."

"They're happiness."

"Would you like to add sprinkles?" the guy behind the counter asks Austin.

Austin rolls his eyes as I grin.

"Sure, chocolate, please," Austin says.

"Now you're being a rule breaker," I tell him, taking another bite of my ice cream.

"You're the one breaking rules, Chlo. Ice cream *before* dinner?" Austin snickers and pulls out his wallet to pay for our cones.

"Oh, I got it," I say, trying to balance my cone and dig into my purse for my wallet.

"Stop."

I look up. "Austin, I dragged you to—"

"Quit it, Chlo." He hands over a twenty-dollar bill. "It's sprinkles."

I grin and he smiles and for a second, it's like we're kids again, riding our bikes to the park and stopping for an ice cream cone on the way back.

"Thanks, Aus."

"Don't mention it." He hooks an arm around my shoulders and steers us out of Maebelle's.

I don't know if it's the familiarity of Martha's Vineyard, the bump of Austin's arm against my shoulder as we walk along the beach, or the fact that I've gotten the dreaded meet and greet with Steve and Brittney out of the way, but I finally relax. After weeks of feeling like I was on the cusp of falling apart, I find my footing. My shoulders dip the smallest amount, my inhales are easier to draw, and the world doesn't look quite as hopeless as it did yesterday.

The balmy ocean breeze ruffles through my hair. The ocean waves lap gently at the shoreline. The sunset colors the sky with brilliant strokes of orange and pink. Butter pecan melts on my tongue and my toes dig deeper into the sand.

Something shifts. Something small but significant and this time, when I glance up at Austin, a swell of gratitude rises to my lips.

"Thank you, Austin."

He grins down at me, wrapping an arm casually around my waist. "You're going to be okay, Chlo."

I nod, believing the words for the first time since I learned the truth about Steve and Brittney.

You're going to be okay.

He's right. I am.

AUSTIN and I are the talk of the engagement party. While I briefly worried that Marissa would feel overshadowed, the pure joy on my friend's face when she pulled me into a hug dashed that concern.

"He's perfect!" Marissa whisper-shrieks.

I blush but when I glance at Austin, chatting amiably with Adam, I can't deny Marissa's observation.

"It's so romantic, how you guys reconnected after so many years," she continues.

I nod along with her version of recent events because it's a perfect backstory and close enough to the truth.

"Adam is angling for a bromance," she adds and we both laugh. "You look happy, Chloe."

"I am happy," I say, relieved that I actually mean the

words. In this moment, right now, at an engagement party in Martha's Vineyard, in the same room as Brittney and Steve, I am happy. My gaze darts to Austin again and I don't want to read into how much his presence here is responsible for my current emotional state.

Marissa squeezes my hand. When I look up, her blue eyes are solemn. "What Steve did to you was shitty. Brittney too. Adam and I talked about it and—"

"You don't have to explain."

"I want to," she sighs. "It's stupid and I shouldn't care but with Steve working for Adam's dad and—"

"Honestly," I squeeze back, "I'm okay. It doesn't matter anymore. I'm here for you and your marriage to Adam. Yes, seeing Steve with Brittney hurts." My eyes flit back to Austin. He meets my gaze and lifts his chin, silently asking if I'm okay. I smile and dip my head yes. "But not as much as I thought it would."

It's true. I thought seeing Brittney in Steve's arms would feel like a knife in my back all over again. And yeah, it sucks. A lot. But witnessing his betrayal firsthand and coming to terms with the fact that I could have been legally bound to a broken relationship, is slowly starting to penetrate my hurt and humiliation. It's making me feel…better.

"Good." Marissa shifts her weight so we're both looking at Austin and Adam. "Because Austin is a much better man than Steve."

I glance at my friend, surprised by the sincerity in her tone. She's known Austin for two minutes and Steve for years. Realization dawns. Did Marissa know about Steve and Brittney's affair?

She glances at me and there's no guilt in her expression.

No. And even if she did, does it matter? She knows enough to surmise that the man I brought to her engagement party is so much worthier than the man who once placed a diamond on *my* finger.

"You're right," I agree.

She bumps her hip against mine. "Thanks for coming this weekend."

"Of course," I respond automatically.

Marissa smiles softly. "It can't be easy, Chloe. And I know I stuffed an entire year of wedding events into a single summer."

I snort because that's the truth.

"But you're making it look a hell of a lot easier than it is. I appreciate you being here. I'm happy you're happy and I hope to see Austin at the wedding in August."

I smile, not confirming his presence just yet. Even though Austin and I agreed to be each other's summer dates, I know firsthand how everything can change in a moment. Marissa's wedding is still two months away and as much as I *want* to bring him, as much as I'm *planning* to bring him, I don't want to jinx it.

"Let's get a drink," I say instead.

"Let's," she agrees, linking our arms together.

On our walk to the bar, we pass Brittney and I note the color high on Marissa's cheeks. The truth is, Marissa is an amazing friend and Brittney is a shitty one. While I know Abbi would strongly object, I decide to make this easier, better, for Marissa and her wedding season.

"Brittney, we're taking a bridesmaid shot. Come on," I offer as we pass.

She looks up, her mouth dropping open. I feel Steve's gaze on my cheek and Austin's glance on the center of my back but I don't turn to look at either man. I'm doing what's right for me, right now.

From now on, that should be my guiding principle. I'm going to do what is best for me, my life, and my relationships. Marissa's friendship is one I'd like to keep and so, I'll do what I can to make sure she has the wedding of her dreams, even if one of her bridesmaids doesn't deserve the honor.

"Um, okay," Brittney stutters, linking her arm with Marissa's.

The three of us line up at the bar, putting on one hell of a show of solidarity for all the party guests who know our sordid history. But when the tequila hits the back of my throat, more of my anxiety, more of my doubts and insecurities, fade away.

I smack my lips and smile. Coming to the engagement party was definitely the right thing to do. But bringing Austin has made all the difference.

As if he can read my thoughts, the hockey heartthrob appears behind me, his arm snaking around my waist.

"How many shots have you had?" he murmurs, his breath skating over the shell of my ear.

I turn in his arms, my back pressing into the ledge of the bar. Instead of backing up, Austin shuffles forward a half step, until our chests are nearly touching. In my peripheral vision, I note the way Brittney and Marissa are staring at us. Brittney with envy, Marissa with excitement. But when my gaze latches onto Austin's, everything around me fades into the background. Everything grows out of focus except for him and the intensity in his sapphire eyes.

"Enough to want to dance," I admit.

He grins, slow and lazy, like the sun peeking out from behind a cloud.

As if on cue, Ed Sheeran's song "Hearts Don't Break Around Here," floats through the room.

I snicker as Austin's grin grows.

"You requested this, didn't you?" I ask.

He takes my hand and leads me to the dance floor, right in the center. For a moment, we're the only two in the space but slowly, it fills up, with Marissa and Adam taking a place beside us.

Austin tugs me into his arms, his hand settling on my hip the way it did so many moons ago. A shiver skates up my spine, just like it did when I was fourteen. Then, I wanted to cry because my date kissed another girl. Now, I could almost care less that my ex-fiancé recently cheated on me.

I inch even closer to Austin, until the warmth of his skin seeps into mine. He grips me tighter and I melt into him.

"Just be happy it's not Madonna's 'Like A Virgin,'" he jokes, reminding me of the drinking game we played just last weekend.

"You wouldn't get up in this crowd and sing karaoke," I say, even though I'm pretty sure he would.

He pulls back and fixes me with a look that calls me out. I chuckle.

"Don't dare me," he says.

"I won't," I say. "At least, not yet."

Austin's hand slides from my hip to my lower back and I arch into him. The look in his gaze changes, the amusement giving way to a seriousness I've rarely seen in him. "You look beautiful, Chloe."

"Thank you."

"And he's definitely jealous." He spins me out before bringing me back into his embrace, even closer this time.

I gasp, both from his words and his dance moves. "Steve?"

Austin nods, his hand splaying wide in the center of my back. His pinkie finger slips beneath the material of my dress and drags down my skin slowly. "Hasn't taken his eyes off you once," he murmurs, an edge to his tone. I start to pull back but Austin holds me closer. "Don't look, Sunshine. Just let me dance with you."

My heart beats rapidly at his words, at the meaning underneath them. Is he telling me this to make Steve more jealous? Or because he likes holding me just as much as I'm enjoying being in his arms?

The song ends and I start to pull away again. "Ed's done singing."

Austin shakes his head as another slow song starts. "But we're not done dancing."

My throat dries and my skin tightens as awareness blazes through me. I don't know when this stopped being about Steve and my saving face but it did. Because right now, I don't care what anyone thinks except Austin. Two deep pools of blue hold my gaze and I dive into them, savoring this moment, this dance, the way I feel in Austin's arms.

I feel eerily like I'm at home, which is crazy. Absurd.

My heart flutters in my chest and my stomach twists.

I have butterflies. When was the last time I had them? Over three years ago now. Is that how long it's been since I've felt…desired? Cherished?

The way Austin's looking at me right now makes me feel both. He makes me feel more beautiful in this moment than Steve ever did.

"You really don't mind that everyone here thinks we're dating? A couple?"

He shakes his head, flashing a lopsided grin. "I started that trumor, didn't I?"

"Trumor?" I question.

"A true rumor," he explains. "We will be each other's dates a lot this summer."

I snort. "Only you." I slide my hand up and around his shoulder. "And you really want to come to the wedding in August?"

He rewards me with one of those leisurely, knowing smiles. "You're too late, babe."

I frown, pulling back to look up at him.

"Adam already invited me," he explains, dipping me.

I chuckle as he pulls me back up. "Oh, really?"

He nods. "But I told him I'd bring you as my plus one."

I laugh, loudly. We draw looks from nearby dancers. Where Steve would have been embarrassed, Austin grins.

"On one condition," he continues.

"What's that?" I ask, waiting for some ridiculous rule.

"You tell me, for real, if our trumor becomes too true. Too real for you." His eyes hold mine, serious.

I nod slowly, clearing my throat. What if it did become too real? What if the spark of feelings I'm already having gave way to something *more*? Is he worried I'd be clingy? That it would ruin our friendship? I close my eyes for a moment, pushing the thoughts away. Austin and I made a deal and I know where we stand. I just need to stick to it. "We're really doing this? All the summer dates?"

Austin nods, his hands linking at the base of my spine, cradling me. His expression is a mixture of serious and playful. "I think our trial run has been pretty successful."

I glance over his shoulder, noting the several guests who avert their gazes. "I'd have to agree."

Austin guides me through one more spin before pulling me flush against his chest. "So say yes, Sunshine."

"Yes."

CHAPTER 9

AUSTIN

"Someone's in a good mood," my sister announces as I step into our parents' kitchen.

"What are you doing here?" I ask Claire.

"I could ask you the same thing."

I hold up a sack of laundry my mother, angel that she is, did for me.

"Jesus," Claire scoffs, jabbing the tines of her fork in my direction. "Mom still does your laundry."

"When I'm in a pinch," I admit sheepishly.

"What pinch? You're not even working."

"You're here eating lunch. What's the matter? Don't feel like cooking?"

Claire dips her head and I grin. Leaning over the table, I pull the glass container of lasagna over and swipe a fork before taking a big bite. "Too lazy to put it on a real plate?"

Claire flips me the bird. "How was Martha's Vineyard?"

At her pointed question, disguised in an innocence I know better than to believe, my guard goes up. "Fun."

Claire sighs and pulls the container back. "East told me Scott's hosting a BBQ this weekend."

I sigh, knowing where this is going. Scott Reland, our

team owner, hosts a BBQ every summer. It's a chance for the whole team, management, coaches, to socialize in a relaxed atmosphere since we're technically not in training yet. It's also a chance for players to bring around their families, children, significant others. It's casual and fun and the perfect place to break in a new girlfriend to hockey life. "It's Friday."

"I know; I'm going."

"Then I'll see you there." I swipe another bite of lasagna. Jeez, our mother is really the best. Lasagna and laundry on a Wednesday afternoon.

Claire sighs again, heavily like her life is unbelievably overwhelming. I keep my gaze averted. "You should invite Chloe."

My head snaps up. "Why would I drag Chloe into the lion's den? You and I both know that the BBQ is the first step to declaring a relationship status."

Claire raises her eyebrows. "And?"

"And," I say pointedly, "Chloe and I are friends. Just because I started a trumor this weekend doesn't—"

"A true rumor?" She rolls her eyes. "Thank God you're an athlete."

I take a massive bite of lasagna in response to that dig.

"Hey," my sister whines, pulling the container closer to her. "All I'm saying is, if you guys are going to be each other's summer dates—"

"To real events," I clarify, picking up Claire's can of Diet Coke and taking a swig. There's no need to admit that I'm not opposed to the idea of bringing Chloe around my teammates when it's something I've always avoided in the past. "To events Mom would have tried to set me up for. Or weddings that Chloe needs a date to. Not a friendly, team BBQ."

"Oh, it'll be *friendly* all right," Claire mutters.

"What's that mean?" I narrow my gaze.

She shrugs. "Panda invited some girls for Friday."

"Some girls?"

"Are you going to repeat everything I say?"

"What girls?" I sigh, knowing full well that any girls Luca Pandatelli invited will be of the puck bunny variety. Panda is a notorious player with a new flavor of the week, every week. Every season, I wait for one of his flings-gone-wrong to blow up in his face but the guy is a savage. He somehow manages to never turn a one-night stand into a two-night stand and still remain surrounded by beautiful women. "Christ, he's going to corrupt Sims," I say, referencing one of our rookies from last season.

Claire wrinkles her nose, tilting her head. "I'd say Sims has already been sufficiently corrupted."

My eyes narrow but Claire holds up a hand, stopping me from asking more about Sims. Instead, I lose my patience and growl out, "What girls?"

"Tamara, Elise, Megan..." My sister ticks off women on her fingers like she's listing ice cream flavors. But all the women she names, while nice people, are kind of like team groupies and have spent several nights in the beds of several different players.

I sigh. They've also all been hounding me since we won the Cup. The offers are endless and while generous, I'm just not interested. Not that I can admit that without looking like a massive pussy.

"So, if you and Chlo are planning to spend the summer flirting around a *trumor*, then you should have no problem inviting her to Scott's BBQ. Unless you want to get *friendly* with some other woman on Friday night," my sister concludes, her gaze watchful once more.

Shit. I don't want to be *friendly* with any of those women and worse, my sister knows it.

I swear and Claire grins. She nudges my phone closer to my hand. "Call her. I'm sure she'd love to meet the team. Besides, if you guys are just friends helping each other out this summer, then you should introduce her to James." She casually drops the name of our longest-playing defenseman now that Torsten retired and moved to New York. James Ryan lost his wife nearly a year ago and while he hasn't started dating yet, a woman like Chloe—serious, committed, thoughtful—would be better suited to a man like him, with two kids and a house, than me, a bachelor with commitment issues and raging anxiety.

A wave of anger burns through me at the thought of Chloe with any of the guys on my team. With any guy, period. It was bad enough having to witness douchebag Steve's eyes trail her all weekend but if I had to watch any of my teammates look at her with lust on their faces, I'd knock them out.

Is the team BBQ an event? Because we did agree to help each other out for events...

"I can't stand you," I tell my sister, picking up my phone.

Claire blows me a kiss. "I'm your fave."

"Pain in the ass."

"Call her."

I shake my head and shoot off a text instead. A text message is more casual. It's...safer.

AUSTIN

Hey Sunshine. How's your week shaping up?

She texts back within minutes and I can't stop the grin that spreads across my face.

"Aww," Claire sing-songs. I ignore her.

CHLOE

Icing.

AUSTIN

What?

CHLOE

A delaying tactic in hockey

AUSTIN

Are you studying hockey rules?

CHLOE

I'm adding a hockey term to this week's crossword.

I chuckle.

AUSTIN

Missing me that much?

CHLOE

Thinking of you isn't the same as missing you.

My eyebrows rise at her honesty.

AUSTIN

Isn't it though?

CHLOE

(shrugging emoji) I had fun this weekend.

I smile again, shifting my weight as Claire practically throws herself across the island to read my messages.

AUSTIN

Me too. Interested in doing it again this weekend?

CHLOE

Sara's wedding is next month.

AUSTIN

I have a team BBQ at the Hawks owner's place on Friday. Come with me?

CHLOE

As your date?

AUSTIN

You're going to make me really ask, aren't you?

CHLOE

Duh.

I smirk.

"What's she saying?" Claire whines. "I need details. My life has been dull since Indy got knocked up and Rielle married Torsten of all people."

I reach over to flick her ear and she yelps, pressing both hands to the side of her head.

AUSTIN

Sunshine, will you please be my date to a team BBQ on Friday?

CHLOE

I'd love to.

AUSTIN

Pick you up at 3.

CHLOE

What do I wear?

I snort, exasperated. The woman could wear a rucksack and stun.

AUSTIN

It's casual. Be comfortable.

CHLOE

I'll call Claire.

AUSTIN

No need. She's pretty much dangling off my arm for information. She'll call you.

CHLOE

(laughing emoji face) Mimi is all over me for details about this weekend too.

AUSTIN

Did you bring her more doughnuts?

CHLOE

All jelly filled. I'm her favorite grandkid.

AUSTIN

I have no doubt. Just so you know, you coming on Friday means the team is going to think we're a thing.

CHLOE

Our trumor is spreading.

AUSTIN

I'm not mad about it.

CHLOE

Me neither. I'll follow your lead. I'm game for however you want to play this.

AUSTIN

You're really are the perfect woman, you know that?

CHLOE

Yeah. You told me that the last day of sophomore year.

I laugh, recalling the moment she's referring to.

Claire's eyebrows nearly fly off her forehead. "Laughter and banter," she muses.

AUSTIN

You needed a ride to school for a final exam so you filled my gas tank. Which you didn't have to do.

CHLOE

Just reminding you what a perfect female specimen looks like.

AUSTIN

(winking emoji) Trust me, I've always known it was you. See you Friday. Hit me up if you need more hockey lingo.

CHLOE

See you Friday.

"She's in." I turn to Claire, placing my phone back on the counter.

Claire rolls her eyes. "Right. Like she was going to turn you down after you stuck it to her ex-fiancé."

"Call her. She doesn't know what to wear."

"Fucking Steve."

"Huh?" I pause, my fork piercing the lasagna at the mention of Chloe's ex-fiancé.

"I hate how he messed with her head. Now she questions her own intuition, doubts herself."

I cross my arms over my chest, forgetting about the lasagna. It's something I noticed too but maybe Claire can shed some additional light on Chloe's self-consciousness. "What do you mean?"

Claire lifts an eyebrow. "When did Chloe ever worry about wearing the wrong thing?"

I flip through a handful of mental images, recalling how Chloe was often called out for not dressing trendy enough. Still, she never cared and she rocked everything with a confidence that fit her. "Never."

"Exactly."

"He really did a number on her, huh?"

Claire nods, giving me a pointed look. "Look, Austin, I know you and Chloe are joking around about your trumor.

But if you're going to be Chloe's date to all these events and vice-versa, just make sure you're careful with her feelings."

"Of course I'm careful with her feelings. The only reason why I agreed to Martha's Vineyard was to *protect* Chloe's feelings."

"I know." Claire holds up a hand. "It's just, well, her feelings over Steve are raw. And you and Chlo always had a connection, a close relationship. This summer, we need to help build her back up, not make her feel worse."

"I'd never—"

"I know. Not on purpose." Claire cuts me off and shrugs. "All I'm saying is be smart about it."

I nod, turning my sister's words over in my mind. Her observations aren't far from their mark. Chloe is fragile right now. I noticed it at the engagement party. I cringe recalling what she confided in me about her and Steve and their lack of a sex life.

What a dick.

As if any man wouldn't be the luckiest SOB on the planet to run his hands over her curves, to kiss her fluttering pulse at the base of her throat, to slide inside of—

"Mom's home." Claire hops off the top of the island, interrupting my wayward thoughts.

I clear my throat, mentally berating myself for having such ridiculous thoughts to begin with. Chloe is my friend. My oldest friend. That's it. This summer, we're helping each other out. We're making her ex jealous and warding off the puck bunnies that have been swarming since the Cup win. If we can have some fun and laughs while we do that, awesome.

But there will be no kissing of throats or sexy times between us.

I won't allow it.

Because in the short amount of time I spent with Chloe, I learned just how much she yearns to be someone's priority.

And my priority will always be my team, hockey. I don't have room in my life for a serious commitment which is why I've avoided them for so long. I don't want to consider what a disappointment I'd be to her when I have to choose hockey first. I sure as hell don't want to hurt her. The thought alone makes my chest tighten and my anxiety spike, until drawing a deep breath is impossible.

I don't have the ability to be the kind of man Chloe yearns for and so all I'll ever be is a friend. Her friend.

I just need to keep reminding myself of this very important fact so my thoughts don't run wild imagining her in overly *friendly* ways. No matter how much parts of me crave Chloe, Claire is right. This summer, we need to build her back up, help her find her way back to the strong, confident, breathtaking, and kickass woman who never used to second-guess herself.

Tangling underneath the sheets with her is a surefire way to ruin the only female friendship I've ever managed to maintain.

Some rules are better left unbroken.

CHAPTER 10
CHLOE

"You look perfect. Beautiful," Austin greets me on Friday afternoon.

I roll my eyes but my grin gives away just how much his words please me. How could they not? Have you ever had a man who looks like he stepped out of an underwear ad stare at you like you rival the sun? With sparkling blue eyes and a devilish smirk? If not, you can't possibly understand just how off-balanced I feel under Austin's unwavering gaze.

I hold up the pastry box instead of responding. "I got doughnuts."

He laughs, shaking his head at me, and his eyes flare with humor. God, I love his laugh. It's so deep and rumbly and genuine. "The guys will be proposing to you by the end of the night. Tell them all no." He takes the box from my hand. "You didn't have to bring anything. I got a couple bottles of wine in the car too. You ready?"

I smooth my hands over my hips, the fabric of my sundress rippling. "All set."

I'm relieved Mom and Dad are over at Austin's parents' house so they aren't peeking from the windows, watching as Austin and I slide into his SUV and back out of the driveway.

If they were, they would be concocting ideas. Ideas that they would fill my head with and under current circumstances, I just may want to believe them. But I know better than to think this BBQ is anything but what Austin presented it as: a team event where he doesn't want to go single.

At least, that's what I think until we show up in the beautiful, expansive backyard, and I witness the sharp gazes and crestfallen smiles of a handful of gorgeous women. For a beat, it's like high school all over again. A horde of women desperate for Austin's attention and me, standing at his side, as the friend, the shield, the person keeping the hockey legend from his adoring fans.

My stomach sinks as the realization fills my mind.

Austin didn't want me to accompany him today so he wouldn't have to be the only single guy. He wanted me to come so he could send a clear message to all the women trying to hook up with him. What are they called? Puck bunnies, I think Savannah once said.

Disappointment coats my stomach but I'm not sure why. Isn't this what we agreed on? To be each other's dates so we wouldn't be set up with other people?

And yet, a silly, naive part of me was starting to hope for…what? Things between Austin and me to mean more than friendship? It's an insane notion since that's all we've ever been.

I hate that the disappointment flaring to life in my body proves that yes, a part of me was starting to think that maybe, just maybe, things between us could be more. The more that I never had with Steve or any other romantic relationship in my life.

"Hey, you okay?" Austin frowns at me.

One of his teammates lifts a hand in greeting. "Hey Cap!"

I nod, gesturing toward his friend. "Fine. Let's do this."

Austin's frown deepens but he follows as I walk in the direction of his friend, a smile pasted on my face. I need to get my errant thoughts and twisted feelings under control and stick to the rules. Especially because Austin is going to be my date to Marissa's wedding. I *need* him to be my date to the wedding so I can't let him know how complicated my feelings for him are becoming. It will ruin everything.

"Hey," the guy waving to Austin greets me, sticking out his hand. "I'm Panda."

"Panda?" I quirk an eyebrow, placing my hand in his.

He shakes my hand casually but there's a glint in his eye as he glances at Austin before checking me out. I blush under his perusal and feel Austin straighten beside me.

"Luca," the guy says sheepishly, smiling back. And jeez, he's a looker. In fact, almost every female in the backyard without a ring on her finger, and some with bling larger than my head, are checking him out. "Pandatelli."

"Ah, got it. The goalie."

Surprise flares in his expression. "You've heard of me."

I chuckle at his shock, enjoying his sincerity. "I have. I'm Chloe Crawford."

"And you came with Cap," he surmises, giving Austin a ruddy grin.

"We're old friends," I explain before Austin has to lie to his teammate.

Panda nods, biting his lower lip as if to hold in laughter. Something tells me he doesn't believe me for a second but that's fine, sometimes, I don't believe me either.

"You want a drink, Chloe?" he asks, dipping into a cooler.

"I got it," Austin says hastily, knocking his teammate out of the way.

Panda moves over easily, shooting me a wink.

I snort and shake my head, tipping it to Austin in thanks when he passes me a bottle of Blue Moon. "My favorite."

"I know," Austin says sharply, causing Panda to snicker.

"You made it!" Claire appears at my side, bumping her hip against mine.

"Hey Chlo. Guys." East swoops in, smacking Panda on the back, banging his fist against Austin's shoulder, and brushing a kiss over my cheek.

"Welcome, fellas." A man smiles warmly, his hands held out to his sides. "I'm glad you could all make it."

"Thanks, Scott." East shakes the man's hand and I surmise that this man is the team owner.

I shuffle back half a step, behind Austin and Panda. I don't know what I was expecting the Hawks owner to look like, but it definitely wasn't the tanned, fit, forty-something-year-old with salt and pepper at his temples and bold green eyes. What the hell? Is everyone Austin associates with drop-dead gorgeous?

I must be staring for a minute because the man shuffles, peering around Austin. "And you are?"

I blush before finding my footing, vowing to not embarrass my oldest friend. "Chloe." I step forward, arm outstretched. "Chloe Crawford."

"Well, it's nice to meet you, Chloe. I'm Scott." He shakes my hand warmly.

For a heartbeat, I'm swept up in the moment. Chatting and laughing with Austin and his teammates, with Claire and her boyfriend, and suddenly, it feels like I belong here. The tension that always existed when I would accompany Steve to work events doesn't exist. My nerves and worries float away like magic.

"What do you do for work?" Scott asks politely.

"I write crossword puzzles for *The Brooklyn Gazette*."

His eyes widen in surprise and Panda's mouth drops open.

I giggle as Claire explains, "She's smarter than all of us. We've got another Indy on our hands."

Scott grins. "That must be a very interesting profession."

I shrug. "It's solitary but I like the autonomy. Thanks for having me today. You have a beautiful home."

"You haven't even seen it yet," Claire gushes, shooting a look at Scott. "If you are open to a home tour, I volunteer."

Scott laughs and gestures to have at it. Claire clutches my arm, about to steer me toward the massive home when Austin drops the box of pastries in my hand and the wine bottles in Claire's. "You can drop these in the kitchen," he explains.

"You didn't have to bring anything, Aus," Scott scolds him.

"The doughnuts are from Chloe," Austin adds and I glance at him over my shoulder. He didn't have to tell Scott that but—

Scott turns to me, gratitude in his expression, as if he's surprised again. "Thank you, Chloe. You really didn't have to bring anything. I'm happy you could make it."

I dip my head but my eyes catch Austin's when I respond. "Happy to be here."

Claire tugs me toward the house but right before I turn around, something shifts in Austin's face. His expression is less guarded, more open. His eyes peer into mine, searching. A moment passes between us but…what does it mean?

Claire's voice pulls me back to the moment. "Scott's just surprised because Austin never brings a date to these things."

"Really?" I turn my attention to her as we take the steps up the deck.

Claire nods. "Really. He's known to keep his personal life quiet but…" She shrugs, pulling open the sliding door.

"But what?" I stop her with a hand to her forearm.

She winces. "Listen, Chlo, I adore my brother. But he has never been boyfriend material. I mean, he could be. He would be the best boyfriend ever if he let himself. But he's always put hockey, the team, before everything else."

"I know. He said as much."

Claire grasps my wrist loosely. "I know you guys are

helping each other out this summer and you're friends and it's fun but…"

"But?"

"I don't want you to get hurt. Or for him to get hurt either."

"I would never, we aren't," I sigh. "We're just friends, Claire."

Claire bites the corner of her mouth like she wants to say more but thinks better of it. She blows out a sigh. "Okay." She steps into the house. "Wait 'til you see this kitchen."

I frown at her quick subject change but the moment I step into the house, my thoughts are sidelined by the most beautiful kitchen I've ever stepped foot in. "Wow. This is—"

"Amazing."

I nod, glancing around. "And spotless."

Claire laughs. "Scott hardly cooks. Like, ever."

"Really?" I ask, a sadness hanging around my words as I run my palm over the gleaming marble countertops. What a shame to have a kitchen like this, outfitted with industrial appliances and a walk-in pantry and not utilize it.

Claire steps up to the espresso maker which definitely costs a mint. "Want one?" she asks, pulling open a cabinet for espresso beans.

"Are you sure Scott won't mind?"

She shakes her head. "Not at all. He's seriously the kindest, most generous guy. A few months ago, during the playoffs, one of the defensemen, Torsten Hansen, had to go back to Norway for a family emergency and Scott was totally cool with it. Granted, he knew it was Torsten's last season and Torst was injured but most owners wouldn't be as understanding as Scott. He looks out for all the guys, more than as just an owner, you know?"

"He seems really invested in the players. Even to do this." I gesture to the backyard where the BBQ is unfolding.

"He is. It's a shame he's single. Indy keeps telling him

she's going to set him up but he just laughs and says her friends are much too young for him."

I grin. "Indy fancies herself the matchmaker, huh?"

Claire groans. "You have no idea. After she convinced Easton to let me move in with him, she pretty much declared herself the matchmaking queen."

I snort, accepting the oat latte from Claire. I take a sip and moan. "This is amazing."

"Right?" Claire asks just as the sliding door opens.

Indy steps inside and shakes her head at us. "I knew I'd find you guys in here, hogging all of Scott's good stuff."

"Want one?" Claire offers.

Indy shakes her head, her hands landing on her baby bump. "No, thanks. The baby is kicking up a storm today. I think any caffeine would be dangerous to my internal organs."

Claire snickers.

"How are you feeling?" I ask.

"Pretty good." Indy slides onto a barstool. "Hey, I didn't even get to invite you but you have to come to my baby shower."

"I'd love to," I agree, pleased to be included.

"Yay! It's the third weekend in July. I'll send you the invitation." She rolls her eyes. "Torsten made them."

"The defenseman?" I ask, since Claire was just talking about him.

"Do you know all the guys' positions?" Claire asks.

I shrug. "You just mentioned the guy from Norway."

"True," she agrees, taking a sip of her latte and leaning back against the kitchen counter. "He married my best friend, Rielle. They're living in New York now and will split their time between the States and Oslo. But—"

"He's throwing me a baby shower!" Indy gushes, bouncing in her chair.

I laugh, glancing between my two friends. "Torsten? Not

you"—I point to Claire—"or your Mom?" I glance back at Indy.

"Well, we're having our own family shower, which you also have to come to," Claire explains. "But Torsten is hosting a team shower for Indy and—"

"He throws the best parties!" Indy squeals, waving her hands. "I'm so excited. He just has the best taste and isn't afraid to go overboard."

I raise an eyebrow. "Indy, you're one of the most understated people I know."

Claire nods in agreement.

"It's different," she explains, glancing down at her baby bump. "It's not for me. It's for my little."

Understanding washes over me as I enjoy seeing this side of Indy. She always had her head in a book, it's nice to see her out and excited about a party.

"So, you'll come to my baby shower?" she asks.

"Wouldn't miss it."

The door slides open again and we all turn to see Panda step inside. His eyes flash with amusement when he sees the three of us huddled around the kitchen island, drinking lattes. "Are we that boring?" he asks, pointing to the backyard.

Indy rolls her eyes. "We were being considerate."

"How so?" Panda asks, quizzically.

"Wanted to save you from hearing any more details about my baby shower."

Panda laughs and glances at Indy's bump. "Torsten messaged me the other day to ask me if—"

"No!" Indy's hands fly to her ears. "I want to be surprised."

Panda shakes his head, bewildered. "I will never understand these traditions."

"You will. One day, when you get a woman pregnant," Claire offers.

Panda blanches and I chuckle at his expression.

He looks at me and winks again, tipping his head to the door. "You better get out there and save your boy."

"My boy?" I ask.

"Austin," Panda says.

Indy hums in approval and Claire shoots me a look.

"We're just—" I begin to explain but Panda cuts me off.

"Women are falling all over him, practically begging for a ride on his—"

"Vomit. Vomit in my mouth," Claire says loudly, covering her ears.

Indy grimaces.

I frown. "What women?"

"The ones he brought." Indy points at Panda.

Panda shrugs, swiping Claire's latte off the counter and taking a sip. "Competing with Cap is hard work."

Claire rolls her eyes.

Indy looks at me. "Don't listen to him. He's just jaded."

Panda chuckles, slipping onto a barstool, unbothered that the women he brought to the BBQ are currently chatting up his team captain. He glances at me, as if waiting for me to react.

I suck in an inhale. Am I supposed to go out there? Is Austin enjoying the attention? But why would he ask me to come today if he knew—

"I think he'd want you to save him," Panda offers, reading my mind.

I glance between Indy, Claire, and Panda. Then, I steel my shoulders and move toward the door. Sliding it open, I step out onto the deck and hold my hand over my eyes to shield the glaring sunshine. I squint, scanning the yard until I find Austin, smiling and nodding politely to a group of women, all twirling their hair and watching him with hearts and moons in their eyes.

Suddenly, I'm back in high school, saving the popular athlete from his attentive, female fans. Jealousy, an emotion I was very unfamiliar with until recently, snakes through me. But it's more than that. When I was fourteen, I used to snicker at Austin's fanbase and pull him away with a well-timed joke. It didn't feel like competition and I sure as hell wasn't *comparing* myself to any of them. A ripple of uncertainty trickles through me and I bite my bottom lip. I can't let Austin know seeing him with these women is twisting me up. I need to be casual and cool.

I start in his direction, keeping my expression blank. But inside, my heart rate triples and a now familiar sensation tightens in my chest. Inadequacies, doubts, insecurities that leave me reeling in anxiety take root. It wasn't until I dated Steve that I ever felt less-than. It wasn't until Steve and Brittney that I ever felt smaller than a speck of dirt. My desire to hold Steve's attention led me to shrink my whole world and now, I'm struggling to grow it again. At the very base of my self-doubt is overwhelming envy that I despise. Austin and I are *just friends*.

I repeat this over and over in my mind the nearer I grow to Austin and the women.

When I'm a few paces away, he glances up. When he spots me, his expression relaxes and his eyes soften.

"Chloe." He holds out his hand. "There you are."

I place my hand in his and suck in an inhale as he tugs me to his side, positioning me so that my back is pressed into his chest. His arms wrap around my waist, holding me possessively.

The girls don't miss the intent behind his hold and two of them frown while the third backs away and the fourth scoffs.

"Ladies, meet my…" Austin pauses, clearing his throat. He rubs his lips over the top of my head. "My Sunshine."

My heart nearly beats out of my chest.

CHAPTER 11
CHLOE

"My Sunshine?" I laugh at him as he places another beer in my hand.

"It just slipped out," he admits, laughing along with me.

"Jeez, I can't take you anywhere," I joke, gesturing to the women who have moved on to a different player.

"You weren't supposed to just leave me like that," Austin says accusingly.

I shrug. "Your sister made me an oat latte."

Austin laughs. "I think Scott just keeps his coffee maker around for her. She's obsessed."

"And Indy invited me to her baby shower," I add, watching him carefully. For what? It's not like my friendship with Claire and Indy is contingent upon my relationship—or lack thereof—with Austin.

He grins and my chest warms. "Good. Torsten is way too invested in planning it."

I smile back. "I heard."

Austin kicks back in the chair beside mine. "You hungry? Scott goes all out for BBQs."

"I'm getting there," I admit.

"Thanks for coming today. I know this can't be much fun for you."

"More fun than Marissa's engagement party must have been for you."

"Nah." He shrugs, glancing at me over the rim of his beer bottle. "I had a good time with you."

"Today isn't bad. I like watching you squirm under the attention of your female admirers. It's like high school 2.0."

Austin snickers and shakes his head. He takes a long swig of his beer and smacks his lips, glancing at me again. "It's more intense now. I've had two women sneak into my hotel rooms before."

My mouth drops open. "No way! That's, that's insane."

"Tell me about it. At first, back in college, it was fun, you know? Hell, it was an ego boost like no other. The attention, the beautiful women, and the things they just…offered up… made me feel like I was on top of the world."

I take a pull of my beer, hoping it washes away the sourness that turns my stomach at Austin's words.

"But too many nights being stupid catch up with you, you know?"

I frown, my eyes latching onto his. I recall his expression when we were at the bar in Martha's Vineyard and I know there's more to his story than he's sharing. "What happened?"

He winces, his face stricken for a moment. He shakes his head and some of the panic in his eyes clears. "It was a long time ago. It's just, now, I don't play those games. I date, casually. I see women in a way that's mutually beneficial. But I'm straight up right from the start. And I don't do this." He gestures between us.

"Friendship?" I deadpan.

Austin guffaws. "I don't bring women around. Not to team events or family events," he clarifies, peering at me. "But it's different with you, Sunshine."

"Because we're friends."

"Because being with you is fun. Easy."

I nod, knowing he means the words as a compliment. And yet, they feel a bit like a smack to the soul. Because I am so firmly in Austin's friend zone—*where you should be*—and parts of me wish I could be more than that.

Claire's warning buzzes around my mind and I clear it away by taking another pull of my beer.

"Here you guys are." Noah spots us, walking over to where we're sitting behind a tree. "Come on, grab a plate. Scott went all out."

"Nice," Austin says, standing. He extends a hand and I take it, letting him pull me to my feet.

As I follow him and Noah to the massive table, laid out with an impressive spread, I remind myself that this isn't my life. I'm not Indy or Claire. I'm not dating a Hawks player. I'm here strictly in a friend capacity. I'm here to help Austin fight off the attentions and affections of women a million times more glamorous than I'll ever be.

Noah passes me a plate and I thank him, eyeing the trays of pulled pork, ribs, and brisket. There's mashed potatoes and yams, veggie burgers, and pasta salad. Everything looks amazing. My mouth waters but my stomach twists, tying itself into knots that only tighten when Austin places his fingers in the small of my back and nudges me forward.

Maybe Claire was right. Maybe we are playing with fire. Maybe I am going to end up hurt, or worse, hurt Austin, when he realizes that I'm incapable of having the same friendship from over a decade ago.

Panda jostles me from the other side when I reach to add salad to my plate.

"Here," he says, lifting a heaping spoonful and plopping it down on my plate, next to the veggie burger.

"Thanks," I say, gratefully.

"Hey, you guys need to come to Taps after this. The team's

going for a round or two and we convinced James to come," Panda continues, glancing at Austin over the top of my head.

"We'll see," Austin says noncommittally.

Panda lowers his voice and leans closer to me. "Convince him to come, Chloe. James rarely comes out with us. Besides, you'll have fun. I promise."

I arch an eyebrow and glance up at him. His smile is all charm and playfulness. "You remind me of Drew."

Panda frowns. "Who's Drew?"

"My brother," I admit, drawing more similarities between them. Fun, engaging, flirtatious, but loyal.

Panda chuckles and tosses me a wink. I'm starting to think it's his signature thing. "Get Cap to come out, okay?"

"I'll do my best," I agree, liking that Austin's teammates like hanging with me too.

Panda squeezes just above my elbow before moving to the other side of the table. I begin to move forward but Austin's hand on my back applies more pressure and I stop, turning toward him.

His eyes are narrowed, his jaw clenched. "What'd he say?"

"Panda?" I ask, confused by his reaction.

Austin nods.

I shrug. "That we should head to Taps after this. It'll be fun."

"That's it?" he asks as if he doesn't believe me.

"And that James rarely joins so we really should go."

Austin nods once, glancing over his shoulder. I look up and spot another guy, perched on the armrest of a chair, a forkful of pasta salad making its way to his mouth. Two kids run up to his side, tugging on his arm. He smiles at them but a sadness sweeps his expression.

"Is that James?" I ask softly.

Austin nods. "He lost his wife a little over a year ago."

Something twists in my chest, watching this man I don't even know interact with his kids. It turns even deeper when I witness the anguish in Austin's expression, as if he feels everything his teammate is experiencing.

"Would you mind going to Taps?" Austin asks, turning back toward me.

"I'd love to go." I tell him the truth.

His fingers brush down my back again. "Okay. Then we'll go."

"Okay," I agree, snagging a brownie off the table. Some of the knots untwist in my stomach and I take a big bite, letting the chocolate, fudgey goodness center me once more.

TAPS IS LOUD AND LIVELY, welcoming and warm. The moment I enter, I understand why the Hawks like it so much. It's laid-back, friendly, and super casual.

"What's good, Pete?" Panda lifts a hand in greeting to the bartender.

"How's it going, guys? You're not going to believe this but the backroom is rented tonight." Pete points to the back and Panda's mouth drops open. "A bachelorette party," Pete adds and Panda's expression instantly shifts. A smile worms its way across his face.

I snort and hit him in the chest with the back of my hand. "You're so obvious."

He grins and glances down at me. "So are you, Ms. Crawford." He steps to the bar and looks at me before turning back to Pete. Except Pete has disappeared to the end of the bar and a different bartender, a petite brunette, stands in his place. "Line 'em up." Panda bangs a hand on top of the bar, grinning at the bartender. "Patron. You new?"

The gorgeous brunette laughs lightly and shakes her head. "I'm just filling in for Selina tonight. I'm Bella."

"Beautiful," Panda says.

Bella rolls her eyes. I snort and glance up at Austin, who's hovering behind me. "Is he telling her the meaning of her name or commenting on her looks?"

Austin shakes his head and smacks Panda on the back of his. "Jackass," he mutters. "You're not Torsten."

Panda shakes him off. "I miss Big Daddy."

East snorts and rests his elbows on the bar next to Panda. "We all do. I'll take a club soda with lemon please."

Bella nods and fixes Easton a drink before lining up a row of shots.

"You don't have to take one," Austin murmurs in my ear.

I shoot him an incredulous look over my shoulder and swipe up a shooter. "What if I want to?"

A slow grin spreads across his lips. "Then have at it."

I pass him a shot. Next to me, Panda lets out a cheer and Claire giggles. We all raise our glasses and clink them together. But Austin's eyes hold mine as I toss back the tequila, wincing as the strong alcohol hits my taste buds.

It's been a long time since I was out in a rowdy bar with friends, with people who make me feel welcomed and accepted, drinking tequila. I bite into the lime wedge Austin holds out for me and smack my lips together. I'd be lying if I said I wasn't enjoying this.

Austin shuffles closer, his body framing mine as I turn back toward the bar. Bella is leaning over the bar to hear whatever James is saying. When she leans back, she laughs and James smiles and for the first time today, he looks at ease. Not wanting to interrupt their exchange, I flag down Pete and order another round of shots.

"I like you." Panda jostles my elbow and passes Austin and me shooters.

Austin mumbles something under his breath but I'm too busy laughing at Panda's antics. He's like a little puppy, playful and amusing and fun to be around. The more I watch him engage with the crowd, the more I miss my brother. I'm glad I'll see Drew next month at Sara's wedding.

After I take another shot, I tell Austin I'm heading to the bathroom.

"Give me a second, I'll walk you," he says as Easton asks him a question.

"I'll be fine," I laugh. "I'll be back in a minute."

A line forms between Austin's eyebrows but he nods and turns back to Easton. I make my way through the crowd, noting it's a lot busier now than it was when we walked in. The music is louder with groups of friends singing along to lyrics and exchanging stories in loud voices. I grin at the people I pass, trying to remember the last time I felt so much a part of my surroundings. Not in Hoboken, not with Steve and his friends. The only time I've ever truly belonged was with the Merrick family and Abbi.

I'm so caught up in my thoughts, I'm not paying attention to where I'm going and I walk straight into a guy.

"I'm so sorry." I throw out an arm to catch myself but he wraps an arm around my waist to keep me from going down.

"Are you okay?" he asks, steadying me.

I look up into deep brown eyes and a concerned expression. The man who I slammed into drops his hold and peers at me, waiting for a response. He's attractive in an understated but familiar way.

"I know you," I blurt out even though it can't be further from the truth. I definitely don't know this man and yet—

He laughs and shakes his head. "I'm a musician."

"A musician?" I wrack my brain. "Derek Reiner?" My mouth drops open. "You were a clue in my crossword puzzle last month."

The man, Boston-bred lead singer for *The Burnt Clovers*, shakes his head in disbelief and laughs. I blush, partly from embarrassment and partly because I'm talking to a real musician. In a bar. In Boston. I don't recognize my life anymore.

"What crossword puzzle?" he asks after a moment, scrubbing a hand across his face. The facial scruff he's rocking would look unkempt on anyone else, but on him, it just works. Must be the musician vibes. He places his hand in the small of my back and nudges me toward the bar. Half in shock that this exchange is even happening—I am obsessed with *The Burnt Clovers*—I move toward his group of friends.

"The Brooklyn Gazette. I, um, I write them."

His face swivels toward mine. "You write crossword puzzles?"

I nod.

"No shit." He laughs again. "You may just be the most interesting woman in here tonight."

I blush harder, not hating this ego boost. "My best friend, Abbi, and I love you guys. Your new single, 'Safe in Summer,' is incredible."

"Thanks," he says easily, gesturing to Pete for some shots.

"Oh, I'm fine. I'm just—" I point toward the bathroom. "It was nice bumping into you," I say lamely, wishing I was a lot less awkward but also not caring because ohmyGod, I just walked into Derek Reiner.

Derek smirks and shakes his head. "Let me buy you a drink. It's the least I can do after almost taking you out."

I bite my lip and point to the bathroom again. I don't want Austin to think I'm ditching him. Even though we're *just friends*, it's still a shitty friend thing to do. "I'm good. But thanks for the offer and—"

"Chloe." Austin's voice sounds behind me.

"Derek?" Claire asks.

"Derek," Easton sneers.

I freeze, trying to read the undercurrent of emotions in all of their voices. Slowly, I turn toward my group of friends. The tequila is buzzing through my veins now, making me feel a little out of my league. I know something is off but I can't quite put my finger on it.

"Hey ya, Claire," Derek says easily, moving in to kiss Claire hello.

Easton steps in between them and grips Derek's shoulder.

Derek snorts and steps back, raising his hands. He turns back to me. "You sure you don't want that drink?"

I shake my head. "Sorry for bumping into you."

"Don't sweat it, sweets." He glances at Claire again. "I have a few things I want to run by you for our new single cover. Call you this week."

She nods as Easton scowls.

Austin wraps his hand around my waist and tugs me firmly against his chest.

Derek catches the movement and his eyes light with amusement before he turns back to his friends.

"Come on," Austin says, moving me back toward Panda and James and the rest of the Hawks.

"I still have to go to the bathroom," I mutter.

Easton chuckles and tips his head. "We'll walk you. I don't remember you being this much of a troublemaker, Chlo."

My mouth drops open. "I'm not, I wasn't—"

"Relax." Claire links her arm with mine and steers me toward the bathroom. "He's just messing with you. I used to date Derek and—"

"You dated Derek Reiner?"

Claire nods, glancing over her shoulder. I follow her line of vision, noting how Austin's gaze is zeroed in on me. His mouth is pressed into a thin line and his arms are crossed over his chest. He looks pissed.

I frown and his expression softens. He lifts his chin at me and I nod just as Claire pulls me around a corner.

"It was casual. I got swept up in him and it was a mistake. As you can tell, Easton can't stand him but I still do some design work for *The Burnt Clovers*. And he's not a bad guy. He just makes bad choices."

I nod along, still trying to process everything that just

happened on top of my two shots and an afternoon of day drinking.

The bathroom door closes behind us and Claire fixes me with a look.

"What?" I ask, glancing at myself in the mirror.

"I thought my brother was going to punch Derek in the face. That's why I came over with him."

"Austin? Punch Derek..." I murmur, my speech slightly slurred.

Claire's eyes narrow. "You holding up okay, Chlo?"

I nod.

Claire tips her head toward the bathroom stall. "Go ahead. I'll wait for you." She shakes her head. "Not counting hockey, I haven't seen Austin look that angry in years..." she says to herself.

I open my mouth to ask what she means but think better of it. I really need to pee and my mind is still reeling from meeting Derek Reiner, learning that Claire used to date him, and witnessing how protective Austin is over me.

Wait 'til I tell Abbi....

CHAPTER 12

AUSTIN

"Fucking Derek Reiner," Easton murmurs next to me.

"I can't believe my sister ever dated him."

Easton nods, rolling his lips together. "He's a dick."

"He would have liquored Chloe up real fast," I agree, hating how easily she fell into step next to him. Did she want to have a drink with him? Did I just…what? Cockblock her? I cringe at the thought. I shouldn't be messing with Chloe's romantic life but fuck if I let her cozy up with Reiner. Not a chance in hell.

"I think she was just shocked," East offers. "Especially if she's a fan. Imagine if you randomly ran into *One Direction* or some shit."

I flip him the middle finger and he chuckles.

"For real, what's the deal with you?" Easton asks.

I shrug, glancing at him. "What do you mean?"

"You're clearly into her as more than just a friend."

"What clearly? I've known her forever. Of course I care about her more than some girl I just met."

East makes a sound in the back of his throat, a cross between laughter and swearing. "All right, man. All I'm saying is, if you're into her, you better lock her down sooner rather than later. Because a woman who looks like Chloe, with her brains and her sweetness"—he shakes his head—"she's not going to be on the market for long. Especially once she realizes most guys aren't as douchey as her ex-fiancé."

My hands curl in anger at the mention of Steve. God, I hate that guy. Hate that he once occupied Chloe's mind and heart. Can't fucking stand that she looked at Reiner tonight with damn hearts in her eyes. And don't even get me started on Panda and his relentless flirting. If he touches her one more time… Christ, what the hell is wrong with me?

"Grab a drink, Aus. Take the edge off," Easton murmurs beside me, sarcastic as ever.

I groan and my best friend laughs.

"It's not like that," I repeat but I'm not even convincing myself.

Easton's laughter grows. He straightens as the girls come around the hallway and reenter the bar. Easton smacks my shoulder. "We're getting out of here. After witnessing that bullshit, I need to remind Claire exactly what—"

"Stop talking and go," I grind out. At times like these, I wish that my best friend wasn't dating my baby sister.

Easton keeps laughing, walking over to Claire with his unchecked swagger. My sister practically melts into him and blows me a kiss goodbye as she follows Easton toward the exit.

Chloe sidles up beside me and I drape my arm around her shoulders, wanting her close. It's irrational and on some level, I know it's wrong, to want to claim her as mine when I have no intention of making her mine. But right now, I don't give a fuck. I want to deck the next guy who makes freaking googley eyes at her—whether she wants the attention or not.

I brush my fingers over her bare shoulder, the feel of her soft skin settling me some. She shuffles closer to my side and I hold her tighter, liking how she fits beside me. Liking having her with me more than I thought I would.

What the hell did I get myself into? This was supposed to be easy, a fun summer without the usual dating drama I avoid at all costs. For sure, being with Chloe is a hell of a lot more fun than any of the other women I've dated in recent years. But I also feel too much when I'm with her. I watch out for her, concerned and anxious and desperate to know where she is at all times. That's not normal, is it?

And if it is, it can't be *my* normal. In a few months, I'll be back to my hockey lifestyle, practices and games and travel. As team captain, I can't afford to have my attention diverted away from anything that's not the team. The game. I've already experienced firsthand the type of devastation that can occur when a player's, a captain's, head isn't in the game. In a split second, a career can end, a life can change. I can't handle that type of guilt again; I'm barely handling the pressure now.

We make it back toward our spot at the bar. James is engaged in conversation with the bartender, Bella, again. I grin at my friend, happy he decided to come out tonight. The past year has been shit for him and it's good to see him engaging in conversation—as innocent as it is—with a woman in a social setting. I snort when I see last season's rookie, Sims, chatting up three women with a finesse I didn't think he possessed. Claire was right, Panda already corrupted Sims. Yeager, most likely one of next season's starting defensemen now that Torsten's retired, is passing out another round of drinks.

He passes one to Chloe and she glances up at me before hesitantly accepting it. A lump swells in my throat. Fuck, did I make her second-guess being here? She shouldn't walk on eggshells because I'm being moody. Instead of building her up the way I promised Claire I would, my reaction to her chatting with Reiner only added to her insecurities. Shame floods through me and I shift my arm from her shoulder to wrap around her waist instead.

Chloe didn't do anything wrong by bumping into Reiner

and then being a little starstruck by his presence. I watched the whole thing unfold and saw she wasn't openly flirting with him.

And if she was, so what? She's allowed to flirt…

The lump grows larger and my stomach knots. Of course she's allowed to talk to any guy she wants but I don't fucking like it. I can lie to myself and pretend it's because I've known her forever and want to look out for her. But that's what it would be. A lie.

My hand fans out across her hip, my fingertips brushing against the material of her sundress. I dip my head and speak into her ear. "I'm sorry. I just, I worry about you, Chlo."

She shifts her weight, tipping her head back to peer up at me. "I really wasn't expecting it to be him, you know? I'm a big fan of *The Burnt Clovers*." She shakes her head. "Abbi is going to flip out when I tell her."

I smile at the enthusiasm in her voice, the delight in her expression at meeting a musician she likes easing some of the frustration still buzzing around my head.

Chloe laughs. "I can't believe Claire dated him."

Yeager lifts his shot glass and our little group follows suit. I clink mine against Chloe's. "Thanks for coming with me tonight."

"I said it already, Aus. I'm happy to be here." Her tone is sweet and sincere. Just like her and it only makes the lump in my throat grow. Swallowing against it is difficult and I toss back the shot to ease the emotions bubbling up.

The noise of Taps, an often-welcomed distraction, grows overwhelming. Too loud. The giggling of a dozen females grates on my nerves as Sims, Panda, and Yeager chat them all up. The tequila begins to throb in my temples. Suddenly, all I want to do is get out of here and take Chloe someplace quiet. Someplace where I can enjoy her company. Enjoy her…

What am I thinking? I glance down at Chlo again, surprised to note that she's still staring up at me. Her green eyes are wide, watching me with a carefulness I dislike. A delicate pink blossoms in the apples of her cheeks. Her lips are so full and they part the tiniest bit. Fuck, she's mesmerizing.

I hate that Easton was right. There's no chance in hell men won't clamor for Chloe's attention, for a ray of her light. She's breathtaking and intelligent and sincere. Being with her is as natural as breathing and I'm beginning to look forward to our time together more than I'm supposed to.

This time, Chloe lifts a lime to my lips and I bite into it slowly, my eyes trained on hers. I don't give a fuck that we're in the center of Taps, where anyone can see us. I don't care that Panda is watching me curiously, with a shrewdness that annoys me. I don't give a shit about anything except Chloe and being with her right now. I bite into the lime and the sour tartness explodes in my mouth. The corner of Chloe's mouth ticks up, slowly. Almost seductively even though I know that's not her intent. My skin feels too hot, too tight.

My head is buzzing with thoughts I don't want to consider, thoughts I want to act on. Her hand drops away with the lime and I shift closer, my grip on her waist tightening. My fingers brush over her belly button, my hand settling even lower on her stomach. She sucks in a sharp inhale, her eyes darting to mine. I meet them and fall into two green pools, not wanting to blink this moment away.

Right now, I want to kiss my oldest friend. I want witnesses to see me kiss her. I want Chloe.

The room spins and it's got nothing to do with alcohol. I search Chloe's gaze for a clue about her thoughts. Does she feel this? The chemistry between us, the push and pull and need that seems to grow with every exchange? Does she think about me as much as I think about her?

If I kissed her right now, would she—

Panda swoops down, jostling me back half a step as he says something I can't make out. Chloe's head swivels toward him and she snorts at whatever he says, amusement rippling over her expression.

And I snap.

Knowing I need to get the hell out of Taps before I knock Panda out, and hitting a teammate is never a good look, especially for the team captain, I bend down, wrap my arm around the backs of Chloe's knees and toss her over my shoulder. She squeals, surprise and delight and the sweetest laughter I've ever heard.

Panda's eyes widen in surprise but instead of looking pissed, he looks pleased, which only makes me want to deck him more. Yeager lets out a "yeehaw" and James, always quiet and observing, laughs along with Sims.

I flip my teammates my middle finger which only causes their laughter to swell, rising and cresting like a wave before it breaks over me. I turn on my heel, careful to keep the hem of Chloe's dress pinned underneath my forearm, and stride toward the door. The crowd parts, people with shocked expressions, wide eyes, and opened mouths, taking us in. Others are laughing and pointing, amused and delighted. A few flashes go off and I know tomorrow, this moment will be on social media accounts across the city, maybe even the country, but I don't care.

Right now, I just want to get the hell out of here and I want Chloe by my side.

She's banging on my back to let her down, her knees rubbing against my chest. But she doesn't sound angry, only surprised. And I don't give a shit either because right now, I just want her in my arms.

We clear the door and the heavy summer heat hits me. When we're out of the parking lot and on the street, I shift Chloe and let her slide down my body until her feet are firmly planted on the ground.

She gapes up at me, her eyes swimming with confusion. She shakes her head, her hands fisting at her sides as she opens and closes her mouth several times, although no words come out.

Then, she does the only thing that could surprise me more than my own actions. She grips the collar of my shirt and tugs me down. She glares at me for a full breath before pulling me toward her and kissing me with a ferocity that nearly knocks me on my ass.

Thank God for quick reflexes because I recover. My right hand finds her hip, my left lands in the center of her back, and I pull her closer, until her chest is flush with mine.

Her grip on my shirt relaxes and her hands slide up over my shoulders, twisting at the back of my neck. Her lips part and my tongue dips inside, meeting with hers. I kiss her back with an intensity that surprises me and as her frustration morphs into want, my need for her skyrockets.

My hands explore her curves, wanting to touch every inch of her. Her fingers thread through my hair and tug. My mouth trails open-mouthed kisses down her neck as she arches up into me, panting. And Christ, she's gorgeous. Her eyes are hazy with want and my fingers ache to slip the delicate straps of her dress clear off her shoulders. Right now, I want her, any way she'll let me have her.

My mouth finds hers once more and I kiss her hard before she pulls away.

She adds two steps of distance between us and glances at me, bewildered. She presses a hand to her chest, the heat of a second ago morphing into a chill I want to melt away.

I step toward her but she lifts a hand and shakes her head.

"Chloe," I say, my voice desperate. Fuck, what was I thinking? I just ruined everything, didn't I? A friendship, a connection, a—

"Jesus, Austin," she breathes out. "I just kissed you." Her tone holds an accusation that makes me want to smile but I bite it back, knowing it will only anger her.

"I kissed you back," I point out.

"But did you mean it?" she asks directly, a vulnerability I wasn't prepared for flaring in her eyes.

I open my mouth but nothing comes out. Of course I fucking meant it. But do I tell her that? How will she react? What will she—

She swears, disbelief wrapped around the curse word. "Austin, I can't do this again."

My eyebrows pull together as I wait for her to explain herself.

She steps toward me and places her palms on my chest. She slides them up and brushes them over my shoulders once, shaking her head. When she meets my gaze, her eyes are guarded, her expression uncertain.

"Chloe—"

"Figure out what you want, Austin. And when you do, give me a call." She turns on her heel, walking toward the corner. She pulls her phone from her bag and taps on the screen.

Panic blazes through me as I walk after her. "Wait. What's that mean? Where are you going?"

She chuckles and shoots me a look over her shoulder. After another second, she drops her phone back in her purse and heaves a giant sigh. "It means, you need to decide what you want. Because that"—she points at Taps—"was all mixed signals. I kissed you first but you responded, Austin. That"—she stops walking and spins, jabbing her finger toward the street corner where I just kissed her like my life depended on it—"was only more mixed signals piled on top. I'm beyond confused, Austin. I don't know what this means." She gestures between us. "And I don't know what you want. So, ball's in your court, big guy." She tilts her head, an expression I can't decipher crossing her face. Her eyes soften, a tenderness filling them. "But that was one hell of a kiss."

I choke on a laugh, confused and surprised and just

wanting her. I reach for her again but she shakes her head as a car pulls up next to the curb. "This is me."

"You're taking an Uber?" I ask, annoyed that she's going to slip inside some stranger's car instead of coming home with me so we can…talk about this.

"It's a Lyft." She opens the back door. "I had a great time today, Austin. Really. I just, I can't be an afterthought again. To anyone." She slides into the car and pulls the door closed behind her.

I watch as the car pulls away from the curb, the taillights growing smaller.

Fuck. I reach up and grip the back of my head. What the hell just happened? What was that kiss? What were all those feelings that exploded in my chest when I held Chloe?

And who the hell was the confident, sassy woman who just served me with an ultimatum and managed to make me laugh while doing it?

I grin at the empty street, knowing full well that everything just shifted. Changed.

And I'm not mad about it. Not at all.

CHAPTER 13
CHLOE

For two days, I don't hear from Austin. It's enough time to make me question everything and eat most of Mimi's doughnuts. Was I too direct? Did I push him away? Was kissing him a mistake?

My fingertips travel over my lips. No way. How could anything that felt that good, that…explosive, be a mistake?

"He'll call," Mimi says with certainty I don't feel. She places another doughnut on my plate.

"I already had one."

"Have another."

"Mim." I tilt my head. "How did you know that Pop was the one?"

"Oh." She leans back in her chair. Her eyes take on a faraway look that's both distant and not as a sparkle glimmers from their depths. "He stood me up."

"What?" I ask, leaning forward in my chair. For all the stories I've heard about Mimi and Pop over the years, this is new. Pop passed when I was in third grade so my memories of him are few and faded. But I do remember how he doted on Mimi.

"Can you believe that?" She turns toward me, smiling. "My big brother Andrew wanted to beat him to a pulp."

"What happened?"

"Well…" She picks up her mug, drawing her story out for dramatic effect. It works because I forget about the doughnut on my plate. She takes a sip of her coffee and sets the mug back down. "Turns out, he'd been in an accident."

I gasp.

Mimi nods, her face serious. "Yep. His father had a farm, you know?"

I nod.

"And that night, one of their goats, Lucky Lucy, gave birth. It all happened suddenly and your pop was needed to lend a hand. He'd been raised on a farm for crying out loud but when Lucy began to rock around, Pop slipped on a patch of mud or wet grass or something and he went down." Mimi pauses to chuckle, wiping a napkin across her eyes.

I smile at her, wondering if her tears are from laughter, nostalgia, or a mixture of both.

"Oh, he went down and knocked his head on the corner of a shelf in the barn. Passed out cold."

"No."

Mimi snorts. "Oh yes, had an egg the size of the moon on his noggin."

I laugh and Mimi's eyes crinkle as she smiles. "What happened?"

"Well, you can imagine his family ribbed him good for that one. Called him all sorts of names for passing out at the sight of new life being brought into the world. You can't begin to guess at the jokes that circulated when I was pregnant with your mother."

"Oh, I can," I say, recalling some of my family's more creative jokes that I've heard over the years.

Mimi waves a hand. "Anyway, later that night, Pop showed up on my father's front porch with a sad-looking bunch of flowers and a bruise on his forehead. After we heard his sob story, we all had a good laugh and my brother decided he shouldn't kick a dog when it's down."

I sputter on my coffee.

"Besides, I told Andrew that night, 'I'm going to marry that man one day.' And I did."

"But how'd you know?" I press for an answer. As much as I enjoy Mimi's stories, they often lack the wisdom I'm searching for.

"It was the look in his eyes when he knocked on the door. Oh, he was embarrassed for sure. He felt guilty. Silly. All sorts of emotions. But when he saw me, that look, all those insecurities, they just disappeared. He looked at me, in my house coat with rollers in my hair—can you imagine?—like I was the most beautiful thing he'd ever seen. Even more beautiful than witnessing life come into the world." Mimi's tone turns wistful. "And I just... I knew."

"When you know, you know," I mumble.

"That's what they say," she agrees.

I sigh and take a big bite of my doughnut.

"Didn't help you, did I?" she asks.

I shake my head and Mimi laughs.

My phone rings and Mimi's eyes light up. "It's him," she says.

I swipe up my phone, my heart hammering in my chest. Austin's name flashes on the screen. Whatever Mimi reads in my expression confirms her lucky guess because she clucks her tongue. "Told ya so."

"Yeah, yeah," I mutter, feigning casual when I really feel like dancing around Mimi's kitchen. Turning away from her sharp eyes for a modicum of privacy—yeah, right—I answer the call.

"Hey," I say slowly.

"Chlo." Austin's voice is gruff, laced with a hint of surprise. Did he think I wouldn't answer?

"It's me."

He breathes out a shaky exhale and I can picture him running his hand over the top of his head the way he does when he's nervous, feeling out of his element. "I meant it."

I remain silent but my fingers grip my phone until my knuckles ache.

"I wanted to kiss you," Austin continues. "I've wanted to kiss you from the moment I opened my parents' front door and saw you standing on the porch. But I don't know how to do *this*. With *you*."

Now I breathe out a shaky breath. Questions ping around my mind but I hold them all back, knowing that Austin needs time to sort out what he's trying to say. If I interrupt him now, I may miss out on hearing what he's trying to tell me.

"I like you, Chloe. I've always liked you but I really like being with you. You're not just some random girl I can hook up with and forget about."

My heart gallops in my chest, so loud and frantic, I bet even Mimi can hear it without her hearing aid.

"But I also can't be all in the way you want, the way you need. The season's starting up and my first priority is the team, the game." His voice cracks and he swears. "I'm not letting a kiss, even if it was hot and made me think of a million things I shouldn't think about doing with you, ruin our friendship. You're stuck with me, Sunshine. But I don't know where we go from here."

Little bubbles of nerves pop in my stomach. Because Austin definitely just tossed the ball back into my court. I bite my bottom lip and lean back in the chair.

Mimi waves her arm beside me, grabbing my attention. I glance at her, raising my eyebrows. She points to the doughnut.

What am I supposed to do with that?

What? I mouth.

She moves the doughnut to the side of the plate and taps

her fingernail against the center of the plate. An image of a wedding dress and tuxedo are stamped into the ceramic and I roll my eyes.

"Chloe? Help me out here…"

"Come with me to Sara's wedding," I blurt out.

"Of course I'm coming," Austin responds automatically. "I'd never back out on our arrangement."

I blow out a deep breath, steel my shoulders, and say what I really want. "Come with me as my date, a real date. Not because of our summer agreement. But because you—"

"I want to. I'd love to."

I close my eyes, my hand nearly numb from clutching the phone so tightly against my ear.

Austin chuckles.

"What's so funny?" I ask.

"I think you just asked me out, Sunshine."

I grin. "I think so too."

"Not gonna lie, I feel a little bit like a pussy right now."

I burst out laughing. "You should."

Austin laughs with me. "You were right. I need to man up."

"Then do it," I challenge him, liking this playful side of him.

"I'm taking you to your cousin's wedding next weekend, Chloe."

"Okay."

"And we're going to dance every—"

"Ed Sheeran song," I interrupt.

"And eat all the—"

"Lobster," I finish his sentence again.

"Fancy cocktails."

"There's a weekend itinerary."

"Sign us up. One hotel room."

I gasp, opening my mouth to remind him that my entire

family will be present at this wedding and our mothers will be gossiping up a storm if we share a hotel room.

"One," he repeats, knowing where my thoughts have turned. "I'm going to dazzle your family."

"They already adore you."

"And at the end of the night, when *I* kiss *you,* you'll know just how much I mean it."

I squirm under Mimi's watchful gaze as Austin's words register in my mind.

"Date me, Chlo."

My mouth drops open.

"I found my balls," he laughs and I snort. "So date me for real. And let's see where this goes."

"See where it goes," I repeat, a little dazed at the sharp turn this conversation has taken.

"I can't give you more than that. I won't lie and say that hockey isn't my priority. This season, coming off a Cup win, being captain…the Hawks are my life. I want you to be part of it but I can't give all of it up either."

"I'm not asking you to." I frown. Doesn't he realize it's not all or nothing? It's blending the two aspects of his life into one. It's not making one thing his everything but making several things his all.

"I can't stop thinking about you."

I bite my bottom lip. I know Austin is being honest with me, completely straight up. Can I even ask for more than that right now? Indecision wreaks havoc on my nervous system. My body feels jittery, my heart thumping at an erratic pace. Every part of me wants to say yes, to give in. But am I giving in? Giving up? Settling for less, the same way I did with Steve?

Austin isn't Steve. Anyone with a pulse knows that.

"One date, Chlo. And if you're not feeling it, we'll be friends no matter what."

"Yes," I say, meaning it with every fiber in my being.

"I'll pick you up for the wedding on Friday. But on Saturday, it's just me and you."

"Okay," I agree, a thrill shimmying down my spine.

Across from me, Mimi reenacts the wave.

When I hang up with Austin, I grin at Mimi. "I have a date."

"You have much more than a date, Chloe Ann."

"YOU'RE DATING YOUR CHILDHOOD BESTIE," Abbi declares through the line later that evening.

"We're not dating. We're going on a date," I clarify.

"With a professional hockey player."

"Yes."

"Who also happens to be one of the most celebrated athletes in the entire state of Massachusetts at the moment."

I huff out a breath. "Yes."

"And you want me to be chill about this?" Abbi exclaims.

I snort and kick my feet back up on my bedroom wall. I'm splayed across my bed, not hating the view of the ceiling as much as I did a few weeks ago. Who knew so much could change in such a short amount of time? Just last month, I was sobbing my eyes out into a watered-down margarita. And now, I'm going on a date with Austin.

"I can't believe you're already bringing him to a family event. A wedding is a serious thing," Abbi continues.

"My family already loves him."

"That will make it trickier if things don't work out."

I drop my feet and sit straight up. "Why do you say that?"

"Shit. Sorry. I didn't mean, I don't know, I—"

"Abbi Walsh."

She sighs. "I just—promise you'll be careful, Chloe?"

"You're the one who kept saying the best way to get over Steve was to get under someone else," I accuse.

"You're going to have sex with him?" Her voice squeaks.

I swear and flop back down against my mattress. "I don't know yet."

Abbi's silent for a long moment and I wait it out.

"I don't want you to get hurt, Chlo. That's all. Steve *broke* you. Austin's been totally upfront with you from the start. But when you go in, you go all in, with all of your feelings. I just—I don't want to see them get hurt again because you want more than what Austin can give right now."

I don't respond because that's…annoyingly accurate.

"And yes, you should have fun, wild, hot sex," she continues.

"Damn straight."

"But I meant with a stranger. Not your childhood best friend who you have history with, whose sisters you adore, who you're bringing to a family function as your *date*."

I work a swallow, noting the truth in her words even if I don't want to admit it. "You have a point," I begrudgingly admit.

"Just…be careful. That's all. Enjoy the moment and take things at face value without reading into them. Other than that, I'm really freaking happy for you!" She squees again and I grin at the excitement in her tone now that she got her warning over with. "Does he have any friends?"

I laugh now and tap my heels against the wall. "Claire, his sister, is dating his best friend, Easton, and Indy, Austin's cousin, is dating Easton's brother, Noah. They all play for the Hawks."

"Jesus Christ," Abbi guffaws. "That's some incestuous shit right there."

"Tell me about it," I laugh. "But…there is one guy, Panda."

"Panda?"

"The goalie."

"Hang on, I'm Googling."

I roll my eyes.

"Holy shit! He looks like Zeus had sex with a Victoria's Secret angel."

Huh? I frown, trying to follow her train of thought. "He's good looking," I agree.

She snorts, the sound derisive. "He is more than good looking, Chloe. He's…an Adonis."

Now I laugh. "You may change your tune when you meet him."

"Am I meeting him?"

"Are you still coming to visit?"

"Be there tomorrow."

I chuckle. "Simmer down. He's not going anywhere. When you come, I'll introduce you."

"I'm holding you to it. The weekend of Marissa's bachelorette. Why do you think I'd not be into him after meeting him?"

"He reminds me of Drew."

At that, Abbi laughs. "I like Drew."

I groan and her laughter grows louder. But after a moment, I join in. It feels good to laugh with my best friend again after so many nights of crying on her shoulder.

Suddenly, everything seems brighter, better. Hopeful.

CHAPTER 14
AUSTIN

"You look so handsome," Mom gushes as I run through the front door.

"I just need—"

"Your black dress shoes." She holds them out to me.

"How'd you know?" I stop short and take the shoes from Mom before kissing her hello.

She pats my cheek. "You left them here after one of your dinners for winning the Cup."

"Thanks." I tilt my head toward the front door. "Not to just barge in and leave but..."

Mom laughs and walks me back to the entrance. "But Chloe is waiting for you and you're staying at the Fairmont Copley Plaza."

"We are." I glance at Mom, trying to read the twinkle in her eyes.

"One room," she states, not bothering to even pose it as a question.

I snort and shake my head. "You and Diane are bad news."

"Oh." Mom swats my arm. "We're the best. And don't

think Diane and Greg and *Mimi* aren't going to be watching you closely tonight."

I chuckle. "Mimi will just want to make sure she wins whatever wager she bet on Chloe and me."

Mom laughs, knowing I'm right. She pulls open the front door. "All right, Austin." She kisses my cheek. "Have fun this weekend."

"I will, Mom." I kiss her goodbye and bound back down the steps to my SUV.

When I first agreed to help Chloe out, my intentions were purely altruistic. I hated that Steve played her. I felt awful that one of her trusted friends would hurt her this way. But what bothered me the most was the way my friend, always so confident and sure of herself, seemed to falter. The way she dipped her head and tucked her chin and hid behind a curtain of hair when she used to hold eye contact and say whatever she was thinking.

I pull out of my parents' driveway and head toward Chloe's house.

But now, everything's changed. I mean, I felt it from that first night, sitting in my parents' backyard, playing drinking games, and later on, having her hand my ass to me in a game of Scrabble. The connection, the pull, the natural chemistry that you can't fake or fabricate, even when you wish you could. It's just there, like a flicker, begging to spark into a flame.

Being with Chloe in Martha's Vineyard hit me like a slap shot. Fast, unexpected, and hard as fuck. The old memories I'd half forgotten about rose to the surface. The anxiety I've been struggling to control eased. And the string of women I've had in and out of my bed for the past few years stopped seeming so convenient and more than a little pathetic. Pitiful really.

Have I really gone this long without a meaningful romantic relationship in my life? I slide my palm along the steering wheel, my throat tightening as I remember that night. College. Carly Edwards with her pretty blonde hair and seductive blue eyes. The drinking and the partying and the kicking up trouble. Waking up in the wrong bed at the wrong time and showing up to our scrimmage too hungover to see straight. Coach had every right to bench me but we were scrimmaging against our fiercest competition of the season. The goal was to feel each other out and get our heads in the right space for the start of hockey, the one thing that would fuel all of us for the next seven months. But I fucked up.

I drank that extra shot. I joked around that extra hour. I followed Carly into her dorm room when I should have bounced and slept in my own bed. And the next day, I was benched and a freshman was put in my place. Coach wanted to teach me a lesson and he did. Because when Chris went down in the second period with a severe concussion and a spinal cord injury, I wished I was the lifeless body lying in a heap on the ice. He was carried off in a stretcher and the rink was so quiet I could hear Mike Rice breathing at the other end of the bench.

In that moment, my entire world shifted. I sobered up and felt the crushing weight of Chris's injury land on my shoulders. If I wasn't horsing around the night before, he never would have played in the scrimmage. If I hadn't spent the night getting lost in Carly, the woman I was dating, I wouldn't have needed to learn a lesson.

If I had just been the team leader I wanted to grow into, Chris wouldn't have spent the next three years of his life in physical rehabilitation.

I turn on to Chloe's street and feel some of the pressure in my chest settle. I flip on the radio just for some noise to clear my head. That scrimmage was years ago and still, the sound of Chris hitting the ice haunts me. After that day, I approached hockey, my team, my responsibilities, with a different outlook. I no longer broke rules; instead, I made them.

Until now, I've always stuck to them too.

But taking Chloe to a wedding, dating her, exploring if this thing between us is for real, that's allowed, right? I'm not a college kid anymore. I'm not going to lose my head, get distracted, or hurt my team by being with a woman who makes me feel a thread of that reckless invincibility again, am I?

I stop in front of Chloe's house and blow out an exhale.

It's just a date. It's just a wedding. It's just exploring what comes next.

Squaring my shoulders, I exit my SUV and walk the steps to Chloe's front door. I knock and a second later, the door swings wide open.

"How are ya, fucker?" Drew greets me like he used to, when he was seventeen and I was fifteen and I didn't yet know the agony of causing someone life-changing heartache.

"Fuck, man, how are you?" I ask, smacking my hand in his.

He chuckles, the same shit-eating grin on his face. "Doing well. Can't believe you're coming to this wedding."

I shrug. "And here I thought you were going to give me shit for dating your sister."

Drew pauses and leans back to stare at me. "You and Chlo? For real?"

"I knew it!" Mimi calls out, stepping into the foyer. She's already dressed in a cobalt blue pantsuit, her eyes shimmering and her hair coiffed.

"You look stunning, Mim." I kiss her hello.

"Oh, my handsome boy." She pats my cheeks with both of her palms.

"I'm still here, Mimi," Drew reminds her. "I'm your grandson, remember?"

"I do but you didn't lead Boston to a victory," Mimi shoots back.

Drew laughs. "Welcome to the family, man." He smacks me on the back and his words don't frighten me as much as they should. "What's the deal with you and Chloe?"

"She really didn't tell you." I glance at Mimi.

She shrugs. "I had my suspicions."

"You're playing it coy, aren't you?" I joke.

Mimi's eyes light up. "It's my specialty."

Drew and I laugh.

"Whatever dude, as long as my sister isn't still wearing a ring by the douchebag, she can date whoever she wants." He glances at me. "To be honest, I'd rather it be you than some fancy-ass suit from New York. At least I know you won't hurt her."

"Thanks," I say, knowing he means it as a compliment. But coming off of my recent thoughts of Chris, his sentiments land differently. I won't hurt her, right? I know she's scared of being an afterthought but I can balance dating with hockey, can't I? With being the leader the team needs me to be? With being the guy Chloe wants me to be?

"There you are," Diane greets me hello. "Chloe and Greg will be down in a minute and then we can head to the hotel. We're already checked in so we can dress and be ready for the wedding at six."

"Sounds good, Diane. How's work going, man?" I ask Drew, who's stationed at Fort Hood in Texas.

"It's okay. I'm gearing up for—"

But I stop listening to him because Chloe appears at the top of the stairs. Her brown hair is already curled and pinned back in the front. Her makeup is subtle but her green eyes pop. Her lips are mouthwatering and I have the sudden desire to taste them again. To kiss her, even though her entire family is looking on like tourists in Time Square.

She's dressed simply, in a navy, linen sundress that ends

just below her knees. A garment bag is draped over her arm and her rolling suitcase is next to her on the floor.

Drew moves to grab her suitcase but I beat him to it, practically scrambling up the stairs. I hear Drew snicker behind me.

"Hey," Chloe says as I reach down to grab her suitcase.

"Hey yourself, Sunshine." I lift the suitcase and kiss her cheek. "You look gorgeous."

She blushes but I can tell my words please her because she smiles and it's soft and tender. Sweet.

"And so it begins," Greg booms behind Chloe and we both jump.

When I look up, he's smiling widely.

"The boy next door and—" Greg begins but Chloe groans.

"Dad, please. Don't tell me you've been listening to Mom's romance books again."

Greg shrugs, not even bothering to look sheepish. "She listens to the audiobooks while she's cooking. Those friends-to-lovers are my favorite. Oh, and the rom coms." He brushes past us and bounds down the stairs. "Drew, want to help me load the cars?"

"Was that a real question?" Drew asks, picking up Mimi's suitcase and garment bag.

"Nope, just thought it was polite to pose it as one," Greg answers cheerily, pulling open the front door.

I chuckle.

Chloe rolls her eyes. "Honestly, it's a relief you already know how insane my family is. Could you imagine trying to introduce a guy to this…circus." She gestures to her family below us, all calling out last-minute reminders and instructions.

I wrap my arm around her waist and gesture for her to take the stairs. "Trust me, I can relate."

"I know." She glances at me over her shoulder. "You sure about this?"

"A hundred percent."

Chloe smiles that tender smile again and it rolls over me, familiar and comforting.

"Besides," I add, "I wouldn't want Mimi to lose her bet."

A HANDFUL OF HOURS LATER, I stand by Chloe's side as her cousin Sara walks down the aisle. The ceremony, taking place in the Fairmont Copley Plaza, is beautiful. Everything is white and gold and simultaneously ornate and personal.

Chloe draws in a sharp inhale next to me and I watch as wistfulness crosses her face. She's beaming at her cousin and I can read the genuine happiness in her expression. But her eyes are still shadowed with memories of a previous life. With thoughts of a happily-ever-after that never happened.

With hopes and wishes and dreams she thinks she may never have.

The realization—of the life Chloe wants, of the future she desires—descends on me like a curtain. Slowly, gradually, but by the time Sara clasps hands with her groom, Mark, I know it in my bones.

Chloe Crawford is the woman you marry, the one you straight up wifey and never put second.

I don't know if I'm the man who can ever measure up to that role.

But I want to be.

CHAPTER 15
CHLOE

Between the ceremony and reception, something changes.

I'm not sure exactly when it happens but when Austin grasps my hand to lead me into the Grand Ballroom, his touch is more certain, his eyes less guarded. He smiles at me like I'm the most beautiful woman he's ever laid eyes on—*more beautiful than witnessing life coming into the world*—and a reassurance I didn't realize I wanted wraps around me.

I smile back and together, as a real couple, we enter my cousin's wedding reception. Gold and white, silk and lace, flowers, high vaulted ceilings, and unbelievable splendor, greets us.

"I feel like we just stepped back in time," I admit to Austin.

"You're the belle of the ball," he jokes, plucking up the name card with our table seating.

Mr. Austin Merrick and Ms. Chloe Crawford, Table 5

I like how our names look in the bold strokes of the calligraphy. I like how they look next to each other too, like Austin and I are a unit. I lead him to Table 5 where Mimi and Drew are already seated, champagne in hand.

"Not wasting any time, are you?" I lift an eyebrow at my brother.

"Not when they're serving Dom Perignon," Mimi responds quietly.

Austin and Drew bark out their laughter and I fight mine as I sit down next to my grandmother.

"Sara looks mesmerizing, doesn't she?" Mimi asks, her eyes bright. "Like an angel."

"She does. She's beautiful. Happy," I agree, realizing just how much tonight means to Mimi. After living a very full life with Pop, raising her children and greeting grandchildren as they entered the world, she truly enjoys celebrating our milestones with all the pomp and circumstance. Sometimes, I think she's extra but right now, dressed to the nines in a lavender gown, a champagne flute dangling from her fingers, I realize what an exciting, truly happy life my mimi has lived.

Sentimentality washes over me and I wrap my arm around her shoulders, tugging her into my side and kissing her temple. "Love you, Mim."

"Me more, dear girl." Her gaze darts to Austin. "And I think he might too."

I snort, shaking my head. Leave it to Mimi to fill my head with my own wishful thinking.

I chance a look at my handsome date, still hanging by Drew's side talking, and my throat dries. God, he's perfect. Blue eyes deeper than the ocean, cheekbones that could cut glass, and a steel jawline. He has the tiniest dimple in his chin that my brother used to tease him about when we were younger. His hair is styled, pushed away from his face in a way that should look severe but suits him well. He catches me staring and a slow grin moves across his lips. Tenderness sweeps his expression and he stares at me like, like I'm *his*.

Next to me, Mimi fans herself and passes me her flute.

I take it wordlessly and drink it as Austin chuckles.

"That's how a man should look at you, Chloe," Mimi murmurs.

I nod, realizing she's right. Steve never looked at me like that, not once in five years. Suddenly, I don't even care. Because when Austin looks at me, I feel beautiful, cherished, *confident* again. I realize everyone was right; I dodged a bullet. Not marrying Steve was the greatest thing that ever happened to me. Because it brought me back to Austin.

It brought me *home*.

THE WEDDING RECEPTION kicks off with a bang. Sara and Mark have impeccable taste and it shows in all the details of their wedding. But they also have a great love for fun and adventure. Within thirty minutes of their entrance and first dance, the music is bumping and the drinks are flowing.

My family has barely left the dance floor and I don't remember the last time I smiled so hard for so long. Before dinner is served, Ed Sheeran's "Perfect" comes on and Austin slips an arm around my waist, turning me away from my cousins and into his chest.

I hear one of my cousins sigh as Austin's arms wrap around my frame.

"What is it with you and Ed?" I ask, tilting my head up.

"His music is sincere," he answers honestly, holding me in his arms as we begin to dance. "I like that he writes a lot of the lyrics too."

My cheeks ache from smiling so big but I can't help it. "I never would have thought that big, tough, Hawks Captain Merrick could be so sentimental."

Austin lifts an eyebrow. "Really?"

I laugh. "I mean, knowing you have two sisters, maybe."

He spins me before guiding me back to his chest. He holds my wrist against the pocket of his suit jacket, his other arm still wrapped around my waist.

"But, I don't know, Savannah told me you only date models and these badass CEO women." I shrug, feeling a blush spread up my neck and over my face. "I didn't think you'd be into slow songs and wedding dances."

Austin's gaze flickers over my face for a long moment. "Well I am, with the right woman."

"The right woman?"

He nods. "I hate that Steve managed to fill your head with so much doubt. The Chloe I remember didn't care what anyone thought. She knew how wonderful she was, she knew how much she offered, she knew how much her friends adored and respected her…" He spins me again, his smile lopsided when I face him. "I remember the day you decided you wanted to join the debate team and the advisor told you there weren't any spots left."

I cringe, the memory of his story bubbling up in my mind. But a moment later, I flash him a smile.

"You told him that you'd debate the entire team and if you didn't win against each opponent, you'd walk away. But if you did, then he needed to add a spot for you on the team. Everyone tried to talk you out of it."

"Except Mimi."

"Except Mimi," Austin agrees. "We all thought you were going to get your ass handed to you but you didn't care. You said you were going to be the first freshman to make the team."

"And I was," I say saucily.

Austin chuckles. "And you were. You're the type of woman who doesn't back down from a challenge, Chlo. You make things happen; you create change. You're the kind of woman who can make a man do all the things he thought he never would. You always have been, but you need to believe in that girl again too."

My breath lodges in my throat at the truth in his words, at the depth of feelings in his eyes. I stop swaying, standing still in the center of the dance floor, and stare at the same blue eyes I've been losing myself in for years. "Do you really think I could be that woman again?"

"Not again." He shakes his head and my stomach sinks. "You're still her, Chlo." He dips his head and brushes his lips over mine. It's our second kiss and it couldn't get any more public than this moment.

Outing us to my entire family, I kiss him back with an intensity I've never felt before. My hands find the tops of his shoulders and even though I'm rocking some sexy heels, I push up onto my tippy toes for leverage.

Austin's arm around my waist tightens and the hand clasping mine releases it so he can cup my cheek. He tilts my face and deepens our kiss, his tongue slipping into my mouth. He kisses me passionately for one, two, three seconds before he pulls back and grins.

Ed's voice fades as the next song picks up but I don't even register the melody.

"Just be you," Austin says. "You're already perfect." He takes my hand and leads me back to Table 5.

And I want to swoon. Because who thought this guy, the same one who pantsed me as an awkward adolescent, could be so damn sweet?

As we move through the tables, I receive confirmation of Austin's swoon-worthiness in the expressions of guests I pass. The knowing glances and open shock on the faces of my aunts and cousins cause my blush to deepen. But Austin walks with his spine straight, his head held high, and after a second, I emulate him. Why shouldn't I be kissed in the center of a dance floor by the man I'm now dating? Why shouldn't I revel in it?

I giggle to myself, accepting another glass of champagne from my mom.

"That was some kiss," she whispers, her tone laced with humor.

"Austin's some man," I answer.

"Amen to that," Mimi does the Sign of the Cross and we all burst out laughing.

Dinner passes with easy conversation. Dad, Drew, and Austin talk hockey. Mom, Mimi, and I discuss our summer plans, with me reminding them that Abbi will be visiting soon for Marissa's bachelorette and staying with us. The other guest at our table, my great aunt Millie, fills us in on family gossip during the lulls in conversation that have us all gasping in shock or rolling with laughter. Needless to say, Table 5 is where it's at and I imagine the rest of the wedding guests are jealous they aren't sitting with the Crawfords.

After dinner, dancing resumes. As does drinking.

"Shots! Cousin shots!" Drew demands, circling his finger in the air to round up all the cousins and our dates. He picks Sara up, her laughter loud, and carries her over to the bar, plopping her down on top of it.

Mark, already accustomed to our family insanity, having dated Sara for years, trails behind, grinning.

The bartender fills sixteen shot glasses with—

"Fireball Cinnamon Whiskey!" my cousin Marie cries out. "I hate you, Drew."

Drew blows her a kiss and passes her a shot glass. "Come on guys, I never get to come home and see you all."

"True." My cousin Calvin, the most reserved of all the cousins, taps Drew on the back. "But not all of us are military men, able to hold our liquor, like you."

"Fair enough." Drew grins, placing a shot glass in Calvin's hands. "But you're still drinking that, Cal."

Marie and Sara cheer. Mark steps up to the bar and plants an arm around Sara to keep her steady. Austin shadows my back, his hand on my hip. I lean back against his strong chest, liking the feel of him against my back, of his strength supporting me.

Austin points at Drew. "If we do one—"

"We do two," my brother agrees, and I'm reminded of some old, teenage thing they used to do with shotgunning beers in Mom and Dad's garage.

Austin asks the bartender to line up another row of shots.

Calvin groans and Sara claps her hands.

"To Sara and Mark." My brother raises his shot glass and we all follow. "May you find all the love, happiness, and adventure you're searching for."

We all echo Drew, lift our shooters, and toss them back. The Fireball blazes a path of heat down my throat, hitting my stomach like a punch before fanning out and warming my limbs.

I smack my lips together, shooting a look at Austin. "I've drunk more since reconnecting with you than I have in the past two years."

He grins, his lips passing over the shell of my ear as he whispers, "I'll take your second shot if you're not up for it."

I shake my head, even though I appreciate the offer. "No way. I'm just letting you know, you may need to carry me up to our room later. Put me to bed."

Austin's eyes gleam and a cheeky smile curves his lips.

I snort and smack the back of my hand against his stomach. "Get your head out of the gutter."

"You put it there," he accuses.

Marie hands us shot glasses, glancing between us. "You guys are cute together."

"Thanks, Marie," Austin responds.

"Okay." Drew raises his second shot glass. "Now, can we just take a second to applaud the man who brought Boston back from the brink with a Stanley Cup win!" he shouts, lifting his glass in the air and pointing at Austin.

Austin groans next to me, dipping his head in embarrassment. I shoot Drew a look but the grin on my brother's face says he knew exactly what he was doing. He wanted to put Austin on the spot the way he did all throughout our childhood.

Austin takes the cheers and applause in stride, thanking everyone while flipping Drew the middle finger to even more laughter. We all take our next shot.

Drew places his shot glass on the bar. "Come on, man. You're dating my sister. I need to mess with you a little."

"I know, I know," Austin agrees.

"We love you, Aus." Sara claps.

"Just wait 'til he sings us a song later," Drew announces.

Austin's and my heads swivel toward Drew.

My brother chuckles, amusement in his gaze. "Oh yeah. Claire told me all about your drinking game last month. She promised that you can give Easton a run for his money. I never knew you had a thing for Madonna, Aus."

I tip my head back and laugh. A few hours later, as the wedding winds down, Austin entertains my cousins and some of the straggling guests with a rendition of Madonna's "Like a Virgin." He goes all in, with dance moves and sexy hip gyrating. Drew jumps in as back up and even Cal, definitely feeling his alcohol, lends his lack of talents to the performance.

Mimi's face lights up like a Christmas tree. Pure delight shines in her eyes as she claps along, checking several times that Mom is recording it all on her phone.

But I can't tear my gaze away from Austin. He makes me feel all the things I always desired: whole, cherished, beautiful, and happy. He makes me laugh and centers me. He listens and embraces my wild family and all their antics.

And when he carries me over the threshold of our hotel room, he makes my body tighten with unrivaled anticipation.

CHAPTER 16
AUSTIN

With pink cheeks, parted lips, and dark eyes, Chloe Crawford unmans me. I've never been so desperate to be inside of a woman as I am Chloe.

"God, you're fucking gorgeous," I murmur, my fingers fumbling with the clasp on her shoes. After two attempts, I snort. "A little help?"

She grins and quickly removes her shoes.

"How drunk are you?" I ask her.

"Sober enough to want every single thing we're about to do and tipsy enough to not be embarrassed admitting it to you."

I nearly groan at the confidence in her voice. Damn, I've missed it. Somehow, I've missed her without even knowing it. "Don't ever be embarrassed to tell me anything. Especially what you want right now." I run my fingers over the soft skin of her arm before finding the small zipper hidden in the seam running down the side of her body. I drag it down slowly.

Chloe shimmies out of the straps of her dress, a deep purple that looks mesmerizing on her, and lets the material rush down her body and pool at her feet. She kicks the dress to the side and stands before me in a black strapless bra and black lace panties that hide nothing but conceal enough to be sexier than if she was naked.

My mouth dries and I force myself to meet her eyes.

"Like what you see?" she asks, a hint of nerves in her eyes even though her voice is composed.

"Love everything about you," I answer truthfully, popping the bottom on my suit pants. In a handful of seconds, I'm standing before her in nothing but my boxers.

Chloe bites her bottom lip and raises an eyebrow. "Are those Spanx?"

I snort, making a strangled sound of laughter and impatience. "They have a men's line and they're comfortable. Are you going to give me shit about everything?"

She tips her head back and laughs, the sound rich and sincere.

"Get over here." I hook my fingers under the side band of her panties and drag her toward me. "You're trouble, Chloe Crawford."

"Funny." Her eyes flare. "That's what they used to say about you."

I capture her lips in one long kiss. "Now what do they say?"

"That you're a rule follower. A rule maker."

I nod, noting the truth in her words. "But I'm about to break them all tonight."

Her brow furrows, confusion swirling in her eyes. Not giving her a chance to ask any questions, I walk her backwards toward the bed until she sits down on the edge of the mattress. My body presses into hers as I kiss her slowly, soulfully, until she relaxes enough to lie back. I waste no time crawling up her frame, my fingers tracing every curve, my mouth fused with hers.

I kiss Chloe like I'll never get enough. In a handful of seconds, I realize I won't. Her eyes flutter closed as I drag the backs of my knuckles up her cheekbone. She tastes like cinnamon and desire. She smells like violets and vanilla. And she feels like the first day of spring, full of possibility and wonder.

I deepen our kiss, enjoying her soft mewls and elevated breathing. Her hands track my back, running over my shoulder blades and up the side of my body. I kiss my way down the column of her neck, loving how she arches into me. Pulling down the cups of her bra, I drag my lips across her chest, pulling one pert nipple into my mouth and sucking its sweetness.

"Oh!" Chloe gasps, her fingers threading through my hair and hugging my face to her chest. Her legs encircle my waist, pulling me closer.

I'm so hard, so desperate for her, that I groan when my dick presses against her core. She moans from the contact, the sound encouraging me to travel south, until I pull her panties to the side and drag my tongue up her center.

"Austin," she moans. "Austin."

"Shh." I nibble the inside of her thigh. "I got you, baby." I drag two fingers through her center, spreading her arousal around her clit. At my light touch, she bucks against my hand and I recall our conversation from the beach in Martha's Vineyard.

About how Steve didn't pleasure her the way she deserves. About how he never made her body quake and quiver with want and need and delicious relief. How the hell didn't he do that when she's this responsive, this beautiful, this fucking perfect?

Fuck that. I commit to filling my Sunshine up with so much pleasure, she breaks apart on my fingers, my mouth, on *me* before the sun rises. I drop my head again and drag my tongue over her core, locking in on this moment. On the sounds falling from her sweet lips. On the tension in her thighs as they clasp around my head. On the arch of her back. Her shallowed breathing. Her deep moans that fill me with so much goddamn desire, I pulse for her. She shatters, calling out my name in a tone that fills me with so much pride, it nearly rivals winning the Stanley Cup.

"Oh my God," she whispers, her eyes wide and hazy and fucking beautiful when they bore into mine. "That was, holy shit, Austin. I never, that never, I, wow."

Puffed up like a damn peacock, I lose my boxers. I run my hand over my shaft twice before rolling on a condom. Chloe breathes in when she catches sight of me. "Let me make you come again, baby," I tell her. When I drag my dick through her glistening folds, her eyes nearly roll back in her head and she collapses back against the mattress.

I grin cockily at her response but the moment I slide into her, my grin dies. Because holy fucking shit, she's tight, gripping my dick in a way that has me crying out. I pull out slowly before plunging back in.

"Christ, Chloe, you're fucking perfect," I tell her, rocking into a rhythm that has us both breathing heavily. The sounds of our bodies joining together, slick and needy, fill the silence of the room. The scent of our arousal scents the air. My body tightens, more desperate than it's ever been for release. I stare into Chloe's wide, jade-colored eyes and realize that my old friend is now my everything.

"Oh God, Austin," she says when she's close.

And fuck, so am I. My body trembles for release, the sounds Chloe makes pushing me higher. I grit my teeth, determined to hold on for a few more seconds. I conjure up the most awful and depressing things I can think of until Chloe quakes around me. Then, I release inside of her, hard and fast and so fucking relieved. "Baby, you're incredible." I collapse, rolling us so she's nestled into my side.

I hold her against my chest, our skin sticky. Chloe's hair tickles my arm, her breath fanning over my skin.

"Austin," she says after a minute.

I shift to peer into her eyes.

"It's never been like that for me," she admits. "I just—I want you to know that I've never felt this good before."

I grin, her words their own kind of gift. "For me either," I admit.

"Shut up." She smacks my chest, not believing me.

I shake my head, holding her tighter. "I'm serious, Chloe. No one's ever made me feel as good as you. When I'm with you, all the noise stops."

She smiles softly, almost shyly, and I plant another kiss on her mouth.

"Is it always noisy in your mind?" she asks, her gaze searching.

I nod slowly, my fingers tracing lazy eights over her skin. "Since college," I admit, knowing it's time to truly confide in Chloe. If we're going to try to make this work, if we're going to have chemistry like *this*, then she should know what she's dealing with when it comes to my anxiety. With my past.

"What happened?" she whispers.

I sigh, looking down at her and pressing a quick kiss to the tip of her nose. "It was my junior year of college. It was the first time I was really dating a girl. We weren't a couple or anything, but everyone knew we were hooking up. Anyway, one night, there was a party. I got carried away with the drinking, big surprise there." I glance at Chloe but she's watching me intently, her eyes devoid of judgement. Just colored with curiosity.

"I drank way too much and when Carly invited me back to her place, I went. Even though I knew we had a tough scrimmage the next day. At that point in my life, I thought I was on top of the world. There was no way Coach would bench me because I was the leading scorer. But when I showed up to the scrimmage hungover as fuck, reeking of booze..."

"He benched you," she supplies.

I nod, dropping my head closer to hers. She turns in my

arms until she's facing me, her fingertips pressed against my chest.

"He put a freshman in my spot. It was a big moment for the kid, Chris. A chance to step up and prove himself. He was nervous and I was pissed off but he skated onto the ice and did his best." I blow out a sigh, hating that I have to admit this next part to Chloe. Will she see me differently? Will she resent me the way I resent myself for taking a kid's life, the only life he knew, away from him? "He took a tough hit in the second period and went down hard. It was a concussion and a...a spinal cord injury." I wince, closing my eyes.

Chloe's hands press flat against my chest. When I open my eyes she's staring at me with pure compassion. "I'm sorry, Austin. That must have been...well, I can't imagine how hard that was for you to see. But it's not your fault."

"It is," I argue. "If I wasn't goofing off, being irresponsible, Chris never would have played in that scrimmage. He never played hockey again. He spent the next few years in PT, relearning how to walk." I work a swallow. "That day changed everything for me. I can't let anyone down like that again. I won't let my team down."

Chloe nods slowly, snuggling closer. "Your team is lucky to have you for a captain. You're so dedicated and I can tell how much you truly care about the guys, about what's going on in their lives. It's not just about hockey but about them, as individuals."

"Thank you."

"But you're still human, Austin. That day was a mistake, a stupid mistake. But it's not on you."

I shake my head. "Maybe not all of it, but I still feel responsible."

"Is this why you're always thinking about the future? Anticipating a fallout?"

I nod. "I don't know how to balance it all. Hockey and life and relationships." I try to smile but it slips. We're having a serious conversation right now. This is the most I've ever opened up to anyone in my life. I don't want to be glib about it. Not with Chloe. "I don't want to let anyone down. I don't want to disappoint anyone."

Chloe tilts her neck back until she can brush a kiss over my lips. "You won't. The fact that you're even aware of that means you'll do everything in your power to make sure you show up for the team the way you want to. Need to."

My hand squeezes her side as I admit, "I don't want to disappoint you either."

At this, she smiles. "Impossible."

I smile back. "You'll tell me though, right? If I'm not... enough for you."

Chloe winds her arms around my neck and pulls her body flush against mine. "Austin Merrick, we didn't even have our first date yet."

I chuckle.

"Don't worry so much about the future and just, enjoy the now. Be here with me."

"Okay," I whisper, kissing her back.

"And yes," she murmurs against my lips, "I'll tell you. But thank you for confiding in me, baby."

Her acknowledgement of what I need eases some of my concerns. I kiss Chloe slowly, languidly. I explore her body with soft touches and she lets me, doing a bit of her own exploring.

Silence stretches between us. It's heavy with our need but also lighter now, because of the truth I shared.

Chloe turns in my arms again, her back pressed into my chest, her hands hovering over mine as I cup her breasts. "Can we sleep in tomorrow?" she asks, like someone would ever say no to that.

"Of course."

Her eyes flutter, a yawn escaping her lips. "Thanks for

being the best wedding date in the world. And thanks for trusting me with your past."

"Thanks for being you." I kiss the side of her neck.

She lifts our joined hands to press a kiss to my wrist. When she releases her hold, my fingers brush over her nipple. My other hand travels down between her legs again. I play there, slow and languid strokes. Chloe sucks in a breath, her breathing ticking up as I dip my fingers inside of her, pull them out, and circle her clit. I repeat the pattern, keeping the pace slow. The sound of her arousal turns both of us on and it doesn't take long for me to grow hard again.

"Austin," she murmurs, her hand finding my dick, still sheathed in a condom.

"This is about you, baby," I whisper, dragging my nose along her jawline.

She whimpers as her body locks down and then, she shatters, coming hard against my palm.

"Austin."

"Shh, I got you, Sunshine," I tell her, keeping her bundled against my chest.

She makes a small murmur, her eyes fluttering closed. Sated and satisfied, she drifts off to sleep. I smile, kissing the spot below her ear.

I watch her for several minutes before I get up to clean myself off. I wet a hand towel and clean her up as best as I can. Then, I crawl back into bed beside Chloe and hold her until the sun rises.

I never knew being with a woman could feel this good, this real, and I don't want to take a second of it for granted.

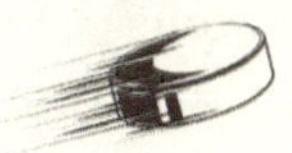

"HOW WAS the rest of your evening?" Mimi sidles up beside me in the coffee line the next morning.

"You're not getting any information out of me, Mim." I fill a coffee for her, adding a ridiculous amount of cream and sugar because that's how Mimi likes her coffee. When I was younger, I thought it was disgusting. To be honest, I still do, but the smile she shoots me when I pass her the nearly white coffee makes up for it.

I fill a coffee for Chloe. Her family, all the cousins and aunts and uncles, are seated in little clusters around the dining area of the hotel, ordering breakfast plates and filling up coffee mugs.

"Did you have fun last night?"

I grin at Mimi, bringing my coffee to my lips. "You know I did. Did you?"

"Oh yes. I haven't heard that rendition of 'Like a Virgin' yet. You were spectacular."

I snort out a laugh, thanking her, before gesturing that I need to bring Chloe her coffee.

Marie waves Mimi over to sit with her and I take off, searching for my girl.

My girl.

I never thought of a woman like that before but the title fits Chloe perfectly. I find her, laughing at something Sara is telling her and Drew, at a back table near a window.

"There you are." Sara waves me over. "I just wanted to say goodbye. Mark and I are heading to the airport."

"Where are you honeymooning?" I ask, handing Chloe her coffee.

"None for me?" Drew asks.

"Get your own damn coffee," I tell him cheerily, slipping into the chair across from Chloe.

Drew grumbles but stands up. He kisses his cousin goodbye and makes his way over to the coffee station.

"Hawaii," Sara responds.

"Nice," I say. "Enjoy it. Congratulations again."

Sara gives me a goodbye hug. "Thanks, Aus. And thanks for coming to my wedding. I hear your late-night performance was a hit."

Chloe laughs as we wave goodbye. When Sara stops at the next table, Chloe turns her attention back to me. "Good morning."

"Morning, Sunshine. How'd you sleep?"

She blushes. "Better than I have in months. Maybe even years."

"Maybe we need to have more sleepovers." I raise my eyebrows.

She smiles, big and wide, and real. "I like your thinking, Austin."

"You always were on my side, Crawford."

She takes a sip of her coffee, her eyes dropping closed for a second as she enjoys the taste. "You know, that's the truth."

"I know. But before we have a sleepover…"

Her eyes pop open.

"I need to take my girl on a real date."

"Your girl?"

"We have a dinner date tonight."

She beams. "Not wasting any time, are you?"

I shake my head. "Not where you're concerned, Chloe. I already wasted years."

She wrinkles her nose. "I know the feeling. And I'm excited for dinner."

"Good," I say just as our breakfast plates are served.

Drew reappears, drawing his sister into conversation. I pull out my phone to shoot Noah a quick message.

AUSTIN

Hey, can you hook me up with reservations tonight at The Ivy?

NOAH

> Nothing like short notice.

AUSTIN

> It's for Chloe.

NOAH

> Wedding went well?

AUSTIN

> A hell of a lot of fun.

A few minutes pass before my phone buzzes again.

NOAH

> You're set for 8 p.m. Enjoy it. You deserve it, man.

AUSTIN

> Thanks.

I don't respond to his "deserving it" comment because something about it strikes me. I never realized that I've spent the past few years thinking I wasn't deserving of a good woman, one like Chloe. But I guess I never allowed myself the opportunity to really click with a woman because I knew I could never measure up. Not without losing some of my focus on hockey and I vowed to never let that happen again.

Chloe's laughter draws my attention and I stare at her, memorizing her facial expressions and holding on to the happiness in her eyes.

I deserve her, this. And I can balance it all. I have to.

CHAPTER 17
CHLOE

"Wow, being banished to Boston sure does suck, huh?" Abbi asks when I call her after the wedding to fill her in on all the details.

Mainly just Austin.

"Fine, you were right. It's not all bad," I admit, grinning in spite of myself.

"I can't wait to meet him."

"Next weekend." I'm looking forward to Marissa's bachelorette party a lot more now. In a few weeks, my entire outlook has changed. Sure, life threw me a curve ball and I landed flat on my ass. But right now, my luck seems to be changing and it feels good to believe in good things again.

"I want one night out with the hockey gods," Abbi says, sighing dreamily.

"That's easy. Consider it done."

"Look at you! A wedding and a hot date this weekend, a bachelorette party and your best friend's visit next weekend. You've got this, Chloe. This summer is turning out a hell of a lot better than you thought."

"As much as I resisted, you're right," I admit. Spending time with Mimi and catching up with Mom and Dad, after living apart for more than a decade, has been grounding in a way I didn't realize I needed. Plus, Austin.

I smile, unable to stop myself from touching my lips, remembering his kiss. It seems like I keep coming back to him but it's more than that. Being around the Merricks again, being back in Boston, has reintroduced me to the girl I was when I lived here. The nerdy, self-assured, no-bullshit chick who could dish out side-eye as easily as a compliment. Back then, I *knew* who I was. I'm realizing that with Steve, I began to view myself more as an extension of him, his dreams, his goals, and less of my own person.

The thought is depressing, especially since I used to scoff at women who wrapped themselves up in men like a security blanket. How the hell did I become the person I swore I'd never become? What's worse, how did I not realize it was happening?

"Have fun tonight," Abbi's voice pulls me back to our conversation. "And message me with all the deets."

"I will."

"Love you, Chlo."

"Love you too. Can't wait to see you next weekend."

She squeals. "I know, me too! It's going to be epic!"

I agree and end our phone call. Then, I slide open the door to my closet and consider my summer dresses. I flip through the hangers, recalling how just last month, I did the same exact thing before dinner at the Merricks. But now, I'm hopeful, I'm happy. I'm *excited*.

My closet is fuller than it was then and I settle on a floral dress that flares out from my waist and ends just above my knees. It's a twirling dress and I feel feminine and pretty wearing it. I pair it with some simple espadrilles and dangling earrings. I pull my hair into a ponytail and keep my makeup simple, with a bold pink lip color.

I'm just stuffing my credit card into my purse when the doorbell rings.

"Chloe," Dad bellows from the bottom of the stairs. "Austin's here."

I chuckle to myself, my heart rate increasing. It's ridiculous really. But I have the same butterflies as high school, with my dad calling me down the stairs to meet my date, and a night of unknown conversation waiting for me. For a moment, it feels like fate has intervened. That even though Austin and I missed our chance to do this—date—in high school, we're getting the opportunity now.

I was never supposed to fall for troublemaker, boy-next-door Austin. But maybe I am supposed to fall for rule-maker, hockey legend Austin.

I give myself one more glance in the mirror before going to meet my date at the door.

Dad and Austin are chatting in the foyer. I hold back for a second, taking in Austin, his casual posture, the ease with which he and Dad joke and talk. My mouth dries as I drink him in. Dark jeans that curve to his ass and hug his thighs. They're distressed to look casual but one glance at them and you know they cost more than most people's monthly rent. A black dress shirt, buttoned down but rolled up on his forearms. And Gucci loafers that make me smile because they are a far cry from the boy who wore oversized hoodies and backwards baseball caps. But damn do they look good.

His hair is styled, the tiniest shadow of a beard coating his cheeks. As if he senses me, he glances up. Our eyes connect and I draw in a breath, loving the way his eyes widen, the way his words falter on his tongue and a smile crosses his face. I smile back and lift my hand in greeting as I descend the stairs.

"You look beautiful, Sunshine." He kisses my cheek hello.

"You clean up nice yourself."

Dad guffaws, clasping Austin on the shoulder. "Have fun tonight, kids." He glances at me. "Should we expect you home?"

I choke on my own saliva but Austin chuckles, amusement evident in his expression. "No sir, you shouldn't," he answers for me and Dad bellows out a laugh.

"Good night, Daddy." I kiss his cheek goodbye, giving him side-eye that makes him laugh even harder.

"See you tomorrow." He waves before closing the front door after us.

I glance at Austin as we walk from my parents' porch to his SUV. "No tact, I swear."

Austin chuckles, his fingers finding the small of my back. "Honestly, with our parents, it's amazing we turned out relatively normal."

"I know, right?" I agree, thanking him as he takes my hand and helps me up the one step into the passenger seat. "Thank God it's you and you know them."

Austin winks and I feel it in the pit of my stomach. "I feel the same. You ready?"

I nod and he closes the door, rounds the front of the SUV, and sits in the driver's seat. For a beat, the space between us charges. We stare at each other, realizing that everything is changing, shifting, evolving.

Austin's eyes are unreadable, a tightness around his mouth that lends a gravity to the moment. I smile at him softly and the tension in his expression eases, the corners of his mouth flipping up.

He extends his hand to me and I take it, threading my fingers with his.

"We're really doing this." His voice is nearly a whisper, laced with awe and nerves.

I squeeze his hand. "We're really doing this."

He lets out a deep breath and his grin grows. I like seeing this side of him, the vulnerable streak when he's almost always collected, his thoughtfulness when he rarely gives his feelings away.

"Okay," he says, turning on the SUV, his swagger reasserting itself, "let's go then."

He drops my hand and backs out of my parents' driveway.

"I've never been to The Ivy," I tell him on our way to the posh, downtown restaurant.

He laughs. "Most people haven't and you've just been back in the city for weeks. I've only been for events, like Torsten and Rielle's wedding, but never on a date."

I bite my bottom lip, tucking that little morsel of truth away. "You trying to impress me, Merrick?"

He glances at me, his palm sliding over the steering wheel. "Always, Crawford."

By the time we pull up in front of The Ivy and Austin valets his ride, we've settled back into our skins. The easygoing, joking, ribbing, laughing that we've always shared, but this time, there's an edge of awareness.

I notice how his biceps tug the material of his dress shirt and recall the strength of his arms when they're wrapped around my body. A thrill dances down my spine when we're escorted to a table and heads turn in our direction, whispers breaking out, a few guys even lifting their drinks in Austin's direction in thanks. The color that spreads high on his cheekbones makes me giggle because Austin, embarrassed?

I slip into the chair across from him as he settles himself.

"Your fan club is growing," I tease.

He snorts and gestures to our server, who approaches our table and runs through the list of special cocktails for the evening.

"Can I start you with something to drink?" she asks.

Good thing I was scanning the drink menu while she was talking because there are too many delicious, sophisticated cocktails to choose from to revert to my trusty old friend, wine.

"I'll take an old-fashioned," I order. Austin lifts an eyebrow and echoes my order.

Our server nods and leaves us to look over the menu.

"It's going to be one of those nights?" Austin leans back in his chair, his gaze scanning my face.

I grin cheekily. "Gonna be one of the best nights."

He smiles and it's one of his real ones. One that transforms his entire demeanor and offers glimpses of the boy from my youth.

"I really am happy we reconnected, Chlo."

I blow him a kiss and he snorts. "Me too, Aus. Thank you for taking me here."

He shakes his head. "Thank you for agreeing to be my date." He leans forward again, his elbows resting on the table. "I know we started this as a way to help each other out with our summer obligations."

"Mostly mine," I remind him.

He shrugs. "And we drummed up a pretty good list of rules."

I nod, wondering where he's going with this.

"Can I add one?" he asks, uncertainty back in his tone.

"Of course."

He reaches across the table, his fingers tracing the backs of my knuckles. "I've never done this before."

"Dated?"

He ducks his head. "Not for real. Not since college."

His admission hits me square in the chest and for the umpteenth time in my life, Mimi flickers through my mind. Maybe she was right about Austin all along. Maybe she read him a hell of a lot clearer than I ever did.

Austin glances back up. "I don't want to mess this up with you. What we have going, it's real."

My throat tightens and I nod, flipping my hand to clutch at his.

"But in order for that to work, I need you to be honest

with me. Real honest. And I'll do the same. We can't play all those mind games I've watched my friends and teammates navigate like freaking land mines. You're coming off a pretty big life change, I have hockey season starting back up..." He shrugs. "We need to be honest."

Everything inside of me turns to goo at the expression on his face. Trust and vulnerability and a desire to do the right thing, to be the right man. All of this on top of his confession last night hits me hard. He really is *trying*. I nod. "I like this rule."

He bites the corner of his mouth. "Even more than singing Madonna?"

I tip my head, as if weighing my options. Austin grins.

We both break out in laughter just as our drinks are delivered to the table. We thank our server and lift our drinks.

"To summer shenanigans and real-life dates," I say.

Austin's smile widens. "To you, Chloe."

The sweet sentiment nearly bowls me over again.

"I don't know what to do with this side of you, Austin," I murmur, clinking my glass with his and taking a small sip.

He cocks his head, raising an eyebrow.

"Sweet, sentimental." I gesture at him.

"Hardly. But I know a good thing when I see it and I don't want to ruin this, Chlo."

"What did we agree on? About being in the moment?" I glance around the restaurant. "We're on our first date."

He snickers. "See, I'm already ruining it."

I smile, tipping my head for him to continue.

He schools his expression. "We've been friends for a long time, have a long history. I just don't want to lose you."

"You won't," I say with more confidence than I've felt in a long time. "I won't let you."

"Promise?" he asks, and I'm reminded of last night's conversation all over again.

"Swear it."

"I knew it." I shake my head. "Mason freaking Kinner."

Across from me, Chloe giggles. God, she's beautiful. Her cheeks have been stained pink the entire evening, probably because of how much laughing we've done. Her eyes shine like emeralds, all glitter and wonder. I have to force myself to keep my eyes trained on her face because the way her dress wraps around her curves would distract me from dinner in an instant.

Not for the first time, I both despise and am grateful to Steve. What an idiot. He's going to regret losing the love of a good woman like Chloe for the rest of his life. And, as much as I can't stand Mason Kinner from high school, at least I can admit his good sense in kissing Chloe at Homecoming our freshman year.

Chloe wrinkles her nose. "I was pretty old by the time I had my first kiss. Honestly, I would have given it to anyone just to get it over with."

I laugh and pick up my wine glass. We changed to wine for dinner but I know the night is far from over and I'll be ordering another cocktail soon. This night can easily stretch to dawn and it wouldn't be enough time to learn all the things I want to learn about Chloe.

"Who was yours?" she asks.

I duck my head.

"Oh no," she groans, and I can't imagine all the faces flipping through her mind.

"Allie Canes."

Her mouth drops open and she jabs her pointer finger at me. "Savannah's best friend!"

I snort, rolling my lips together as I nod.

"Was it Truth or Dare?" she asks.

"Nope. Just a regular night. She was sleeping at our house and we were both up late. Vanny had fallen asleep so Allie and I were just watching a movie and…" I shrug.

"You kissed her."

"*She* kissed me." I set the record straight. "I was so surprised and then I couldn't believe my good fortune."

We both laugh again.

Our server appears at the end of our table and asks if we'd like to order dessert.

"Do you have doughnuts?" I ask before Chloe can order.

Chloe snorts and orders a tiramisu and an espresso martini. I tack on a cheesecake and a Bailey's. Leaning back in my chair, I grin at the beautiful woman sitting across from me.

My whole childhood is tangled up with hers. So sure, I would look at her and feel all sorts of affection and concern. But this summer, it's all changed. She's not just a little girl crying about skinned knees or a pre-teen I pranked on a beach trip. Now, Chloe Crawford is all woman and I want to be the man worthy of her attention and affection.

I want to be man enough for her.

Our conversation continues to flow as easily as our drinks. When I bring Chloe into my bed later in the evening, I do so with the understanding that we're taking another step forward. I've confided in her, she's been honest with me, and our relationship is growing.

Chloe does so willingly, with trust outshining the vulnerability in her gaze, with sweetness overshadowing the sass of her mouth, with all the feelings that usually scare me away, bringing me closer.

AFTER A NIGHT SPENT EXPLORING Chloe's body, a morning feeding her French toast and horsing around over mugs of coffee, I'm on cloud nine.

All the things I've been searching for—acceptance, understanding, *forgiveness*—can be found in her deep green eyes and knowing smirk.

We walk into my parents' kitchen for weekly, Sunday night dinner, holding hands and our parents clap and whistle like I just announced that Chloe's pregnant. Nothing would make my mother or Diane happier than to become grandmothers. At the same time.

Claire grins and passes Chloe a wine glass. Indy's telling anyone who will listen that she'd like credit for setting up yet another perfect couple. Even Easton, who's usually more reserved, lets loose with a loud whistle.

"It's about damn time." Dad clasps me on the shoulder.

"About time? Chloe's been back in Boston since June," I respond.

"I always knew from when you two were kids," Dad says, going on and on about Chlo's and my childhood adventures as if he could have predicted this outcome.

Mom winks when I catch her eye and raises her glass to me in silent cheers.

My family is seriously prouder in this moment than the

night the Hawks won the Stanley Cup. My chest tightens uncomfortably at the thought of the Cup, at the realization that I'll be gearing up for training camps in a few more weeks, at the reality that's waiting for me.

This summer, the events, Chloe, have been one hell of a good time. They've been a much-needed time out from the constant pressure I feel buried under. But now, reality is waiting and I don't want to meet it. I glance at my girl, enjoying how content she is chatting with my sister and cousin.

I take a swig of the beer Noah slid in my hand and grin at my family and friends. I tuck Chloe under my arm and relax a little, try to enjoy the boisterous noise of the Merricks and Crawfords and Scotch brothers surrounding me.

"Oh, Panda will sort it all out," my sister says and I tune back into the conversation unfolding around me.

"Panda will sort what out?" I ask.

Easton snickers. "Your girl's best friend is coming to visit next weekend."

"The bachelorette party," I recall.

"Yep." Chloe smiles. "Abbi can't wait to visit Boston and she wants a night out with all of you guys. Preferably some singles thrown in."

Indy rolls her eyes. "Trust me, Panda may be all the single she can handle."

"Sims will come," Noah tacks on.

"Let's try to convince James," Claire adds. "He needs to get out more."

I nod, biting down hard. My worry increases the moment James Ryan is mentioned. Losing his wife destroyed him. Even though he's been making strides in his personal life, even coming out to Taps the other week, he's been in a year-long struggle to make sense of the senselessness of it all while trying to single-parent twins.

"He was chatting up that bartender the other night," Indy says, catching my attention.

"See? This is why it's good when one of us doesn't drink." Claire smiles. "Did he look happy-ish?"

Indy purses her lips as if she's thinking it over. "He didn't seem so...intensely sad."

"All right, James comes next weekend," Chloe decides. "Abbi pulled me through all the shit with Steve. She's been working her ass off and I owe her an epic, all-out, Boston weekend."

Noah nods. "Consider it done, Chlo. We'll round up the team. When's your bachelorette?"

"Friday night," Chloe responds.

"Then make sure you're not too hungover to properly enjoy Saturday night," Easton snickers.

Chloe grins and raises her glass. "To next weekend."

The whole group cheers and I don't miss the way Mom's and Diane's smiles widen. At everyone's effortless happiness, some of the anxiety I try to keep at bay crawls back in, pulling in my chest.

This seems too good to be true. Too easy, too natural, too damn fun.

I draw in a deep breath and tighten my hold on Chloe. Dropping a kiss to the top of her head, I try to embrace this moment. But still, my worry lingers.

CHAPTER 19
CHLOE

My phone rings and I laugh as I answer.

"Seriously? Cat pajamas?" Austin's chuckle comes through the line. "You couldn't even lie to me and pretend to be in some sexy lace?"

"We said we'd always be honest," I remind him.

"Chloe Ann Crawford, I haven't seen you all week," he responds.

"I know." I pout. It has been a long week. I got buried under deadlines and, after a conversation with my boss on Tuesday, have been exploring some growth opportunities within the newspaper. Austin's been crazy busy preparing for his upcoming training camps which start in two weeks.

"How'd your conversation with Janie go?"

"Good! I don't want to jinx anything but there may be one or two positions opening up. They're both entry-level, investigative journalism but I'd be willing to start at the bottom again for a chance to try it out."

"That's awesome, baby."

"Yeah." I grin. "We'll see what happens but I'm excited."

"Good. I'm happy for you. If you keep pushing in that direction, something will give and work out."

"I hope so. But I'm also excited to see you on Saturday."

"Trust me, I'm counting down the hours. When's Abbi get into town?"

I glance at my watch. "Two hours and fifteen minutes, give or take a few."

"You really miss her, don't you?"

"You have no idea. Abbi Walsh is my person. Through and through."

"I get that. We all need a friend who will have our back no matter what."

"Is Easton yours?"

"Since I was thirteen," he answers easily. "And you're kicking the night off where again?"

I grin at the curiosity burning behind his words. "Why, Austin Merrick, I don't believe I told you."

He laughs. "And you're not going to, are you?"

"No way, man. Bachelorette parties are ladies only."

"It's not like I'm going to crash it," he says quickly. Too quickly.

"That's exactly what you're going to do if I share the details. You'll have me all to yourself tomorrow but tonight… girls only, Aus."

He snickers but agrees to not ask again. "But you'll call if you need anything, right?"

"Like a ride?"

"Like anything," he repeats, his tone harder than it was a moment ago. "Whatever you need, I'm here, okay?"

I roll my lips together, a shot of giddiness rocking through me. I like the possessive edge to his words. I like the way he offers himself up like he's mine. "Okay," is all I say but God, I want to say so much more.

Is this for real? Will you worry about me tonight? Do you think of me as much as I think of you?

"Okay," he repeats. "Well, I'll let you go get ready for your reunion with Abbi. But um—"

"I'll message you when I get home tonight," I reassure him, sensing he wants me to but doesn't know how to ask without sounding needy.

"Thank you."

"'Bye, Aus." I end the call.

Then I flip on some music, slide my closet door open, and try on a ridiculous amount of dress options until the doorbell rings and Mom announces Abbi's arrival.

I fly down the stairs, grinning the moment I see my best friend, with her dark brown hair and light brown eyes. "You're here! You're here!"

"Missed you, bitch!" she shouts back, shooting my mom a glance. "Sorry, Mrs. C."

Mom snorts and gestures between us. "I'll go grab you a bottle of wine."

Abbi laughs as I rush her, the two of us hugging each other like we've been separated for years instead of weeks. "Missed you," I tell her.

"God, you have no idea, Chlo. I need that bottle of wine and then some."

I pull back. "What do you mean?"

Abbi sighs and rolls her eyes. "Nothing. It's just, there's been a lot going on at work. And I need this. A night out with my best friend, a weekend away from my life, just, a chance to let loose."

I grin and thank Mom for the wine bottle and glasses she passes us. "Trust me, you're going to love everything about this weekend then."

"Good," Abbi says, gesturing to the house. "Let me see

your Boston digs."

"I like how you worded that, Abs, as if I'm not still living with Mom and Dad." I grab the handle of her small suitcase.

Mom snorts again. "You say that as if you aren't living rent free with access to all the good stuff." She points to the wine bottle.

Abbi laughs and kisses Mom's cheek. "Thanks for having me, Mrs. C."

Mom shoos us toward the stairs. "I'm taking you both on one of those Duck Tours on Sunday."

"Done," Abbi agrees, following me up the stairs and into my bedroom.

I close the door behind us and my bestie and I spend a solid five seconds just staring at each other, blinking, until we erupt into giggles and screams. We clutch each other's forearms and laugh, half in nostalgia, half in excitement.

"I'm so ready for tonight," Abbi says again.

"Me too."

"And you're totally fine with Brittney being—"

"Brittney who?" I lift an eyebrow.

Abbi chokes. "Savage as fuck," she says, unscrewing the wine cap and pouring us two glasses. She passes me one. "To tonight."

"Hell yeah." I clink my glass with hers and take a big gulp. "To me and you, Abs."

"Always." She smiles and tips back her glass.

Then, we raid my closet and her suitcase, pool our makeup together, and spend an insane amount of time getting ready for an evening we both need. It's the best.

"WOO!" Marissa shouts, tossing back another lemon drop.

Our dinner at Carter's steakhouse, a fancy affair, has given way to downright debauchery as we inhaled margaritas at Jolene's before barhopping across Boston.

Abbi and I are straight up giggling, hanging onto each other's shoulders. I'm having so much fun dancing, celebrating Marissa, being out with Abbi, that Brittney's presence has barely registered on my radar. After my first glass of wine at Carter's, I pretty much forgot all about her and her shitty interpretation of girl code.

It's a powerful feeling, knowing you're so completely past something that once had the ability to cause deep pain. In one summer, I've managed to grow into a much fuller, happier version of myself and while I shouldn't give Austin all the credit (hey, I've been doing the work!), I know it's partly because of him.

I toss back my shot and turn from the bar, slamming face-first into a hard chest of muscle.

When I tip my head back and glance up, I'm surprised to be staring at Panda.

"What are you doing here?" I blurt out.

He chuckles, his hands cupping my elbows to steady me. "It's Friday night in the off-season. What do you think?"

I grin. "Fair enough, Pandatelli. Who's your pick tonight?" I scan the bar.

"Why? You going to warn your friends about me?" he teases, his eyes catching on Abbi.

"I am if you try to kick it to Abs."

"Abs?"

I point to Abbi, dancing solo next to the bar. Her eyes are closed, her arms swaying at her sides. She's rocking a bohemian vibe that's so out of place in the bar we're at, it's impossible not to notice her outright. But then, you can't tear your gaze away once you recognize how effortlessly gorgeous she is underneath her fringed and beaded threads. "That's my best friend, Abbi Walsh."

Panda's mouth drops open the tiniest bit. "My night just got interesting, Crawford." He glances over my head. "Where's Austin?"

I point at Marissa, wearing all white with a tilted crown on her head. "It's a bachelorette party, Luca. Girls only."

A knowing gleam appears in his eye. "Ah, got it. So you're just going to drunk dial him in"—he glances at his watch—"a few hours for a ride home?"

I smack his shoulder. "Don't go ruining all my plans." I stick my tongue out at him because, yes, that's exactly what I'm going to do. In all fairness, my original plan didn't include Austin at all.

But the more drinks I tossed back and the more I watched pretty girls dance in the arms of guys with too much swagger to contain, the more I missed Austin. My guy. The one I want to put me to bed tonight, preferably his.

Abbi spots us and makes her way over to my side of the bar.

"Abs, meet Panda." I gesture between them.

"Luca Pandatelli." She grins.

"You've heard of me?" He sounds impressed.

Abbi and I laugh. "Only through Chloe," she responds. "I don't watch hockey or anything."

"No?" he challenges.

She shakes her head. "I mean, I'm into the players. Just not the game."

Panda snickers but his jawline pulls tight, his eyes narrowing, as if he doesn't like the gist of what Abbi's saying.

"She's not a puck bunny or anything," I throw out, quick to defend her.

Panda shrugs, as if he doesn't care one way or the other. But the way his gaze lingers on my bestie suggests otherwise.

"Chloe!" Marissa grabs my hand and pulls me into her side.

I wrap an arm around her waist, trying to keep her

upright. She's the drunkest of the bunch, as she should be, but I don't want her to fall and bang up her face weeks before her wedding.

"I need to go home," she slurs, shaking her head.

I brush her hair out of her eyes and giggle. Her eyes are blown and she's more than just slurring. "You sure, Maris?"

She nods, passing me her phone. "I had the best time. I love you. I love you so much."

"Love you too. Who am I calling?"

"My brother. He's my desig-desi-des driver for tonight."

I dial Ethan and rattle off the name of the bar when he picks up. I keep my arm wrapped around Marissa, my gaze darting over the crowd to locate the other girls.

We came out as a group of eight but I always knew we'd scatter in different directions once the night got going. Brittney hooking up with Steve kind of ruined the harmony of our friend group. Plus, three of tonight's girls are cousins with Marissa and we just met them through her wedding plans.

Marissa and her cousins are staying at her parents' house. Brittney and another girl are staying at a hotel. And Abbi's sleeping at my parents' house with me.

I turn back to find Abbi. She's deep in conversation with Panda, both of them gesturing with their hands. I frown, wondering what the hell they're talking about when Marissa starts to pitch forward in my arms.

"Whoa. I got you," I tell her. "Let's get some air." I round up Marissa's cousins and herd the girls outside a few minutes before Ethan pulls up.

"Shit," he swears when he takes in his sloshed sister and drunk cousins. "You're seriously leaving me with this, Chlo?" he asks playfully.

"They're all yours." I help Marissa into the back seat of the car and buckle her in.

She grabs my face. "Thank you, Chlo."

"Love you, Maris. Happy bachelorette." I kiss her cheek before closing the door. I glance at Ethan, helping his cousin into the passenger seat. "You going to be okay?"

"This?" He gestures to the car. "I'm all good. It's kind of funny to see them all drunk together again. Reminds me of college."

"Call me if you need anything."

He tips his head back toward the bar. "Go have fun, Chloe. Unless you want a ride home?"

"I'm good." I shake my phone at him. "I got plans anyway."

He grins. "Thatta girl. Be safe."

I wait until he settles into the car and pulls away from the curb before turning back to the bar. Right before I reenter, my phone chimes with a text.

ABBI

> How much would you hate me for going home with Luca?

What? She wants to *go home* with Panda?

CHLOE

> Are you serious?

ABBI

> He's hot. (Fire emoji)

CHLOE

> How drunk are you?

ABBI

> Enough to go home with a hockey player. Not enough to regret it.

Damn.

CHLOE

> Call me in the morning?

ABBI

Duh. You'll be my ride of shame.

I laugh.

CHLOE

Love you. Be safe.

ABBI

Me more, bitch. Now call your man.

I stand in front of the bar, shuffling from one foot to the next.

Should I go back inside? What for? Abbi's heading out and I don't really care what Brittney and her friend are up to. I lean back against the brick, a delicious anticipation pulling low in my abdomen. I miss Austin. It's only been a week but already, I feel desperate for him. Maybe it's the alcohol buzzing through my veins but I doubt it. I dial him.

"Chloe?"

"Austin Merrick." I wince when I realize I sound tipsier than I thought.

"You okay, baby? Where you at?" he asks and I can hear the smile in his voice.

I tell him the name of the bar.

"Do you and Abbi need a ride?"

I chuckle when I think of Abbi going home with Panda.

"Just me," I sing-song. "Hurry up and come get me, Austin."

"Is something wrong?" His voice hardens and in the background, I hear the jingle of his keys and a door closing.

"No," I reassure him. "I just—I need you. *All* of you."

He chuckles. "That so?"

"Mm-hmm."

"How badly?" His voice drops several octaves.

My thighs press together at the promise in his tone. Fuck, I want him to just get here. Now. "What's your ETA?"

"Three minutes. I'll see you in three minutes."

"Hurry," I say.

"I'm already on my way, Chlo. Now tell me exactly where you are."

So I do. And not even three minutes later, Austin Merrick, looking insanely hot in casual sweatpants and a black workout tank, steps from his SUV. My mouth drops open and I swipe my tongue over my lips.

He grins when he spots me, his eyes widening when he takes in my barely-there, very daring dress. He walks over, his hands grabbing my hips. "You look sexy as fuck, baby." He kisses me hard on the mouth.

I wind my arms around his shoulders and hop onto him, my legs wrapping around his hips. He catches me easily, his hands palming my ass. He growls, low in his throat, and I shiver, not giving a damn who sees my flashing ass right now.

"Take me home, Austin."

"I'll take you anywhere you want to go, Chloe." He kisses the side of my throat before depositing me in the passenger seat of his car. He pulls the seat belt across my chest and glances at me, serious like. "Just tell me. Where's Abbi? Are your friends all good?"

The concern in his tone flows through me like honey. God, he's sweet. Thoughtful. How did I get so lucky? I reach for his face and cup his cheek, liking the prickle of his stubble against my palm. How will it feel between my thighs tonight? I bet—

"Chlo?" he says softly, dipping to catch my eyes. "Your friends?"

"Oh, yeah," I breathe out. "Everyone's good." I laugh, shaking my head. "You're not going to believe this but Abbi went home with…Panda!"

I anticipate Austin's laughter but when he frowns, his jawline tightening, I lean forward. "What's wrong?" I whisper.

He shakes his head, his eyes finding mine once more. This time, they're cloudier, swirling with thoughts I can't read.

"Nothing," he responds. "Just fucking Panda."

I wrinkle my nose at him and his expression softens slightly.

"They're adults, Austin," I remind him. "They can make their own decisions. Choices."

He sighs and runs a hand over his hair. "I know. I just—I worry."

I widen my eyes at him. "Even right now? When I'm desperate for you to take me back to your place and—"

He silences me with a kiss. It's hot and intense and full of dirty promises I want to lose myself in. I reach up and grasp the material of his shirt as his tongue slips inside my mouth and duels with mine.

"No." He pulls back, breathing heavily, his forehead pressed against mine. "Not right now. Let's go home, Chlo."

I smile and kiss him again. "Hurry."

CHAPTER 20
AUSTIN

A breathless, trusting, yet determined Chloe who looks at me with big eyes and parted lips, is my undoing.

For a beat, she stands next to my bed with a stricken expression, that causes a wave of worry to flood my chest. Her eyes dart to mine.

I frown, pausing three paces away, and hold up my hands. "Are you feeling okay? We don't have to do anything."

One side of her mouth pulls up and she shakes her head slowly, her fingers dragging down the zipper along the side of her dress. "It's not that," she says, right before the slinky fabric ripples down her body.

Jesus. I stifle a groan.

Of course she's not wearing a bra. How could she in that painted-on dress? But her panties are lace, a bright tangerine color, when I would have guessed white or black or nude. And yeah, she's sexy as hell, an endless canvas of smooth skin and mouth-watering curves. But the thing that really causes my heart to beat frantically, my throat to dry, and my desire to flare to life is her confidence.

She wears it effortlessly, proudly. She's not rounding her shoulders or dipping her chin. She's standing tall and steady, no hesitation in her expression or doubt in her gaze. It's sexy as hell.

"What is it then?" I ask, closing the space between us.

My fingertips glide over the skin at her hips, skirting along the edge of her lace panties.

She pulls back slightly, tipping her face up to mine. "I know it's too soon. I know it, Austin. But I'm falling for you."

Her words ripple through the space between us, like skipping stones. Concentric circles that expand around us, until we're the center of all these things I've always known but never realized. My heart pounds, my concern from moments earlier melts away, and a joy I've never known rises in my chest. A slow smile works its way over my lips as I drown in her eyes, in her trust, in the beautiful certainty of the woman before me.

"You are?" I ask, humbled yet desperate for her to say it again.

She nods shyly, her hands slipping up my chest and tugging on my shirt before resting on the tops of my shoulders. "This wasn't supposed to happen," she murmurs.

I roll my lips together, studying her. Memorizing the shape of her face, the smattering of freckles on the bridge of her nose, the delicate fan of her eyelashes, the dimple I adore in her left cheek. "I'm happy it did," I reply, my tone deeper than a second ago.

As I say the words, I realize I mean them. Sure, on some level, Chloe's trust in me, her confidence in *this*, sends a jolt of panic through me. But it's quickly snuffed out by a wave of calm. A sense of *knowing*. This is right; we are right together.

I lower my head and brush my mouth over hers. She sighs contently, raising her chin to meet my kiss. I kiss her slowly, thoroughly, our tongues meeting together in sweet caresses and sincere claims. Our breathing rises as one, our bodies melting into each other effortlessly, naturally.

I kiss Chloe like I've never kissed a woman before. With

promise and intent, with thoughts of more than just tomorrow but the entire future before us, with all of me poured in.

She grips my shoulders harder, one of her arms snaking around my neck and I groan, taking the sweet to steamy in a heartbeat. Our kissing morphs into touching, exploring each other's bodies with a need that wasn't there last week.

I lose myself in her, my hands tracing the lines, curves, and dips of her body. I tug on her hair until the column of her neck arches. I lick a path down the side, kissing and nipping, tasting and needing.

Chloe mewls when my hand palms her breast. She pushes into me and I nuzzle the delicate spot below her ear. I love how she fills my palm, as if she was made for me. "You want me, baby?" I murmur, rolling her nipple between my fingers.

"Badly," she breathes out.

Her tone ignites a fire inside of me. My want to savor her transforming into a need to claim her. Because, fuck, I want her badly too.

I spread her out on my bed, taking a moment to appreciate how sexy she looks there. I shed my shirt and pants in record time. Our panting mingles in the air and our eyes stay locked together.

I crawl up her body, kissing her sweet skin as I go. She shivers beneath me, her fingers tracing up my ribs, gliding across my shoulder blades. When we're lined up again, I glance down at her and tell her the truth, one I've never admitted to a woman before because I've never felt the way I feel in this moment. "I'm falling for you too, Chlo. And it scares the shit out of me and lights me up at the same time."

Her eyes widen, a ribbon of understanding flickering through them. Instead of responding, she threads her fingers through my hair and tugs my head down. I go willingly, my lips finding hers once more.

Our kissing turns intense, overflowing with the depth of

our feelings. Our bodies grind against each other, searching. Right before I push into her, I remember something important. "Condom," I breathe out.

My girl shakes her head and kisses the corner of my mouth. "I'm on the pill."

Fuckkkkk. Heat blazes through me at the meaning in her words and I push into her slowly, my entire body clenching up at how fucking amazing she feels.

Her body arches into mine, my frame cages her in, and slowly, we create a centuries-old rhythm that feels brand new. Chloe's lips graze along my skin, leaving an inferno in their wake that only her fingertips can satisfy. Her touch is both torture and pleasure. The sounds falling from her mouth turn me on and I know I need to slow this down, savor it. Pulling out of her, I kiss a path down her body until my head is between her creamy thighs.

Her fingers find my hair and tug just as I swipe my tongue up her center.

"Oh, God!" she cries out, bucking off the bed.

I nip at the inside of her thigh, dragging my mouth back to her most pleasurable spot. Then, I devour her until her pretty thighs shake and she lets out a strangled cry.

"Austin," she moans, her hands clutching at me.

"Shh, baby." I slide back up her body, my dick rock hard and desperate to slide back home. "You good?"

She nods, her tongue swiping across her bottom lip. A lip I desperately need to taste again. So I do. My cock drags through her folds and she moans again.

"Please, Aus. I need you. I love you," she murmurs, the words coming quick and needy.

They fill me with an unprecedented swell of pride as I slide inside and make Chloe my girl. In every meaning of the word. "You're mine, baby."

"I am," she agrees, stating it clearly, without a hint of hesitation.

I rock deeper, setting a pace that increases from sweet to heady to frantic. We crest and crash at the same moment, crying out in unison and floating back to Earth with our limbs intertwined and our eyes locked.

"Jesus," she breathes out. "I've never…that was—"

"You're perfect, Chloe."

Her eyebrows bend together as I pull out of her and tug her body so she's sprawled across mine. I drag my fingers through her hair and let out a chuckle, glancing down at a woman so familiar and yet so different than I imagined. "You're perfect for me," I clarify.

She presses a kiss to my chest and snuggles deeper. "It's funny sometimes how much things change in such a short time."

I roll my head against the pillow, my hand drawing lazy patterns on her back. Seriously, how is her skin so smooth? It's like I can't *not* touch her. "What do you mean?"

She shifts, crossing her arms over my chest so she can prop up her chin. "In June, I was crying to Abbi that I'd been banished to Boston and was pretty much missing out on my own life. Now, it's almost August, and my life is better than I ever could have imagined it."

"Even better than when you were planning your wedding?" I ask, hating the insecurity that wraps around my words. Hating myself for even thinking of, never mind mentioning, fucking Steve while I'm in bed with Chloe. After we did *that*. But still, I wonder. Would she be happier with him if he never got caught with Brittney?

"Much better," she says easily, tilting her head. "I've taken off the rose-colored glasses. I think I thought things were great because we were checking all the boxes, meeting all the milestones. Condo, marriage proposal, saving for a house. But in hindsight, it sucks to admit it, but I was doing most of it on my own. Decorating our place, planning our wedding, thinking about our retirement. Steve was never into it as much as I was and yeah, I'm happy I realized that. Because how awful would it be to go through your entire life being more invested in your marriage than your partner? I don't want to be an afterthought anymore, Austin. I want to be the leading lady of my own life. I deserve to be."

"You do," I agree, tugging her closer so I can kiss her mouth. "You deserve everything, Chloe. Fucking everything."

Her lips curl into a smile against mine and I kiss her again. My hand squeezes her ass while the other one curls around the nape of her neck.

She swings a leg over my torso, straddling me. "I could get used to this, Austin," she murmurs cheekily, nibbling along my jawline.

"I'm counting on that, baby." I roll her over and we begin again, exploring, touching, and tasting.

I make Chloe Crawford come with my mouth, my fingers, and on my cock. It's my favorite fucking hat trick and as I drift off to sleep, I feel lighter than I have in a long time.

I pull my girl closer, wrap myself up in her presence, and stop worrying about hockey, this season, the team. I just let myself be, and man, it's one of the best nights of my life.

CHAPTER 21
CHLOE

I wake up to a view.

Damn.

Austin's naked body is breathtaking. All sculpted muscle, firm lines, and hard planes. He almost looks like he was carved from marble. But the scars from a handful of surgeries, from years of playing hockey, serve as a reminder that he's still mortal.

Hot, breathing, mortal man I want to have for myself all over again.

He whistles low and I snap my eyes to his. His gaze is sleepy but the smirk on his mouth is all-knowing and I laugh.

"Like what you see?" he asks.

"Too much," I tell him, crawling on top of him.

He snorts and grasps my upper arms as I kiss him deeply, attacking him with a mixture of affection and want. My need for him spikes and he senses it, losing no time matching my frantic kisses with his own. He slows down the pace and we settle into languid, lazy, morning lovemaking that I've read about in books and seen in movies but never experienced in real life.

I've been missing out.

Austin's body shadows mine. He thrusts deep, filling me up with pleasure. His eyes hold mine captive and I fall a little bit harder, faster. Everything with Austin Merrick is more and I realize just how empty the last five years of my life have been. I don't want to miss a moment of it.

I wrap my legs around his hips. "I want to be on top," I demand and he acquiesces, rolling us until I'm straddling his waist.

I sink down on his hard cock, groaning as he hits the spot I need.

"Fuck," he breathes out, his palm splayed wide over my thigh.

I plant one hand in the center of his chest, the other gripping the headboard, as I find my own rhythm. It's freeing. For the first time in my adult life, I feel uninhibited. Sexy. Desired. Sure of myself and who I am in this moment, with this man.

I tip my head back, the ends of my hair brushing my back. I increase the tempo, sliding up and down on Austin like my body was custom made to ride his.

"Jesus, baby. That's it. Ride me, Chlo," he groans out, his hands holding my hips.

I ride him hard and fast until my body shatters, a million shards of glass, a thousand droplets of water, a hundred grains of sand. All that is sharp and spiky, sweet and gentle, coarse and determined about me breaks apart in his hands. He follows a moment later, moaning my name.

It's an undoing that somehow puts me back together. I collapse forward and Austin wraps me up in his strong arms. I know the moment that he recognizes everything that just happened is deeper than this moment, more than just sex, everything and yet nothing at all. Because he holds me tighter.

"I love you too," he whispers in my ear.

And I smile. Because I know he *sees* me. And what's more

than that, he loves me just as I am. Dimpled ass, nervous laughter, word-loving me.

"Now let me feed you breakfast," Austin adds.

"Pancakes."

"Anything you want, Chlo."

I press one more kiss to the underside of his jaw and shimmy off of him.

Austin's eyes drink me in like he'll never get enough, like my body is the most desirous thing he's ever seen. He looks at me the same way I look at him and the realization fills me up with happiness.

"Coffee." I raise an eyebrow.

"That too," he agrees, swinging his legs to the side of the bed and standing. Austin stretches and I can't tear my eyes away from his glorious nakedness.

He really is a national treasure. He really is the best man I know.

"This is already the best morning I've had in a long time."

He turns, takes in my expression, and smiles. Walking over to me, his fingertips gently touch my stomach as he leans in to kiss me. "Mine too."

While Austin takes a quick shower, I find my phone and wince at the three missed calls from Abbi.

Shit. I dial her back.

"Chloe Ann Crawford," she answers.

"I'm sorry! I'm a shit friend but—"

"You were having the best sex of your life," she guesses.

"Yes!" I exclaim, relieved she gets it.

My best friend dissolves into laughter.

Oh God, I hope she didn't say that in front of my mom.

"Wait, where are you?" I ask, wondering if she really went home with Panda last night. Is she at his place?

"Waking up in a very masculine—"

"Macho." I hear Panda's voice in the background.

"Macho," Abbi amends, "bed."

"You slept with Panda," I surmise.

"I did. And now I need—"

"Pancakes," I supply.

"And coffee."

I giggle. It's really no wonder Abbi and I are best friends. "I'm going to take a quick shower. Austin and I will pick you guys up for brunch in an hour."

"Sounds perfect, my friend," Abbi says, humor and happiness in her tone.

I end the call just as Austin reenters the room.

"Who are we picking up?" he asks.

"Abbi and Panda."

He winces.

"What?" I ask.

Austin shakes his head. "It's just that, look, Panda's my boy. But I know Abbi's your girl. And if she's thinking that last night with Panda meant—"

I shake my head to stop him. "She's not. Trust me, Abbi is the last girl you have to worry about getting the wrong idea about a hookup. If anything, Panda's going to be begging her for more."

Austin tips back his head and laughs. He laughs so hard, his chest vibrates.

I laugh along with him, raising my eyebrows as I wait for him to offer an explanation.

"I'd fucking pay to see that," he says finally, swiping a hand over his face. Then, he drops his towel and snaps it against my ass. "You going to shower?"

I nod.

"You want company?" he asks slyly.

I grin and nod again, taking Austin's hand and leading him into the bathroom.

An hour and a half later, we pull in front of Panda's condo. I'm not sorry we're late. Not even a little bit.

"WHAT'S GOING on with you and Panda?" I ask Abbi later that afternoon.

She raises an eyebrow. "Me and Panda? What's up with you and Austin? You could hardly stop making heart eyes and kissy faces at each other over brunch."

I snort, rolling my eyes. I collapse in the center of my bed and feel the mattress dip as Abbi lays down beside me.

"I'm in love with him, Abs."

She turns her head toward me, prompting me to look at her. Her gaze is searching, but after a long pause, a smile spreads across her lips.

"You really are." Her words are coated in wonder but her expression is pure happiness.

I smile back. "I really am. He's…he's amazing."

"He's nothing like Steve."

"What the hell was I thinking agreeing to marry him?"

Abbi shrugs, wedging a pillow under her head. "I think it was habit. The next logical step, you know?"

I nod. I do know. Steve and I made sense on paper and the longer we stayed in our relationship, the more natural the next steps—moving in together, merging our bank accounts, getting engaged—seemed.

"You would have been settling," Abbi adds.

"I know," I reply. This time, I *do* know.

"So, you're going to stay in Boston now?"

"I…I want to. I spoke to Janie and some other members of senior management at the paper." I shrug. "There may be some opportunities I could explore here." I bite my bottom lip. "Still, it's only been a couple of months and everything happened so quickly between Austin and me. So unexpectedly."

"That's usually the way of things."

I elbow her in the ribs. "Seriously? Because you have such extensive dating experience?"

"I do have extensive *dating* experience. It's relationships I fail at."

I shake my head, hating that Abbi's built her walls so high, she doesn't allow herself the chance to consider a real relationship with any of the men she casually dates. Deciding not to open that can of worms, I say, "I'm going to see what happens. Give it until the end of the summer at least before I make any decisions. When I'm in New York for Marissa's wedding, I've arranged to meet with Janie to discuss things in person."

"That's a good plan. No need to make big decisions now, when you're still having fun."

I frown and Abbi adds, "I didn't mean that's *all* you're doing," she clarifies, popping up on one arm and staring down at me. "I just meant that you don't need to add pressure or expectations to something so…new."

I nod, biting the corner of my mouth. Abbi has a point. It's just, I can't imagine not being with Austin. Now, when I think about my future, I see him in it. For someone who usually works from home, the thought of relocating doesn't hold the same weight for me as it does for most people. Besides, Boston has more opportunities for me to break into the type of journalism I'd like to explore. Plus, my family, Mimi, are here. It's not like moving to Boston would be a hardship. It would be a new beginning, a fresh start. A homecoming.

"Anyway," Abbi changes the subject, "what are you wearing tonight?"

I snort. "Abs, I need a nap if I'm going to make it out with a rowdy group of hockey players tonight."

She lifts an eyebrow, grinning. "He worked you over good."

"Oh my God!" I blush, hitting her in the face with a pillow.

She laughs. "I'm not judging. I need a nap too."

I groan.

Abbi's laughter heightens. "Let's nap. Then, we'll pick out outfits. But tonight, please, let's have fun."

"Of course we'll have fun. Have you talked to any of the bachelorette girls?"

"Marissa is having a spa day with her cousins and some fancy, family dinner party tonight. Do we care what Brittney and the other girl are doing?"

"Not even a little." I close my eyes.

"Exactly," Abbi says.

But I barely hear her because I'm already drifting off to sleep.

"NO MORE SHOTS!" I hold up a hand, nearly stumbling.

Austin's arms dart out and wrap around my middle, holding me upright. "You okay, babe?"

I nod, sinking against his chest. "Panda's trying to kill us."

He chuckles. "He's got nothing on Torsten. But your girl is keeping up with him."

I watch as Abbi throws back another shot, her ass planted firmly in Panda's lap. "She's going to regret it tomorrow."

"The hangover?"

"Everything. She'll hate herself for being so openly flirty with him." I lift my chin as Panda's hands skate up Abbi's thighs and his lips drop to the sensitive spot where her shoulder meets her neck.

Austin makes a noncommittal sound. "Do you want to go rescue her?"

Now I laugh. "No way. In this moment, she'll kill me for interrupting." We watch as Abbi turns into Panda's touch, their mouths clumsily finding each other.

"Damn," Austin mutters. "Panda's not usually so…open with his PDA."

"Abbi's the same," I agree.

I head over to Abbi and Panda, bumping my hip against their shared seat until they both glance up with hazy eyes.

"We're going to head out." I point at Austin. "Do you guys want to come with?" I direct this question to Abbi.

But of course, she grins at me and shakes her head. "I'm good, Chlo. Swear it."

I lift an eyebrow.

"Don't worry," Panda cuts in. "I'll take care of our girl."

I glance at Abbi for confirmation, not missing the way Panda threw out "our" as if he and Abbi are more than just this weekend. She grins at me and flashes a wink. I stifle a laugh and kiss my bestie goodbye before heading back to Austin.

"They're good," I tell him, snickering at the concerned scowl on his face. "Hey." I slide my hand down his back, not pausing until I pinch his ass.

His face quickly snaps back to mine.

I grin. "Want to get out of here?"

His eyes lighten with understanding. He nods, wrapping an arm around my waist and turning us toward the exit. Dipping down, he asks, "How'd I get so lucky?"

"We're both about to get lucky," I correct him.

His laughter rings out and washes over me, keeping me wrapped up in this moment. I don't ever want it to end.

CHAPTER 22
AUSTIN

"Damn, you've got it bad," Noah says before taking a swig of beer.

"What?" I shake my head, tipping back my bottle.

"I've seen that look before," Easton agrees, smirking.

"Yeah, because you wear it." Noah points at his brother.

Easton flips him off. "Whatever, man. You're about to become a daddy."

At that, Noah's laughter fades and a look of pure joy, of contentment, washes over his face. "I can't wait. I'm happy we decided to hold off on learning the sex, but man, I hope it's a little girl."

I grin and even Easton's expression softens. "I'm really happy for you and Indy," I tell Noah.

"Yeah, man. You guys are going to be amazing parents," Easton agrees.

"Torsten really went all in, making sure you guys have everything you could possibly need," I add, recalling Indy's baby shower.

Noah snorts. "He made a damn registry with Indy. Rielle kept messaging me to ask if I think Big Daddy has baby fever."

East and I laugh.

"It was cool that Chloe came," Noah continues, turning back to me. "Indy's really happy that they reconnected and I've never seen you so invested in a relationship before."

"That's because this is his first one," Easton supplies.

This time, I flip him off.

I shake my head and lean back in my chair, taking another sip of my beer. "She's different, guys. Things between us, they're easy. It's like we bypassed all that awkward, getting to know each other shit because I already know her. I have for years. Sure, she grew up but at her core, she's still the same girl who used to my best friend."

"Damn," Easton whistles. He dunks a corn chip in salsa and pops it into his mouth. "She planning on staying then? In Boston?"

I frown, thanking the server when she drops off our entrees. We're hanging at our favorite Mexican fusion restaurant, not too far from Noah and Indy's place. "I don't know," I say slowly. "We haven't really talked about it. I know she's looking into other options. But for now, we're just...taking things as they come."

"But you guys are for real," Noah states.

I nod, shaking off the tremor of uncertainty I feel from Noah's question. "Yeah, man. We're for real."

"Good for you, man." East nods, wiping a napkin across his mouth. "It'll be different now, you'll see. It's better having someone you can count on, someone you trust, especially once the season starts. I know we always said it'd be impossible to balance hockey and a family life but it's not. Your priorities naturally realign when you find the person you want to share your life with. Of course, hockey is still hockey. But it doesn't come close to having a home."

Noah mulls that over before agreeing and picking up his taco.

I watch my friends as they dig into their lunch but

suddenly, I'm not hungry. Because while the past few weeks with Chloe have been amazing, a turning point in our relationship that has elevated it from a casual, summer fling to a real, life-changing commitment, we've been insulated. Our entire dating experience has been confined to this summer. During the off-season, when I'm not constantly traveling or rushing to practices and workouts. With her here temporarily. With our families pushing us together and our friends cheering us on from the sidelines. We haven't yet managed the balancing of our careers and hectic schedules. She doesn't have a key to my place and hasn't stated what her plans are come September.

All I know is when Chloe told me she loved me, I felt it in every fiber in my being. I felt it deep in my soul and her feelings for me shifted something in my world. But once hockey season resumes and I take up all the responsibilities on and off the ice that go with being the team captain, will I still be worthy of her love? Will I still be the man she fell for? Will I still be able to show her that she's at the center of my world, even on the nights when it won't feel that way?

"You don't like the fajitas?" Noah flips his chin at me, squinting at my plate. "Is that sushi? I thought those were just in the nachos."

I shrug, picking up my fork. "It's a new dish."

"Cool."

"Hey," Easton says suddenly. "You guys want to go to the MMA fight this weekend?"

"You got tickets?" I ask. "They were sold out last time I checked."

"Oh yeah," Noah says. "Jay Rodriguez is fighting out of Cyanide MMA in Chicago."

"Yep." East nods. "It's Connor Scott's original gym, before he launched the Soul Sanctuary franchise. Connor's one of my college teammate's friends. Evan hooked me up with four tickets."

"Nice! I'm in," Noah agrees.

I shake my head, a tiny flicker of disappointment running through me. "I wish, man. But this weekend is that wedding in New York."

"Shit. Already?" East asks.

"Is Chloe worried about seeing her ex again?" Noah asks.

I shrug. "I doubt it. She seemed pretty much over him when we ran into him at the engagement party."

"Yeah." East waves his hand in my direction. "Because now she knows what it's like to be with a real man."

I grin, dipping my head in thanks. It isn't often that East tosses out compliments but when he does, they sure are genuine.

"The fight is Friday night. When are you leaving for New York?" East asks.

"Friday morning," I respond, trying out my sushi fajitas. "These are pretty good."

"I'm going to order them next time," Noah says as I push some onto his plate.

"You'll have a good time," East says.

"Huh?" I look up.

"At the wedding. With Chloe," he clarifies.

"Yeah." I grin. "It's going to be one hell of a weekend."

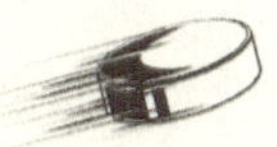

THE WEEK PASSES QUICKLY as I start to prepare for hockey camps and check in on the team. I rev up my workouts, spend more time lifting weights, and realign my diet. But when I'm not training, I'm with Chloe.

It's amazing how different my life feels now compared to the start of summer. Even the tough workouts, the ones where I struggle and feel like I lost my edge, the ones that used to cling to my mind for days afterwards, plunging me into a foul mood, fade into the background as soon as I see my girl.

Being with her makes everything better, brighter. It's the little things too. The small, thoughtful gestures that let me know she's thinking of me. Chloe pops by my place with green smoothies after morning training sessions. She'll forward me an article on a new diet athletes are trying. On the nights when I'm exhausted, she curls up beside me on the couch to watch a movie and my body relaxes, my mind clears, and I feel at peace. Like the weight of my teammates' futures—professionally and personally—aren't sitting on my shoulders.

"Hey baby," I answer her call Thursday afternoon.

"Hey! You ready for this weekend?"

"Tell me about your dress again," I demand, teasing her. My sister and cousin took Chloe shoe shopping and while Claire and Indy have gushed about how amazing Chloe looks in her bridesmaid's dress, I haven't seen it yet.

She chuckles. "And give away my grand moment? No way, Aus. I want to see your eyes widen and your jaw hit the floor and—"

"We'll be late to the wedding."

She laughs again. "I'm just reminding you that our train leaves tomorrow morning at 8:23."

"Why aren't we driving again?" I ask, pouring myself a glass of water. I lean back against the kitchen counter, prepared to make my list of arguments *why* driving makes so much more sense: we'd have a car for the weekend.

"Because we'll sit in traffic for hours, parking will be a nightmare, and isn't it more romantic to take a train ride?"

I snort. "About as romantic as riding in a smelly subway."

"It's going to be fun. I promise! I already got our tickets."

"Okay," I acquiesce. "I'll pick you up at 7:30."

Chloe squeals. "It's going to be the best. I can't wait to take you to Annabelle's on Saturday morning for brunch.

Sourdough waffles are a gift after a night of drinking champagne."

"I can't wait, Sunshine. What are you doing today?"

"I'm heading to Mimi's in a bit. I'm going out to dinner with my parents and Drew tonight."

"Drew's in town?"

"Yes! He surprised my parents for their anniversary."

"I thought their anniversary is next month." Diane and Greg's wedding anniversary is the week after my parents and…a wave of panic grips me. Did I forget Mom and Dad's wedding anniversary? No, Savannah would have said something…

"It is. But Drew couldn't get time off that week so he surprised them early."

"Nice. Okay, well say hi to Mimi and enjoy dinner tonight. I'm going for a run now and then swinging by Panda's place to hang for a bit."

"You mean play video games."

"Correct. See you tomorrow morning?"

"7:30. I'll be on the front porch."

I recall our getaway drive for Marissa's engagement party and grin. "I'll see you then. 'Bye, baby."

"'Bye, Aus."

I end the call and pop in my ear pods. Rolling my neck, I select a playlist and head out for a run.

The sun is shining, my legs are pumping, and I'm ready for the weekend. Who knew being a plus one to a wedding would fill me with such excitement? But I can't wait to have a weekend in New York City with Chloe. And I really can't wait to see her in that dress.

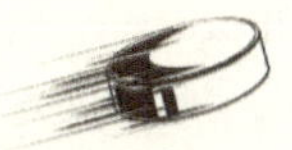

THE RINGING of my phone pulls me from sleep. I glance around groggily, noting that it's still pitch-black outside. What the hell time is it?

I reach for my cell phone, banging my hand against the bedside table until I grasp it.

"Easton?" I answer, my voice thick with sleep. A thought zips through my head and I bolt upright. "Is Claire okay?"

"Austin. Fuck, man. Fuck." My best friend sounds agitated.

"What's wrong?" I demand.

"Aus, I need you to come to Taps."

"Taps?" I pull the phone away from my ear to squint at the time. "It's almost two in the morning."

"Yeah," East says miserably.

Realization slams into me. "Easton, are you drunk?"

"No," he growls out. "No, I'm not fucking drunk, Austin. But Christ, I want to be. Fuck, please, I need you to come get me."

I spring from my bed, looking around for a pair of jeans and my wallet. "Where's Claire?" I ask, not wanting to end our call, not wanting to leave Easton alone with his thoughts.

"We got into a fight," he admits. "It was, it was my fucking fault," Easton rattles on, swearing up a storm.

I pull on a T-shirt and slide into sandals. Locking the door behind me, I hustle out to my ride. "What happened?"

As soon as I'm behind the wheel, I switch East to Bluetooth and head toward Taps.

"Derek, man. Fucking Derek Reiner. Smarmy motherfucker said some stupid shit to Claire."

"Like what?" I ask slowly, taking a left-hand turn.

"Shit about when they used to hook up."

Fuck. "But she shut it down right?"

"Of course she did," he bellows. "She'd never step out on me."

"I know that." I frown, wondering what the hell tran-spired between East and my sister.

"But she's still doing work for him. I told her to cut off all fucking communication with him. If he's going to talk shit to her, mention things about when they… She shouldn't work with him!"

I park in the parking lot and hurry into Taps. As soon as I clear the threshold, he looks up and I stop in my tracks. His eyes are wild, his expression twisted. His shoulders are tense, his foot tapping restlessly against the bottom rung of the barstool. I narrow in on his hands, noting they're wrapped tightly around a glass of club soda. Damn. Even from across the bar, I can feel the anger radiating off of him.

I walk to his side and slip onto the barstool.

Pete, the bartender, shoots me a nervous glance.

"I'll take a Coke, please, Pete."

He nods and fills up a glass, sets it beside my hand, and heads to the other end of the bar.

"What are you doing here, man?" I ask.

Easton looks at me, glances away, and then turns back, his expression fierce. "I want a fucking drink, Aus. I want to drink, man. I can't do this. Who the fuck was I kidding to think I could have a real relationship with a woman like your sister?" He drags a hand over his face, his other hand slam-ming the bottom of his glass against the bar. The club soda spills over, splashing onto his skin.

When it does, I get a whiff of it. "Vodka." My eyes cut to Easton's.

He glares back, his expression twisting into regret, his gaze heavy with apology.

"Did you drink it?" I ask.

"No."

"Not even a sip?" I press.

He clears his throat. "Nothing."

I look to Pete who gives me a slight nod, confirming Easton's version of events.

"How long you been sitting here, East?"

"Too long," he whispers.

"Claire know you're here?" I demand, knowing I need to ease up. My best friend needs me right now, my teammate needs me, but Claire is my sister and…fuck. I take a large swig of my Coke and clear my throat. "Are you okay?" I lower my voice, taking some of the bite out of my tone.

East shakes his head, slowly pushing the glass of vodka over to me. "No."

I close my eyes for a breath, dropping my head. Then, I turn to my best friend and give him my best. "Well, let's get you right again, brother. You want to get out of here?"

CHAPTER 23
CHLOE

I wake up to a text message from Austin.

When I see his name flash across my screen, I smile. Until I realize that it's 6 a.m. and he wouldn't be messaging this early unless something was wrong.

AUSTIN

Hey baby. I'm so sorry. I'm not going to make the train. Explain later. Meet you in New York.

What the hell?

CHLOE

Everything okay?

I frown when ten minutes pass without a response.

CHLOE

Austin, are you okay? Where are you?

I swear when he doesn't respond and pull myself from my bed. I go through my morning routine of showering and blow-drying my hair. I check that my shoes for the wedding are packed and that I slipped the envelope with Marissa's wedding gift in my purse. But every two minutes, I glance at my phone.

There's nothing. No response from Austin. No explanation. Nothing.

Tears prick the corners of my eyes, a mixture of concern and frustration.

At 7 a.m., I text Claire.

CHLOE

Claire, is Austin okay? What's going on?

My phone rings a second later and I swipe right, desperate for information.

"Claire?"

"Oh, Chloe. It's awful," she cries.

My stomach sinks and twists painfully. I sink to the edge of my bed. "What happened?"

"East and I got into a fight. I have no idea where the fuck he is but I'm guessing if you can't find my brother, then Austin is with him." She breathes out a sigh. "That actually makes me feel better."

I frown. "A fight? About what?"

"Ugh. It's so stupid. Honestly, not worth getting into. But Easton stormed out of here around midnight and I haven't heard from him since. I barely slept."

"Are you okay?" I ask, my mind racing.

"Yeah, I'm fine. Just, confused, I guess."

"And you think Austin is with East?" I ask, thinking that it makes the most sense.

"Austin and Noah are the only people Easton would call. But I talked to Indy already and he didn't call Noah. Noah's out looking for him now."

"Shit." I stand back up, nervous energy zapping through my veins. I glance at the time and close my eyes. "I'm so sorry, Claire. Really. Please, let me know when you hear anything."

"Of course. I'm sure my brother will get in touch with you."

"Right," I say. Yesterday I would have whole-heartedly agreed. But now, glancing at my empty messages, I'm not so sure. Unease trickles down my throat and collects in my chest before pooling in the pit of my stomach. "Hang in there, Claire. Get some sleep." After I disconnect our call, I stalk aimlessly around my bedroom.

Worry for Easton buzzes in my head but so does a wave of anger. Toward Austin. Why couldn't he message me *that*? Why couldn't he tell me about Easton? Why doesn't he think it's important to let me know what's up when I'm about to get on a train to New York by myself to go to a wedding solo?

Disgust with myself, for my anger, washes over me, making my guilt rise. Dammit. Of course Austin should be with East right now. Easton's his best friend, most likely his future brother-in-law. And he's been doing so great, trying so hard, to stick to his sobriety. I don't know a lot about alcoholism but I know enough to understand that it's a lifelong struggle, that every day is a series of choices. That it doesn't just magically go away or get easier.

But why does it have to be today? This moment? Why—

A knock sounds on my door and I glance up as Drew pops his head into my room. "You're going to wear out the carpet," he jokes but his eyes are narrowed in concern.

I sigh and plop back down on the edge of my bed. "I need to leave for the train station in fifteen minutes."

"Okay. Is Austin on his way?" Drew closes the door behind him and leans against it.

I blow out a chortle. "Austin can't make it. He's going to meet me in New York."

Drew's eyebrows dip. "Why?"

I shake my head, wringing my hands together. "I don't know. His message was cryptic. But I spoke to Claire and she and Easton got into a fight. She thinks Austin is with Easton."

Drew's frown deepens. "But she didn't say where?"

"She doesn't know."

"Shit," he murmurs, glancing at my suitcase. "Okay, well I'll give you a ride."

I drop my head, muttering my thanks.

"I know you're upset." My brother walks closer, until he's sitting next to me on the bed. His hand rests in the center of my back and I lean into his side, until my head bumps his shoulder.

"I'm disappointed."

"You should be."

"But East needs Austin right now," I manage to admit.

"Yes," my brother agrees. "But so do you."

I look up, surprised by his words. "You don't think I'm being selfish for being…upset?"

"I think you're being human." He tugs the ends of my hair. "You're used to Steve bailing on you and you're used to having to manage those emotions. With Austin, it hurts more because you didn't have the same expectation. Plus, you've got your past coloring your outlook. You gotta give him the benefit of the doubt this time, Chlo. He's never disappointed you before, not even when we were kids."

I huff out a sigh. "I know."

"But it's okay to be upset. I know you don't want to walk into that wedding by yourself, have to see Steve and Brittney together."

I drop my head back to my brother's shoulder. "What if it's always like this?" I whisper, voicing my concern aloud. "He's the captain of the team. He's told me several times that his team comes first, that his team is his life. What if there's always someone else's emergency or need? What if I…" I pause, working a swallow.

"What if you're always playing second fiddle?" my brother asks quietly.

I nod, rolling my lips together.

Drew shifts to wrap his arm around my shoulders. "Then he's not the one."

I close my eyes, not wanting to admit the truth in Drew's words. I can't even consider the possibility that Austin isn't the right guy for me. That I've chosen wrong yet again.

"But," Drew continues, "you making a big assumption on a single incident wouldn't be fair to him. Or to you."

I glance up, staring into my brother's warm eyes. "When did you start giving such great advice?"

The corner of his mouth pulls up. "Yeah, well, it seems I can give it, but not take it myself. Come on." He stands and grips my suitcase handle. "You don't want to miss your train."

I huff out a breath and force myself to stand. I pick up the garment bag with my dress and lay it over my arm. "Thanks, Drew."

"You'll be okay, Chlo. For now, try to enjoy your weekend in New York. At least you'll see Abbi."

"Yeah, I will," I say, knowing he's right. I need to shift my perspective, enjoy this weekend for what else it offers. Like time with my best friend. A meeting with my boss. A chance to be back in the city.

Still, as I follow my brother out of my room, a pit of disappointment swells in my stomach.

When I'm on the train to New York, it grows. By the time I check into the hotel, it's climbing up my throat.

I feel too many things too powerfully. Anger, hurt, betrayal, guilt, frustration.

The only thing I know for certain is I am not in the right frame of mind to celebrate a blissful union. I am not in the mood to dance at a wedding reception. And I am definitely not prepared to see Brittney flash a diamond engagement ring.

I check my phone one last time before the wedding ceremony starts.

Abbi gives me a side look but I shake my head.

There's still no word from Austin. No explanation. No missed call.

It's like he's forgotten I exist at all.

MARISSA AND ADAM have a beautiful wedding ceremony that causes nearly every guest to cry. Including me, although I'm fairly certain I'm shedding tears for the wrong reasons. Because as shitty as it is, I'm crying for myself.

Watching my friend kiss her husband for the first time should be joyous.

Witnessing the union of two people, made in love, is a miracle of sorts.

But as Marissa and Adam throw their arms in the air and walk down the aisle, accepting hugs and well wishes from their family and friends, I catch sight of Steve. He's winking at Brittney and she's smiling like the happiest woman on the planet.

And something inside of me cracks.

Why can't that be me? Not looking at Steve but looking at Austin. Why can't I ever be madly in love with a man who looks at me and doesn't see the rest of the room?

A sob rattles in my chest and I pinch my lips together to keep it there.

Because I am madly in love with Austin Merrick. And he didn't show up. He didn't even give a reason as to why he bailed on today, knowing how important it is to me that he be here.

My man forgot all about me.

"Hey." Abbi appears behind me and I turn. When she reads my expression, she winces. "Want to get drunk?"

I close my eyes and nod. Abbi leads me to the bar and I don't protest when she pushes a shot of vodka in my direction. Instead, I toss it back and wait for the numbness I need to take over.

I'M another two shots of vodka and too many flutes of champagne in when Steve drops his elbows to the bar in the space next to mine.

I peer at him from the corner of my eye, muttering a curse word and tipping back my fourth shot.

His eyes narrow and he twists in my direction. "New man couldn't make it?"

I roll my eyes, hating the fake concern in his tone. Hating that he put me in this position, showing up to an event alone after he bailed at the last minute, several times too. "Fuck you, Steve."

He jerks back, surprised. He should be. I've been waiting months, hell, maybe even years, to say those words to him.

"Jealous?" He tilts his head and I snort.

It's not a delicate or feminine sound. Nope, it's loud and obnoxious and leads to a burst of laughter that pours out of my mouth like a waterfall. My shoulders shake with laughter and I hunch forward, clutching my stomach.

Steve shifts his weight awkwardly.

"Oh God." I breathe out, dabbing the tears from the corners of my eyes with a bar napkin. I turn toward my ex-fiancé, relieved his ring isn't still on my finger. I feel so strongly about it that I tell him as much, ending with, "You and Brittney deserve each other. Really, congratulations. Now fuck off and let me drink in peace."

Steve stares like he doesn't know me. Because he doesn't

know this version of me, it's one I've never showed him. But damn does it feel good to put Steve in his place after all the hurt he dragged me through.

Abbi appears at his side. She clicks her tongue and tips her head, indicating he should get lost. He glances between us and huffs away.

I chuckle. "That was like out of a movie."

We both crack up but my laughter quickly morphs into tears.

"Oh, Chlo," Abbi says sympathetically, angling her body to shield my emotional meltdown from the guests and dance floor.

Fortunately for me, the wedding is starting to wind down and people are already trickling out.

"Has he messaged you? Anything?" she asks.

I shrug, turning back to the bartender. I'm about to order another shot when Abbi intervenes and suggests water.

"I don't know," I answer, stabbing a straw into the water glass. "After the ceremony, I stashed my phone in my hotel room. Otherwise, I knew I'd be the pathetic girl checking it every three seconds and trying to swallow back my disappointment." I sigh. "That wouldn't have been fair to Marissa." I glance down at the beautiful bridesmaid dress. It's a light blush color with a fitted, sexy bodice that flares out into a soft, chiffon skirt. It's sexy and flirty and the first time I tried it on, I felt like a princess.

Too bad I'm worse off than Cinderella.

I'm more like one of her cast-off stepsisters.

I definitely want one more shot.

Abbi grabs my wrist, causing me to look up.

"Austin isn't Steve," Abbi says.

"I know that."

"Do you?" She tilts her head, studying me. "I know at first I had my concerns about him but after I saw you two together… Chloe, the way he looks at you… He wouldn't just bail if there wasn't a good reason."

"Sure." I brush it off.

"Chloe."

"Abbi, I get what you're doing. And I appreciate it. But I can't keep falling for guys who put every other aspect of their lives before ours. Before the life we're supposed to be building together. The only reason why I know he has a real reason for bailing is because I called his sister. Austin hasn't given me anything to go off of except a brush-off."

Abbi sighs, swiping up my water glass and taking a long pull. "I just don't want to see you stop a good thing before it has the chance to take off."

"He's starting training camp soon anyway. Then he'll be back to his hockey life, travel schedule, team captain commitments." I shake my head. "He told me, you know? Right from the start, he told me. I don't know why I expected anything different but… I did. I expected more from him than this." I toss a hand toward the dance floor, where only twenty or so people are left swaying to the music.

Abbi's expression changes, surprise rippling across her face. "Maybe he's delivering anyway."

"What?" I ask, starting to turn to follow her line of vision.

"Austin's here," she says.

I turn fully and gasp, my fingers rising to my mouth.

Austin Michael Merrick stands inside the Grand Ballroom dressed in a simple navy suit. His hands are stuffed in his pockets. A sexy stubble coats his jawline and he bites the corner of his bottom lip, his eyes scanning the space. Until they find mine. Then, they spark and hold. Intensity rolls in their depths, keeping me rooted in place.

He looks exhausted, like he hasn't slept in two days. But affection sweeps his expression when he sees me. His eyes scan my frame, widening appreciatively as they take in my dress, then darkening with regret when they recognize the disappointment in my eyes.

Austin walks toward me and Abbi scurries away, leaving me posted up at a bar with a lineup of empty shot glasses as witnesses to what suddenly feels like a defining moment in my life.

"Chloe," he murmurs.

I heave out a breath and shake my head, partly in disbelief and partly in hurt. "What are you doing here?"

CHAPTER 24
AUSTIN

I'm not prepared for the animosity in her tone.

Sure, I knew she'd be upset. Maybe even angry.

But the Chloe before me, looking like she just stepped off a goddamn runway, is fuming. Red splotches appear on her cheeks and her shoulders stiffen, waves of hurt emanating from her frame.

Shit. I swallow, hoping to ease the dryness in my throat. I reach to grab her wrist but she yanks it away.

"Hear me out, Chlo."

"Why?" She crosses her arms over her chest.

"I'm here, aren't I?" I say defensively. Yeah, it was shitty of me to bail on the wedding but Easton needed me and I thought Chloe of all people would understand that. She's always been caring and compassionate, always one to jump in and help when needed. I mean, here she is, a bridesmaid in a wedding with the woman her ex-fiancé cheated on her with.

She rakes her teeth over her bottom lip, picking up a shot glass and waving it at the bartender.

Damn. Concern blazes through me. Did I cause her to react like this? She's already unsteady on her feet and the gleam in her eyes, feverish and hazy, is a good indicator that she crossed over from tipsy to drunk a while ago.

"Why are you here, Austin?"

My eyebrows snap together. "Because I want to be here. With you."

She shakes her head. "Try again."

"What?" I move closer to her, trying to get a read on the wild expression in her eyes.

It's reckless and exasperated and unlike anything I've ever witnessed in her before.

I have a hell of a lot of experience, too much really, with irate women.

But Chloe's never been irrational…

"You're here because you feel guilty," she murmurs quietly, not picking up the shot glass the bartender placed down before making himself scarce. Smart man. "You promised you'd come to this wedding with me and so here you are. And I appreciate it, Austin. I appreciate the gesture and you being here when you're clearly exhausted. But you didn't show up for the right reason. You didn't show up for me; you showed up for you." She points at me accusingly, her words slurring.

"Baby, that's not true." I grip the underside of her elbow, my tone pleading.

Tears collect in the corners of her eyes and nausea twists my stomach as the full realization of just how much I hurt Chloe rocks through me.

"Chloe, please. Let's head up to the room. It's been a long day. We can talk in the morning."

She lets out another humorless sound. "Right. Because now I'm drunk and emotional and who wants to have a real conversation about real things with the insecure bridesmaid, never the bride." She hiccups.

I stare at her for a long moment, as if I'm seeing her for the first time. Gone is my charming friend. Gone is the confident woman I'm stupidly in love with.

Instead, I see the hurt, scared, somewhat broken woman who Steve knocked down and I just kicked over. I close my eyes, tipping my head skyward as the damage I caused sinks in.

"Sunshine," I reason, "I'm so fucking sorry about today. Okay? I really am. But baby, Easton needed me and—"

"I needed you," she cuts me off. "And I know that's selfish and unfair. I know that, Austin. Admitting it out loud makes me hate myself a little bit. But I'm never anyone's first choice. I'm never anyone's real concern. I'm always the afterthought. I mean, you didn't even message to tell me about East. I heard about everything from Claire. And maybe it's me and my insecurities, but I don't want to be this person anymore." She shakes her head. "Is East okay?"

I nod.

"Claire?"

"They're both fine. Back home."

"Good." She nods and moves to sidestep me. "I'm tired."

"Okay," I say, catching her hand. I walk with her to the elevators, shooting side glances her way. My anxiety spikes, crawling up into my throat and making my tongue thicken, too fat to form words.

Will Chloe forgive me? Can she see past this moment? This misunderstanding?

My heart races and the back of my neck prickles as my thoughts splinter off in different directions. I try to focus on the moment, on Chloe. But her distracted expression only increases my concern.

Her head is somewhere else entirely. Her emotions are twisted up, causing little sighs and sniffles to sound out. But the resignation in her expression, the coolness in her eyes, is what scares the hell out of me.

She's just drunk.

She's just tired.

You'll talk in the morning.

I mentally flip through rationalizations as Chloe kicks off her stunning dress that I waited all week to see her in. She doesn't bother pulling hairpins from her updo or washing her face. Instead, she pulls on a T-shirt, slides into the bed, and ignores me completely.

"Chloe—"

"I'm not in the mood, Austin," she cuts me off, turning her back.

I swear, gripping the back of my neck. Turning away from her, I stride to the window and stare out into the darkness. The windowpane is cool against my palm but it doesn't center me the way I need.

Instead, my worry gives way to anger at Chloe's dismissal. The fatigue I've been battling all day crashes over me. I'm fucking exhausted.

I've been up since nearly 2 a.m. My nerves are rattled, trying to talk Easton off a proverbial ledge. I'm emotionally drained from running interference between my best friend and his sponsor, between Easton and Claire.

Not to mention, I spent over five hours driving from Boston to Manhattan to show up for Chloe. To show her how much I care about her, that I want to be here for her, that I'm committed to our relationship.

And she throws it in my fucking face? Says I'm making it all about me?

"No." I turn away from the window and stride back toward the bed, flipping the lights on in the process.

"What?" She sits straight up.

And fuck, I hate the damn mascara streaks on her face, giving away that she was silently crying while feigning sleep. But I'm hurt too. And angry. And frustrated.

"You don't get to shut me out like this. I spent five hours driving to be here for you. I'm sorry I didn't tell you about

Easton in my message. There wasn't a lot of time and I didn't want you to worry."

"You didn't want me to worry?" She leaps out of bed, surprisingly spright for someone slurring their words so badly.

I know I should let it go. She's drunk and I'm scared. We're both exhausted and pissed off. Whatever we say now isn't going to be well-thought-out and level-headed. No, we're going to hurl angry barbs at each other that are only going to make us both feel like shit in the morning.

But my hockey captain's levelheadedness is irrelevant when I'm dealing with women. Especially with *the* woman. The only one I've ever truly cared about.

"I'm sorry, Chloe! Okay, how many times do you want me to say it? I know I should have been more upfront with you. But I've been trying to call you since 4 p.m. You could have picked up too, ya know?"

Regret flares in her eyes and she glances at her phone, discarded on the desk.

I snort, moving to pick it up before she can. When the screen lights up, I see the list of my unanswered messages and missed calls.

"I left my phone here," she says, crossing her arms over her chest.

"Mature. Real fucking mature," I snap back, raking a hand over my face.

"This was never going to work," she murmurs.

"What?" I narrow my eyes at her. My fingers tremble as an icy coldness slithers down my spine.

"Me and you," she continues. "We fell back into old habits, something comfortable and familiar."

"There's nothing familiar or comfortable about this." I gesture between us, faced off and arguing. "We never fought. Ever. And I've never felt the way I do before you came back into my life. You make me feel like I'm fucking flying. You make me feel…" I trail off, heaving out a sigh. "How did we fuck this up so badly, baby?"

She dashes a tear off of her cheek, some of the fight leaving her body. "I don't know, Austin. Maybe because I'm not ready. Maybe I'm more hurt and twisted up over my past than I thought. Or maybe because you're holding back. And you're not as ready to be in a real relationship as you thought. Or wanted."

I stare at her, witnessing the hurt ripple across her face. It's deep and potent. But her words strike a nerve because she's right. The shakiness of my hands, the sickness roiling in my stomach, is proof of that. Maybe I'm not as ready as I need to be, not for a woman like her. Not for a relationship like ours.

"I want to be," I murmur, clearing my throat.

She nods and compassion floods her eyes. "I know. But sometimes wanting it just isn't enough." She sits back down on the mattress and closes her eyes, heaving out a sigh. When she opens them, she just looks sad. Deflated. "I'm tired, Austin."

"I know."

"No, I mean I'm tired. Exhausted and drained and empty. I can't keep doing this." She throws an arm in my direction before letting it fall limp next to her on the bed. "Part of my reaction today is because of my history with Steve. We both know it." She glances at me and I dip my chin in agreement. She lifts a shoulder and lets it fall, resigned. "This was never going to work."

"Chlo—" I step toward her but she holds up a hand.

"Please, let's just sleep now, okay? I don't want to argue. I don't want to feel like, like this"—she gestures to herself—"anymore right now." Her eyes are pleading when they meet mine and even though I want to hash everything out, convince her that we can fix this, that we can do better, I nod.

She swings her legs back into the bed and pulls the comforter over her shoulders. I flip off the lights and lose my suit pants and shirt. Sliding into bed beside her, an ocean of space exists between us. We both hover on the edges of the mattress, our backs to each other, our silence hovering over the bed like an oppressive weight. Things between us, always so effortless and fun, now seem strained and stressful.

How the hell did this happen? How did I let this happen?

CHAPTER 25
CHLOE

I feel like death.

Even worse really because on top of my raw emotions and old hurts, I'm hungover as fuck. My head throbs, my lips are chapped dry, and my body feels like I've done CrossFit when I really spent the evening slamming back vodka shots and silently fuming.

I crack an eye slowly, closing it the second I catch sight of Austin. He's perched on the edge of the bed, his back to me. His elbows are resting on his knees and he's staring out the window, thinking, or perhaps, silently fuming.

I force my eyes open and shift my weight. The rustle of the sheets has Austin turning and his gaze sweeps over me, guarded. The nausea that rolls through my stomach as I sit up intensifies at his expression.

I fucked up. I feel it all the way down to my toes and yet…did I? I mean, yeah, I definitely, one hundred percent, went about everything all wrong. But is it wrong to want to be an equal in your own relationship? To have your significant other confide in you about what's going on instead of leaving you hanging? To be worthy of more than a text message?

My throat is achingly dry and it takes me a moment to work a swallow.

"Here." Austin uncaps a hotel water bottle and passes it to me.

I accept it, muttering a thanks. His kindness scrapes at me, at odds with my insecurities. Insecurities I thought I had a handle on until last night, when the scabs were ripped off, shining a spotlight on my vulnerabilities. On the hurts I can't fully conceal no matter how hard I tried to bury them.

"I'm sorry, Austin," I whisper, my voice cracking.

His eyes soften slightly. He shakes his head. "Nah, it's on me too. I should have told you what was going on with East."

I shrug, scraping a hand down my face. Makeup smears across my palm and I know I must look like a train wreck. I bite my lower lip, my stomach roiling. I grasp the base of my throat and Austin's eyes narrow.

"Where do we go from here?" I ask.

He shrugs a shoulder. "I want this with you, Chlo. I want to be all in with you…"

"But?"

"But while I admit I should have handled yesterday better, I'm not ever going to bail on a friend, on a teammate, when he needs me." He says the words clearly, a hint of apology in his blue eyes.

"I know. I don't want you to. I love how much you care about your friends and family and team. It's just when you bailed on me at the last minute, without any explanation, it brought up a lot from my relationship with Steve and—"

"I'm nothing like that douchebag."

"I know that. But yesterday morning, I felt the same way I did with him. Unseen, forgotten about."

Austin's eyes flash. "But you know I'd never leave you hanging unless it was something important. An emergency."

I shrug, taking another sip of water. "Do I? Sure, that would be my natural assumption but when you didn't answer my messages or leave me with a real explanation, I didn't have much to go off of, Austin."

"I was worried about this happening," he mutters.

"Worried about what?" I say, much more defensively than I planned to.

He gestures between us. "Our entire relationship has existed in the bubble of Boston. We've been insulated by our families, our history, our past. But in real life? Does our summer together even stand a chance against all these external pressures?"

"I hoped it would," I bite out, wincing on the past tense.

Austin catches it too because his face pales. "What are you even planning to do after summer ends? Are you sticking around in Boston or coming back here?" He raises an arm to the window, to the expanse of Manhattan, before letting it drop.

Shit. I glance at my phone. "I'm meeting my boss in a few hours to discuss options."

"You are?" His tone hardens. "Why didn't you tell me?"

"It was something I was going to discuss with you on our train ride here," I snap back.

Austin grips the back of his neck and swears. "Chloe, I need to get back to Boston this morning. I have a meeting later today with Coach Phillips. Training camp starts next week…"

I nod, feeling the backs of my eyes sting. "I understand."

He sighs. "If I knew about your meeting—"

"It's fine. We both have things we need to do. We should get up, shower, and start our days."

"I don't want to leave you in New York," he bites out.

"Why? It's practically my home." The moment I say the words, I regret them. Because hurt flares across Austin's face and I feel it like a kick to my stomach. "Austin, I, I didn't mean that."

"Didn't you? Is this how you and Steve used to fight? Just throw out barbs to hurt each other?"

I wince, hating myself in this moment. My mind flips back through Steve's and my disagreements and it's like a wakeup call. Because Austin is right. This is exactly the kind of unhealthy, unproductive shit Steve and I used to do.

I frown, recognizing for the first time that I played a much larger role in Steve's and my demise than I previously admitted. Yes, he was completely wrong for cheating on me. But if I really think about it, without hurt-tinted glasses, I wasn't exactly blameless. We didn't have the relationship I tricked myself into believing. We sure as hell didn't have the connection or the chemistry that I share with Austin.

I look at him again, noting the tightness in his jaw, the hurt in his eyes. Unworthiness floods through me. I did this to him. I hurt him. From the first day, Austin has been nothing but open and honest with me. I pushed him into this relationship, knowing full well that his priority was hockey, and now, I'm crying because he stepped up for his team the way he's supposed to?

Shame swirls through my body and I duck my head. "I'm sorry, Austin. Truly." I shake my head, forcing myself to meet his eyes. "You're right. I shouldn't have said that. I shouldn't have dragged you into all of this."

He frowns and shifts closer to me. "Chlo, I want to be here for you. I want to do this with you."

I reach for his hand and link my fingers with his. Just his touch settles some of my nerves, my fears. "I don't know how," I tell him honestly. "I'm emotionally raw. I thought I was ready but the truth is, I lashed out at you because of my history with Steve. If I was done working through all those insecurities, last night never would have went down the way it did. And you need to have your head in the game, you said it straight from the start, not worrying if you hurt your girlfriend's feelings."

His eyes shutter closed for a second and when they meet mine again, they're filled with regret. The air between us shifts, a melancholy resignation. It's stuffy, pressing down on me.

I suck in an inhale. "I should get ready to head to the office. And you need to head out if you're going to make your meeting on time."

"I hate this," Austin's voice cracks and he clears his throat. "It wasn't supposed to be like this for us, Sunshine."

"I know." I squeeze his hand once before letting it go. Offering up a small smile, I add, "This was one of the best summers ever, Aus. So thank you for that."

"Where do we go from here?" he murmurs, glancing at our intertwined fingers.

"I think we both need to take some space, some time. We should figure out what we want, what we need."

He nods slowly, swiping his tongue over his bottom lip. "If you stay in Boston…"

"I'll see you around," I promise.

He leans forward until he can press a kiss to my forehead. His lips linger over my skin and I inhale deeply, breathing him in, memorizing his scent and the brush of his lips.

"If you ever need anything, you call me." He pulls back, looking me in the eye.

I nod, even though I won't call him. From the expression on his face, he knows it too. I lay my hands on his cheeks and he dips his neck to kiss my lips one last time.

It's too short but sweet enough to be one of the most heartbreaking kisses of my life. Because it's filled with regret. Apology. And I know this is goodbye.

I watch Austin change, pack his bag, and leave the hotel room. When the door closes behind him, I succumb to the tears layered in my chest. I cry them all out, a tumultuous river of hurt and heartache, until there's nothing left but my own disappointment in myself.

I drag myself to the bathroom and take a scalding hot shower. Two hours later, after Advil, coffee, and a strict talking-to by Abbi, I step on a subway and head downtown to my office.

When I enter the building, I square my shoulders and blow out an exhale. Five years ago, I stopped chasing my professional dreams because of Steve. Just last week, I considered relocating to Boston to be closer to Austin. Maybe the reason why I have no luck in relationships is because I'm not happy with where I'm at as an individual. As Chloe Crawford.

I push into Janie's office and smile when she greets me hello.

It's time I stop defining myself by my association to others. It's time for me to grow up. One thing I learned from Austin was to put everything on the line.

And right now, that's exactly what I do.

"YOU'RE GOING TO EL SALVADOR," Abbi repeats, her eyes wide.

I nod, blowing on my tea. "I'm going to El Salvador," I say again, still waiting for the news to sink in.

"Janie gave you an assignment, just like that?" Abbi narrows her eyes.

I shake my head, a smile tugging at my lips. "Hell no. It wasn't just like that. It was me basically having a moment in her office where I questioned what the hell I was doing with my life and why I'm always running after a man…"

Abbi's mouth drops open. "And that worked?"

"Apparently. Janie understood because she wallowed through a similar situation. Ben, the guy that was supposed to travel with Marni, had a family emergency and Janie and Marni agreed I could take his place. It's only for two weeks but if I can prove myself, Janie said we could discuss a more permanent shift into investigative journalism. Real reporting, Abbi."

"But you love writing crossword puzzles."

"I do. But I'm ready for something else. Something that makes me feel…more. Alive. Part of something bigger. I spend a lot of time on my own. I've made my world a lot smaller than it should be. Austin showed me that and if I'm honest, being with him gave me the boost to dip my toe in this new pool. I want to give it a shot."

"Then you should. You one hundred percent should."

"Thanks."

"What about Austin?" she asks just as I take a sip of my tea.

I cough and Abbi smirks.

I clear my throat. "Nothing. Austin has hockey. He starts training camp next week. He was clear what his priorities were from the start and I need to respect them."

Abbi narrows her eyes at me, as if she's searching for some secret I'm not telling her. "So, that's it? It's done, just like that?"

I tip my head, unwilling to voice the words aloud.

"And his gala in September?"

I shrug. "That's still weeks away," I respond, also not willing to think that far in the future.

Because if I do, I'll have to admit that I ruined things between Austin and me far beyond repair.

CHAPTER 26

AUSTIN

Yeager slams into me, pushing me up against the boards.

"Fuck off." I elbow him as Coach Phillips blows the whistle.

"Stop horsing around. Get your heads in the goddamn scrimmage," Coach bellows.

I skate to the line and drop into position, forcing my mind back to the play. East gains control of the puck and flips it toward me. I handle it easily, weaving down the ice before flicking it to Noah who has a clean shot on goal. He takes it and scores. The guys throw their arms in the air, cheering. I smack Noah on the back. "Nice shot."

We all skate to the bench to guzzle some water and sports drinks. Coach makes some line changes and calls out instructions. Jerseys and skates whirl around me, both familiar and not.

For as long as I can remember, hockey, the ice, has been an outlet for me. It's the one place that I can go to and everything in my head quiets. The worry I carry in the pit of my stomach dissipates. The unknowns of the future fade away.

Playing hockey has always been my respite from real life. But right now, no matter how much I try to zone in, my head's not in it. My head's not in it because my heart's not in it and I don't know what the hell to do with that. We're four days into training and I feel unbalanced when I should feel focused.

"Yo." East shoulder bumps me.

I glance at him and he raises his eyebrows.

"We got one hour left," he says low, so no one can hear him. It's as if he understands my mental turmoil, can sense my emotional anguish.

I give him a curt nod and skate back to the center of the ice, mentally berating myself to pull it together. But my head feels foggy, my vision unclear. My palms itch and worry for Chloe, losing herself in the streets of El Salvador, spikes. I miss a clean pass, my head caught up on my lost girl, restless energy pulsing through my limbs. Except there's nowhere for it to go because I can't focus the way I used to. My concern for Chloe, my need to learn everything about the adventure she's having, my desire to just hear her voice, overshadows everything else, even my game.

The next hour drags as I make a series of fuckups that should have Coach Phillips benching my ass. When practice is over, I yank off my helmet and skate to the side.

Coach gives me a long, hard look but doesn't comment on my piss poor performance. The team clears out and I stay on the ice, rethinking the shots I missed, the plays I fucked up. I skate up and down the ice several times, the cool air washing over my face, and wait for the sense of peace to flood my body the way it usually does. Instead, more images of Chloe fill my mind and I stop abruptly, wondering where the hell I go from here. Will this agony ever end?

She's in El Salvador. I dropped the phone when Diane told me the news, sounding as happy about it as I felt. Even though I hate that she left, just disappeared from my life, without a real goodbye, a sense of pride swelled in my chest that she was chasing her dream. That she was still putting herself out there in a way that's brave.

But God, I miss her. I miss the way her presence put me at ease. I miss the way her smile lit up a room, bright like sunshine. I miss the effortless way she stitched her life into mine.

"Hey," Easton calls out, tapping the end of his fist against the glass.

I skate over to him and exit the ice. "What's going on?"

"You tell me."

I shrug.

"I fucked shit up for you and Chlo, didn't I?" he asks directly, making me rear back.

I didn't tell Easton about what went down between Chloe and me at the wedding in New York. He doesn't need to carry around misplaced guilt and I didn't want to share shit with anyone because then I'd have to admit that I let Chloe go. Instead of sitting down and having the conversation we should have had, I hustled back to Boston for hockey and she chased a dream she's put on hold for far too long.

"Nah, man. It wasn't going to work out anyway."

"Bullshit," East spits, his eyes narrowed. "If you weren't with me, you would have been with her, and whatever the hell happened between you guys would have been avoided."

"Maybe," I admit, gripping the back of my neck. "But for how long?"

Easton furrows his eyebrows, waiting for me to continue.

"Hockey being my number one priority was always going to be an issue for us," I admit. "And if I'm putting my career first, I can't blame her for doing the same." I drop my arm and bend to unlace my skates. "She's in El Salvador."

"What?"

I glance up. "For two weeks. She comes back next weekend. It's a reporting gig. It's something she always wanted and…" I trail off, not bothering with the rest. "I'm happy for her."

"Bullshit."

This time, my look is sharper. "No, I am. I'm proud as hell that she—"

"Yeah, fine. You're proud of her and you're happy for her that she went after what she wanted. But you're moping around, fucking shit up on the ice, because your head is still tangled up on her. So don't give me some shit that you're happy about you being here and her being in Central America and you guys not being together."

I swear and stomp off to the locker room. East stays on my heels, waiting patiently while I rinse off and toss on some sweats.

When I'm finished getting dressed, I turn to him, leaning up against the lockers with his arms crossed over his chest. "You ready to talk now?" he asks.

"I was honest with her from the beginning," I say, defensive as hell. "I told her that hockey, the team, this season, all of that was going to be my priority."

"Okay."

"It's ridiculous, East. I made one mistake. I didn't show up to the wedding on time and—"

"You missed the entire wedding, Austin. And that's on me."

"No." I shake my head. "It's on me. I should have told her that I was with you. I should have given her some insight as to what was going on. I guess bailing on her the way I did brought up a bunch of her past, a bunch of her shit with Steve, and she pulled away." I swear again, locking onto East's hard blue eyes. "I don't blame her. And I don't blame you. I blame myself. I should have handled it better."

"Stop."

"What?"

"Stop taking the responsibility for everything, man. Just

because you're team captain doesn't mean you always need to go down with the fucking ship. Truth is, we're all to blame in this situation. Me, you, and Chloe. I hate that I came in between you guys, Austin. I'm really fucking sorry."

I dip my head in acknowledgement at his words.

"But if you play like that"—he jabs a finger toward the ice—"you're not helping the team, yourself, or Chlo. So if you want to be with her, if what you guys had was real and from where I'm sitting, it sure as hell looked it, then get her back. Win her back. Prove to her that you can make room for both hockey and her in your life."

"How?" I ask. "She's in El Salvador."

He smirks. "For ten more days. After that…ball's in your court, Aus."

"We'll see," I say noncommittally, standing from the bench. "Come on, let's go eat."

"Come over. Claire's making chicken piccata."

I snort, knowing it's East's favorite. "You guys made up?" A ridiculous grin splits his face and I groan, holding up my hand. "Don't say anything. The chicken piccata is telling enough."

I follow Easton out of the arena and head to his and my sister's place.

Over the next ten days, I throw myself into hockey and training. I accept every dinner invitation my family tosses my way and regularly pass by Panda's place to play video games. I keep myself busy, engaged, and socially active.

None of it helps ease the ache in my chest. None of my efforts pull my thoughts away from Chloe.

If anything, I miss her even more.

CHAPTER 21
CHLOE

"How was it?" Abbi asks me over mid-morning coffees. My flight landed a handful of hours earlier and Abbi and I are already tucked into our favorite corner at our favorite coffee shop.

"I miss their coffee already," I lament, taking a sip of my latte.

Abbi rolls her eyes and leans forward. Her eyes dance with excitement. "Sure, sure. But how was it?"

I grin, loving her enthusiasm. "It was amazing. It was action and adventure. I was thrown into everything and it was a little bit trial by fire but I loved it. I loved every second of it. I'm heading into the office today to—"

"You just got back."

I scrunch my nose. "I know. But Marni wants to finish this story and submit it so…" I waggle my fingertips. "Wish me luck."

"Luck. Will you see Janie?"

I frown and shake my head. "Not today. She's away but we're going to talk when she's back, see if there are any real growth opportunities for me."

"To move into a reporting type of position?"

I nod.

"Here in the city?" she asks hopefully.

"I'm definitely open to it but, if I'm being honest, I haven't closed the door on Boston either." I bite my bottom lip.

"Have you talked to him?" Abbi asks.

I shake my head. "No. What could I possibly say? I didn't even say goodbye before leaving for El Salvador. Besides, he's already in training. I don't want to mess with his head when the season just started. He needs his focus to be on the ice, on the team." A few weeks away definitely helped clear my head and allowed me the space to view Austin's and my demise with a fresh perspective.

One that demonstrated just how messed up I was over Steve's betrayal. One that highlighted the resentment I carried for far too long. I kept blaming Steve, and then Austin, for not making me a priority in their lives when I did a shit job of making me a priority in my own life too.

"I needed to woman up," I tell Abbi. "I needed to go on this assignment to prove to myself that I could do it. That I can still achieve the dreams I put aside. And instead of blaming Steve for that choice, I need to own it. Instead of being angry with Austin for being such an incredible friend, teammate, all around good guy, I need to be worthy of him. And the way I acted at Marissa's wedding was not the woman I want to be."

Abbi offers me an understanding, lopsided smile. "My baby's growing up," she jokes and I roll my eyes. "What about the gala?"

I pause, tipping my head to the side. "What about it?"

Abbi huffs. "Are you going to go?"

"No! Austin and I broke up. I can't just show up to—"

"Yes. Yes, you can and you should." Abbi points at me. "Real talk girlfriend, you both messed up. But Austin was doing his best when he messed up. You were being bitter and judgey because of fucking Steve when you messed up. If anyone should go out of their way to make things right," she sighs, shrugging, "it should be you."

I bite my bottom lip. Abbi's words roll over me, packing a punch with their truthfulness. "You're right," I say finally.

"I know," she replies.

I stick my tongue out at her and she laughs.

"What if he's with someone else? Another date?" I ask, the thought causing my heart to plunge to the floor.

"Then you give him closure and move on. You said it yourself, Chlo, it's time to woman up. So do it," she challenges.

I sigh and take a big gulp of my latte, both loving and hating that Abbi is right. "Help me find a dress?"

"That's our next stop," she says matter-of-factly.

Abbi and I finish our coffees and spend a handful of hours dress shopping. I settle on a champagne-colored cocktail dress with thicker straps that plunge to a deep V in the front and back. The style is very similar to the dress I wore to Marissa's engagement party, to our first summer event. "You look good, Chlo." Abbi's stamp of approval seals the deal and I hurry to my office with the garment bag strewn over my arm.

After an evening of revising our story, Marni and I submit it. Just as I'm about to head out and catch a late-night train back to Boston, Marni eyes the garment bag knowingly.

"Do you love him?" she asks.

"Who?"

The corners of her mouth tip up. "The guy you've been pining over for the past two weeks."

"I didn't, I wasn't." I blow out a sigh. Licking my lips, I admit the truth. "Yeah, I love him."

"Then make sure you hang onto him," she advises, her eyes taking on a faraway glow. "This career path is competitive. It's fast-paced, intense, and never-ending. If you want to make it, you need a real support system. And if you've found a partner who can be that for you, trust me, you don't want to let him go."

I let her words sink in for a long moment before I settle the garment bag on top of my rolling suitcase. I shoulder my bag and nod. "You're right, Marni. I don't. Thanks for everything."

"You did one hell of a job, Crawford. Keep an ear out. I'm sure Janie's going to have news soon."

I smile, grateful for the encouragement. While I wasn't able to connect with Janie today, I feel more settled than I have in a long time. "Thanks, Marni. I hope so."

"See you around, Chloe." She turns back to her computer and I head to the exit.

It isn't until an hour later, when I'm seated on the train, that exhaustion pulls me under. It's intense, as the wave of adrenaline I've been riding on recedes. I close my eyes as the train pulls out of the station. When I open them, I'm back in Boston, holding on to a glimmer of hope that the life I desire is still within reach.

That the man I love will forgive me.

THREE DAYS after coming home to Boston, I look up at the Boston Public Library and release a shaky exhale. My palms are sweaty and I wipe them down the sides of my dress, mentally swearing at myself for already being out of sorts. I haven't seen Austin yet and my heart is beating erratically. Nerves race through my body, zinging around. I feel like I'm teetering on the edge of a precipice. Will I crash or will I soar?

I blow out a deep breath, steel my shoulders, and climb the stairs to the library where the gala is being held. It's absolutely beautiful and for a moment, I'm too caught up in the elegance of the architecture, in the extravagance of the event, to think of my nerves. Austin wasn't very forthcoming about what tonight's gala entailed and it isn't until I'm standing in the foyer of the dazzling library that I learn he's being awarded the highest honor: Most Influential Bostonian.

Tonight's event is to raise funds for youth programs throughout the city but also to highlight the outreach work that professional athletes have undertaken in recent years. There are many framed photographs and blown-up posters but I can't tear my eyes away from one with Austin, surrounded by dozens of kids, cheesing hard for the camera.

"You're here," a voice says behind me and I turn, smiling when I see Easton.

"Hi, East."

He dips his head, brushing a kiss over my cheek. "Claire didn't mention you were coming."

"It was more of a last-minute decision."

"I saw your parents," he admits.

"I didn't even tell them."

"I'm glad you're here," he says, his blue eyes serious.

"Do you think Austin will be?" I ask, my nerves coming back full force.

A small smile glances off Easton's mouth as he nods. "Yeah, I do." He tips his head to a vacant corner and we relocate. "Listen, Chloe"—he turns toward me—"I'm sorry. That night, everything with the wedding, it was completely my fault. Austin was just trying to do the right thing and I never meant for my weakness to come between you guys. Especially when your relationship was so new and you were figuring shit out." He scrapes a hand over his jawline, looking contrite.

I touch his wrist, making sure he meets my eyes before I say, "Thank you, Easton. Really, it's nice of you to say that. But Austin's and my breakup is on me. I was too quick to react and I judged him unfairly. The truth is that Austin's compassionate side, the way he cares so much about people, is one of the things I love most about him. I never should have made him feel guilty for being such an incredible friend."

East clears his throat, shifting uncomfortably. "So, you love him?"

I look at Easton, noting the wariness edged with hope in his eyes. My palms resume their sweating, my heart gallops, and my vision swims. This is it. I'm finally ready to own my feelings, regardless if they're returned or not. I owe it to Austin. I owe it to myself. I owe it to what could have been, what still should be, between us. "I do. I love Austin. A part of me always has."

A gasp sounds behind me and I sense him before I even turn around. When I do, I'm standing directly in front of the man who has owned most of my sleeping and waking thoughts for the past few weeks. Then, I nearly faint because ohmyGodwow, Austin Merrick is perfection. He's the sexiest man in the room. Hands down.

His suit is expertly tailored, making my mouth water. His jawline is just as rugged as I remember, the dimple in his chin popping. A light beard, really a dusting of stubble, coats his chin and cheeks, giving him a bad boy vibe I want to lean into. His eyes, that stormy Atlantic blue, swirl. Intensity radiates off of him, simultaneously tugging me closer while warning me away.

I lick my dry lips, suddenly at a loss for words. I open my mouth but before I can apologize, before I can tell him just how badly I messed everything up, he shuffles back a step.

I freeze, rooted in place.

"I didn't think you'd show," he murmurs.

Behind him, a flash of red. A beautiful brunette in silver stilettos.

Understanding dawns and my stomach drops. "I, I came to apologize. I'm sorry, Austin. For everything."

He glances up, his eyes wary.

The brunette in the red gown grows closer and my heartbeat intensifies, an endless drumroll. "You are the greatest man I know. Even before seeing this"—I gesture to the framed photographs and the Boston Public Library—"I knew it. I wanted to be here tonight because I made you a promise. And before I made a mess of things between us, we were friends. We've always been friends. No matter what, I'd like for that to continue. I'm sorry I hurt you. I'm sorry I wasn't as understanding and empathetic as I should have been. Most of all, I'm sorry I wasn't the woman for you, the same way you've been the man for me."

His eyebrows bend together, his eyes boring into mine. The brunette brushes past him and I hold my breath, nearly passing out from shock when she breezes by. I turn slightly, frowning when she clasps hands with Panda at the entrance.

"Chloe," Austin says and I turn back. "Did you mean what you said to Easton? Do you still love me?"

I let out a breath and stare at the man who measures so far above all the others. "I've always loved you, Austin. I love you now and I've never stopped."

CHAPTER 28
AUSTIN

I *love you now and I've never stopped.*

At her words, I close the space between us. Her confession is the only thing I need to hear because it matches the tenderness in her expression, the truthfulness in her eyes. Placing my hands on her hips, I dip my head to hers. When our lips are barely touching, I pause, hovering for a beat, making sure she wants this just as much as I do.

And she does. Because Chloe tips her face upward and presses her lips against mine with a desire that's all-consuming. I kiss her passionately, with all the regret and apologies of the last few weeks pouring from my mouth into hers. She kisses me back, with a desperate need to make things right.

When she pulls away, her eyes wide and hopeful, her mouth plump and perfect, my world tilts back on its axis. The heaviness I've been carrying around eases. The dullness that's been clouding my vision, and my judgement, fades away.

I place my palms on her cheeks and bring my forehead to hers. "Thank you for being here."

"Thank you for still having me. I know I messed up."

"We both did, baby."

"No." She shakes her head, her hands wrapping around my wrists.

I smile, kissing her again. "Yes. Part of being in a real relationship is sharing the blame, Chlo. We both failed at communicating. We both did a poor job being upfront about what we needed. We need to do better, Sunshine."

She glances up, her eyes latching onto mine. "You mean… you still want this, with me?"

I kiss her a third time, unable to keep my mouth off of hers. Not when it's calling to me like a Siren and I've felt like a drunken sailor for weeks. "I do, baby. I want you and I never stopped."

She smiles, the shadows in her eyes receding as hope colors her irises.

"After this gala, we'll sit down. We'll talk it out. We'll make a plan. Whatever we need to do to make sure we're both on the same page," I rush to explain. "I can come to New York and you can come—"

"I'm coming home," she cuts me off.

"Home?" I frown, remembering how the last time she muttered that word, she was referring to New York.

"Yes. Just this morning, Janie offered me a job in the Boston office. I'm back, Austin. Permanently."

Relief sweeps through me as disbelief rocks me to my core. I chuckle, scrubbing a hand over my face. "You're serious? Jesus, Sunshine," I murmur, my hands squeezing around her waist. "You've just given me the best news of the night."

"You still have an award to accept."

I duck my head at the reminder. "Will you be my date?" I offer her the crook of my elbow.

She slips her hand around my arm and smiles up at me. "I'm your forever date, baby. No more summer flings for us."

I chuckle at her brazenness. Damn, I've missed her confidence. I've missed the version of Chloe I've always been a little bit in love with. Fierce, determined, perfect. "Now you're getting ahead of yourself."

"That so?" she teases me back, falling into step beside me as I guide us toward the main room.

I nod, raking my teeth over my bottom lip and looking down at her. Heat flickers in her eyes, the same way desire colors mine. "Our summer fling was pretty hot."

"Our real relationship will be even hotter," she promises.

I take her hand in mine, lifting the back of her hand to my mouth and pressing a kiss to her knuckles. "Promise?"

She grins then gasps as we step into the main room. It's decorated beautifully, a little over the top, but by Chloe's reaction, I'm guessing the event planning committee met their goal. I barely notice the flowers and candles because my sights are set on the most beautiful woman in the library.

"Swear it, Austin. We can start by celebrating tonight. Your success."

"Our," I amend, guiding her to a table where my family, and her parents, are seated.

When they see us, a cheer of excitement sounds out. Easton winks at Claire and I know he didn't spill the beans of seeing Chloe enter the gala.

"Oh, dear. I'm so so happy to see you," Mom exclaims, holding out her arms for a hug. She squeezes Chloe tightly, pinches my cheek, and turns to Dad. "Isn't it wonderful?"

Dad shakes his head at Mom's reaction but I can tell he's happy that Chloe's here. "It's the best news we've heard all night," he agrees.

"I can't believe you didn't tell me," Mom addresses this to Diane.

"We didn't know!" Diane says, grinning at Chloe. "Happy to have you home, baby girl."

"For good," Greg adds, generating another buzz around the table.

Mimi stands up and holds out both her hands. "I'll accept

my winnings now," she declares and we all burst into laughter.

I guide Chloe to an empty seat, pulling out the chair for her. Dipping down, I whisper along the shell of her ear, "How much do you think they bet on us?"

She shrugs, turning into my touch, goosebumps breaking out along her shoulder. I run my finger over her sensitive skin, already picturing tonight. After the gala. "I have no idea. But Mimi's on doughnut duty. Indefinitely."

I snicker. "Being with you, Chloe"—I kiss her cheek, not even caring that I'm about to be cheesy as fuck—"is priceless."

She giggles and I flash her a grin, settling into the chair beside her. I lace my fingers with hers, keeping our hands clasped throughout the entire dinner. I only let go when I'm called onstage to accept an award that humbles me. Chloe cheers for me loudly, clapping along with our families.

It's a perfect evening. I spend the entire time oscillating between shock that Chloe is really here and disbelief that she's really mine. Of course, we have our work cut out for us but now, I know we're both ready for it.

I'm all in with my ray of sunshine and I intend to spend all of hockey season and more proving that to her.

EPILOGUE

CHLOE

Three Months Later

"Love seeing you in my jersey," Austin says before he captures my lips in a deep kiss and smacks my ass.

"You guys are gross," Claire jokes, perched on Easton's lap.

"But no one could compare to your cuteness, baby girl," Noah coos, holding sweet Emmaline over his head before cradling her against his chest and dropping a kiss to her forehead.

"Agreed." I collapse on the couch in the living room. Just last month, I moved in with Austin and, being the incredible man he is, he agreed to let me redecorate the space.

Easton passed along the number of his buddy Evan's wife, Charlie, who is an interior designer in New York. Through a series of Zoom calls, we managed to transform this space from a bachelor pad to a welcoming and warm home.

Austin hands Indy a fresh glass of wine and sits on the couch next to me, wrapping his arm around my shoulders.

Indy takes a sip and groans appreciatively. "Oh, wine, how I've missed you." But her wine is quickly forgotten as her gaze lands on her husband, whispering lullabies to their daughter, and a wistful smile crosses her lips.

"So," East says, reaching forward to grab a handful of pretzels from the bowl on the coffee table, "we're clearly old."

"Speak for yourself," Austin says, shifting to pick up his beer.

Noah shakes his head. "Nah, Easton's right. We just won our second game of the season and instead of hitting up Taps to celebrate we're—"

"Watching a three-month-old blink," Claire finishes, her eyes trained on Emmaline.

I chuckle, tucking my feet underneath me and snuggling into Austin's side. "I think I like this better than Taps."

"See." East points at me. "Old."

I shrug. "I'm okay with it."

"Me too." Indy leans back in her chair and takes another sip of wine, her eyes fluttering closed. "I'm too tired to go to Taps anyway."

"Want to play a game?" Austin asks.

Claire narrows her eyes. "Want kind of game?"

"Not a drinking one," Noah decides.

Indy snorts. "Sure, now no one wants to drink..."

"Scrabble?" I suggest.

Claire groans. "So you can kick all our asses?"

"Hey! I'm good at Scrabble." Indy perks up.

Emmaline gurgles and Noah walks across the room to the window, pointing to the city below.

"I'm in," East agrees. "Claire can be on my team."

Austin stands and rummages through a cupboard until he finds Scrabble.

I clear the charcuterie board and drinks off the coffee table. We all huddle around, dressed in sweats and hockey jerseys, with fuzzy socks and slippers on our feet. It's definitely a far cry from the start of summer but as I look around the room at the faces of my friends who have become my family, a sense of peace washes over me. Being banished to Boston definitely turned out to be the best thing that ever happened to me.

Austin unfolds the board and I pass around the bag with the letter tiles.

We all set up our tiles and Easton lifts his chin in my direction. "You go first, Chlo."

I grin, glancing at Austin.

His eyes spark as they hold mine.

Slowly, I spell out my word. *Love.*

Claire groans as Easton snickers.

Without missing a beat, my man lays down his tiles, using the o in "love" to make "you."

"Jesus," Indy mumbles, rolling her eyes. "I'm totally going to win."

Under the table, Austin's hand finds mine and I flip my palm up so he can lace our fingers together.

Easton carries on with the next word but I'm not paying attention to the game.

I'm staring into the deep blue eyes of Austin Merrick wondering how the hell I got so lucky.

He leans forward, brushing his lips over my ear. "Love you, Chlo."

"I love you."

Austin's eyes soften. He looks at me like I'm more beautiful than witnessing life come into the world. Like the rest of the room faded away. Like he's madly in love with me.

I bite my bottom lip and stare back, knowing that I'm finally enough.

For me, for him, for us.

THANK you so much for reading *The Rule Maker*! I hope you loved it!

IF YOU WANT MORE hockey heartthrobs and swoon for single-dad romances, don't miss James and Bella's emotional and heartbreaking book. *The Defender* is out now! Turn the page to start reading.

DESPERATE FOR A PEEK of Indy's baby shower? Sign up for my monthly newsletter to snag a bonus scene!

THE DEFENDER
PROLOGUE - JAMES

My shoulders stiffen the moment I enter Taps. I glance around at the patrons, at Pete behind the bar, at the laughing groups of friends and knowing glances between couples.

Panda hits me on the back. "You good?"

"Yeah, man." I force a grin. Because I'm supposed to be good by now, right?

I follow some of my teammates and their significant others to the bar, but I walk slowly, hang back a bit. Noah has his arm wrapped around his pregnant girlfriend, Indy. Easton's muttering something into Claire's ear.

It wasn't that long ago that I was *that* guy. The one in the happy, committed, healthy relationship. The guy who was expecting twins and then, a first-time dad. The guy that liked to swing by Taps with the team for a drink before heading home to my woman, my family, my goddamn everything.

I look down, sucking in an inhale to ease the tightening of my throat. It's been over a year since Layla passed and still, it's hard to visit any place I once went with her. Which means, it's hard to go anywhere. It's even more excruciating to be at the house, in the *space* she made into a home. If my kids, Milly and Mason, weren't so attached to the place, I would have sold it the week after Layla died.

"You want a beer or shot?" Yaeger clasps my shoulder.

I clear my throat. "Whatever you guys are getting into."

"Line 'em up!" Panda calls out, smacking the top of the bar. "Patron. You new?"

I squint as a bartender I've never seen before comes into focus. She introduces herself to Panda as Bella, and the name fits because, God, she's gorgeous. Gorgeous in a way that even strangers on the street would take note of. Her long brown hair is pulled back into a ponytail but some strands have escaped. Her eyes are a startling shade of blue, a contrast against her dark hair and tanned skin.

She indulges whatever lame ass lines Panda spits with a laugh that hits me square in the stomach.

I look away quickly, shame rolling through me. How dare I check her out? How dare I appreciate the curves of her body and the sweetness of her laughter when I once had Layla? But God, is this ever going to end?

The constant anguish? The debilitating second-guessing? The acute loss that I still feel, no matter how I try to cope? Once upon a time, I had my happily-ever-after. I had a loving and giving wife. We built a home and filled it with the loud wails and peals of laughter from two beautiful, silly babies. I was fortunate enough to turn my passion, hockey, into my career. Men like me, men who already had it all, don't get second chances at that type of happiness.

Bella's melodic laughter pulls my attention back to the bar where she's filling up a line of shot glasses with chilled tequila. She talks quickly, joking and smiling, but when she looks up, her gaze slams into mine. I suck in an inhale, recognizing the shadows in her eyes. Pain. Longing. Emptiness.

She holds my gaze for a beat before looking away, her cheeks coloring.

But I continue to watch her because dammit, I *see* her. I see *it.* I have a deep understanding of the void in her eyes because for too damn long, I've worn it. Recognized it in my own reflection.

Bartender Bella wears a cloak of concealment. Everyone who sees her, chats her up, would never suspect that she's not good, not happy. I mean, she's smiling, right? But underneath, there's something. I catch it in the shadow that passes through her eyes when her gaze lingers on Indy's swollen belly. I spot it in the slow exhale she releases when she punches in Panda's order and thinks no one's watching.

Maybe it's the hint of loss that draws me to her. Two similar hurts in a sea of merriment. I accept the shot of Patron. I throw it back, hissing when it collides with my throat. I slip onto a barstool and watch the gorgeous bartender with lonely eyes and a too big smile.

When she turns to me, she falters for one blink. A jolt of surprise, a flicker of worry, a moment. In that moment, something shifts. My world, a cocoon of hurt and loss and grief, opens the tiniest bit. For the first time in over a year, it allows me to smile at a stranger and open myself back up, knowing that I'll never find what I once had. Knowing that I don't deserve to find what I once had, because I already had the best. But also knowing that right now, maybe I deserve just a little bit more than what I've been drowning in.

"Can I get you a beer?" she asks, her fingers curling around the top ledge of the bar. Her fingernails, a deep purple, tap restlessly.

Her nervousness settles me some and I nod. "I'll take an IPA. Whatever you have on tap. I'm James, by the way."

She turns to look at me over her shoulder as she grabs a pint glass. "Bella."

"Good to meet you."

She fills the pint and places it down in front of me. "I've filled in for Selina a few times and these guys always roll through"—she gestures to my Hawks teammates—"but I don't think I've ever seen you here before."

I shrug, picking up my beer and taking a sip. "I don't come out much."

She quirks an eyebrow, partly in question, partly in disbelief. "No?"

"Nope."

She leans forward and her scent, a light floral perfume I'm relieved I've never smelled before, wafts over me. She smiles, biting the corner of her lip. "What changed your mind tonight?"

Is she flirting with me? Is this what flirting is? Whatever the hell this exchange is, I'd be lying if I said I didn't like it. No, I like it too much. The way the blue in her eyes brightens, the scent of her perfume, how her new position pushes her firm breasts forward.

"It seemed like the right time to finally let these guys drag me out." I gesture to Panda and Yaeger, ignoring the delighted expression on Panda's face.

My words cause her expression to shift for the tiniest of moments before she offers a throaty laugh. "Well I'm glad you decided to come. It's nice to meet you too."

She smiles again, more open this time. I feel it wash over me like sunshine, dragging out a smile of my own when I've done nothing but glare for months.

Another guy on the team, Sims, pulls me into conversation that leads to a game of darts. But I keep glancing over at Bella, making sure she's okay as she navigates a full bar with a bunch of rowdy athletes.

Between her presence and the guys ribbing, I drink more than I'm used to. When last call sounds out, a ripple of panic darts down my spine. Milly and Mason are sleeping at my sister-in-law's tonight. They attended the team BBQ with me this afternoon and then I dropped them at Maia's for a slumber party. But I haven't checked in once.

Guilt replaces my worry as I pull out my phone and shoot off a message.

JAMES

Hey, sorry I didn't check in. How are the kids?

MAIA

Hi! Don't be ridiculous. I'm relieved you're not interrupting our movie and sugar marathon with questions.

I ignore her good-natured joking and focus on the more important part of her message.

JAMES

The kids are still awake?

MAIA

No, worry wart. They're sleeping. They are wonderful and we had a great time. Now go hang with your team and HAVE FUN. She'd want you to live your life.

A lump clogs my throat at Maia's words. It hurts because deep down, I know Layla would want me to live my life. But how can I live half a life now that I've already experienced a full one? Maybe I'm resigned to living the bare minimum that life has to offer.

"Hey man." Sims bumps my shoulder. "You good?" He glances at me before turning to look over his shoulder where a redhead plays with the ends of her hair, clearly waiting for him.

I chuckle, appreciating how the guys always look out for me. But I don't want to cockblock Sims so I nod. "I'm good, Sims. Get out of here. Use protection."

He snickers and walks toward the redhead, slinging an arm over her shoulder as he leads her out.

I turn back to my phone.

JAMES

I'll pick the kids up tomorrow morning.

MAIA

I promised them waffles so just message in the morning. No rush, JR. Really.

JAMES

Thanks.

I slip my phone back in my pocket and head to the bathroom. When I reenter the main bar area, I'm surprised that it's nearly cleared out.

"Hey." I stop next to the ledge.

Bella turns toward me, a bar cloth in her hand as she wipes down the well bottles. "Hey."

"Can I settle up?"

She shakes her head. "Panda took care of the team bill."

I mutter a swear. It's customary for one of the guys to pick up the tab but since I haven't come out in ages, I was hoping that tonight, that guy would be me. I dig into my wallet and pull out a hundred-dollar bill, sliding it across the bar.

Bella shakes her head. "Put your money away, James. You want to do something nice for me?"

What? My mouth drops open before snapping closed. Where is she going with—

Bella laughs. "Relax." She tips her head toward a barstool. "I was going to ask if you wanted to hang for a few, have a beer, and then walk me to my car. Pete usually does but he had to leave early." She shrugs, dropping a vodka bottle back into the well and picking up a rum. "Besides, it looks like you could use an ear."

I plop down on the barstool and snort. "Am I that obvious?"

She tilts her head. "You do a pretty good job concealing it."

"It?"

"The hurt."

"Ahh," I agree. "If we're going to have a heart-to-heart, then I'll need something stronger than a beer. I'll take a whiskey. Neat."

She grins, as if my words please her. She pours two tumblers of whiskey and taps hers against mine before taking a pull. "Bad breakup?" she guesses.

I shake my head. "My wife died."

Her face falls, stricken. But instead of feeling awful, the way I always do, a part of me is relieved to admit the truth. To have that part of this conversation already over with.

"I'm so sorry, James," Bella whispers.

I dip my head. "Thank you. Layla passed about a year and a half ago. In March." I look back up, offering a small smile. "And it broke me."

She nods, her eyes wide and empathetic. There isn't an ounce of pity in them, just compassion and a sliver of understanding.

"This is not the same thing, at all," she emphasizes. "But I got divorced almost two years ago and that…" She trails off and a sarcastic laugh twists her mouth. "Well, that fucked me up pretty good."

At the hurt in her expression, at the hardness in her tone, I can tell she's still battling that demon, searching for closure. And man, closure in situations like ours is fickle. It's hard to make your peace when the other person isn't around to help you find it.

"I'm sorry, Bella."

"Yeah," she agrees, refilling my whiskey glass. She leans forward again and I try my damnedest not to let my gaze dip to her breasts. "How are you coping?"

I take a large gulp of whiskey, my head buzzing. "I'm not," I admit on a chortle.

She tips back her glass and smacks her lips. "Me neither."

I watch her for several minutes, the silence between us comfortable, natural, as she closes out her register. When she's done, a bar rag flung over her shoulder, she rolls her lower back across the ledge of the bar and faces me. Her posture is casual, arms crossed over her chest, feet crossed at her ankles. Her expression is unreadable. But her eyes burn, deep blue filled with longing and loneliness that I relate to.

The music playing on the speakers changes to the next song. Brad Paisley's "Whiskey Lullaby" floods the space and I shake my head as she bites her bottom lip.

"Pretty depressing, huh?" she chuckles, pushing to her full height.

I laugh with her, reaching over to press the stop button on her Spotify playlist. The music stops and a new sound, a silence pregnant with unchartered territory, rushes in.

"Does it ever get easier? Better?" she murmurs, her voice threaded with yearning. For what? Her ex? The life they once shared? The elusive sliver of peace?

"I don't know," I admit. "So far, for me, there hasn't been one easy day. Just moments, sometimes stretches of minutes, where I feel like I can breathe."

Her eyes meet mine and hold. She swipes her tongue over her bottom lip and I can't look away. I grip the underside of the bar ledge, simultaneously wanting to bolt for the door and never move from this spot.

My hands want to reach out to touch her. To feel her soft skin, her smoothness. My body wants hers. But my mind, fuck, my mind is racing. *This is wrong. It's too soon. It's too much.*

Still, I can't move. The silence of the bar rings in my eardrums, pulses in my temples. Bella's pain mixes with mine, swelling into something both dangerous and comforting between us.

I breathe in an inhale and hold it in my lungs.

It feels like I'm on the edge of a precipice. The next decision I make is going to redefine my present, shake up my future.

"Bella," I murmur.

Whatever she hears in my voice has a sad smile tugging at the corners of her mouth. "It's okay. Walk me to my car?"

I nod, standing from the barstool. I wait for her to round the bar and we walk out of Taps together. I pause for her to lock up. When we enter the parking lot, my fingers naturally settle in the small of her back. The heat of her skin seeps through the thin material of her tank top and unable to stop myself, I press my entire palm to the center of her back.

She slows and glances up at me, her eyes uncertain in the moonlight.

"Come with me?" I whisper.

She stops walking and turns to face me. Her hands settle on my hips and even though they *should* feel wrong, they don't. They feel right, wanted, *needed*. "Are you sure?"

I nod and clear my throat. I feel like a dick for what I'm about to propose but, "There's a hotel a few blocks over."

Understanding passes through her expression and instead of the anger I expect, relief flares in her eyes. "Yes. I'll drive."

I slide my hand to meet hers, stopping shy of her fingers and grasping her wrist instead. We walk to her car.

"Just so you know, I don't ever, I mean, I don't do this type of thing," she clarifies, clearing her throat.

I smile as she stops beside a red Mercedes Benz. "I know. I don't either."

She unlocks the car doors and we slip inside. I lean back against the seat and turn to look out the window.

Is this okay? Is this allowed?

You're an adult, James. You're allowed to enjoy the company of a woman.

What would Layla think? Will my kids hate me if I date?

Why are you thinking about dating? This is a one-night thing.

But what if it could be more than that? Bella is the only woman in the past year I've even noticed, let alone connected with.

It's too soon. It's been long enough.

Bella eases her car in front of the hotel and passes her keys to the valet. She keeps her back straight as she rounds the car and I reach for her hand again, tugging her against my side as we step up to reception and secure a hotel room.

We take the elevator in silence and as we draw closer to the room, I keep waiting for panic to rush through me. I keep waiting for her to turn around and bolt. But neither of those things happen.

In fact, when I close the room door behind us and turn toward Bella, I feel a flare of that peace I'm always searching for. To date, I've only ever found it on the ice. But at my age, even hockey will soon come to an end. Then what will I do?

My pulse slows, my head clears, and her presence fills me with desire.

My hands grip her hips as she pulls her shirt over her head. She tugs out her hair tie and a waterfall of dark curls roll over her shoulders.

My throat dries, my body humming with awareness and want and a flicker of shame I snuff out. Not tonight. Tonight, I'm choosing peace. Tonight, I'm choosing Bella over my demons.

Her bra is red and sexy, her curves delicious, her skin so goddamn silky.

I slide my hands up and down the sides of her body as her fingers deftly undo the row of buttons on my shirt. She pushes it off my shoulders and pops the button on my jeans.

I cup her chin, angling her face so I can peer into her eyes. "You sure about this, Bella?"

"I'm sure, James. Please, make me feel something good."

I nod, understanding exactly what she means. We're both too broken to be whole but maybe, just maybe, we can be whole together for this night.

I drop my mouth to hers and when our lips touch, I revel in her soft sigh. I kiss her fiercely, months of dormant need unleashing in an instant. Her lips part under mine and my tongue dips into her mouth, exploring. She tastes like whiskey and summertime, like shooting stars and lost dreams. There's something exquisitely tragic in her kiss and I'm drawn to it, to her, in a way I never imagined I would be again. I slow our connection for two heartbeats, savoring the taste of her mouth, the feel of her touch, the naked desire in her moan.

But that sound, her want, snaps something inside of me and my own need takes over. Our bodies come together fast and desperately. There's no time for tenderness, there's no more room for generosity and compassion. We lose ourselves completely, filling each other up with want.

When we're spent, a sweet sorrow envelops us. Bella curls up against my chest and I wrap my arms around her. Right before I doze off, I wonder if I've arrived at a turning point.

Can I date Bella? Can we grab a coffee or even breakfast tomorrow?

But when I wake in the morning, she's gone. Vanished with the sunrise. Just another ghost to haunt my thoughts.

Read *The Defender* now!

HEY READER!

Hi lovely reader!

I hope you loved *The Rule Maker*! Austin and Chloe's story was a joy to write and I hope it added something extra to your summer reading!

It would mean so much to me if you would please leave a review and share your thoughts. If you're loving Boston Hawks Hockey, don't miss *The Defender*, an emotional, single dad romance.

If you're interested in learning more about my books, please sign up for my monthly newsletter. Join now and receive a FREE bonus scene of Indy's baby shower. It's filled with humor, love, and your favorite hockey heartthrobs!

Or, come hang out in my Facebook Reader Group, Gina's Group for Book Gossip.

Thank you so much for all of your support and happy summer!!

XO,
   Gina

ALSO BY GINA AZZI

Knoxville Coyotes Football:

Faked and Fumbled

Surprised and Sacked

Trapped and Tackled

The Burnt Clovers Trilogy:

Rebellious Rockstar

Resentful Rockstar

Restless Rockstar

Tennessee Thunderbolts:

Hot Shot's Mistake

Brawler's Weakness

Rookie's Regret

Playboy's Reward

Hero's Risk

Bad Boy's Downfall

Lock 'Em Down

Boston Hawks Hockey:

The Sweet Talker

The Risk Taker

The Faker

The Rule Maker

The Defender

The Heart Chaser

The Trailblazer

The Hustler

The Score Keeper

Second Chance Chicago Series:

Broken Lies

Twisted Truths

Saving My Soul

Healing My Heart

The Kane Brothers Series:

Rescuing Broken (Jax's Story)

Recovering Beauty (Carter's Story)

Reclaiming Brave (Denver's Story)

My Christmas Wish

(A Kane Family Christmas

+ *One Last Chance* FREE prequel)

Finding Love in Scotland Series:

My Christmas Wish

(A Kane Family Christmas

+ *One Last Chance* FREE prequel)

One Last Chance (Daisy and Finn)

This Time Around (Aaron and Everly)

One Great Love

The College Pact Series:

The Last First Game (Lila's Story)

Kiss Me Goodnight in Rome (Mia's Story)

All the While (Maura's Story)

Me + You (Emma's Story)

Standalone

Corner of Ocean and Bay

ACKNOWLEDGMENTS

All of my love and heartfelt thanks to Becca Mysoor, Erica Russikoff, Amy Parsons, and Virginia Carey for getting this book in tip top shape! Couldn't have done it without you ladies!

All the thanks to the incredibly talented Kate Farlow, Y'all. That Graphic. for designing covers that I love and being an absolute joy to work with!

To MPP for managing all the things and always being a true friend on top of it all!

A million thank you's to Dani Sanchez and her awesome team at Wildfire Marketing Solutions and the fabulous women of Give Me Books Promotions for spreading the word about Austin and Chloe.

All my gratitude to the amazing bloggers, reviewers, and readers. I thank you every day for taking a chance on my words. Hope you loved this read!

And to my home team. Love you always.

www.ingramcontent.com/pod-product-compliance
Lightning Source LLC
Chambersburg PA
CBHW031027310726
48969CB00007B/1892